THE FIRST
SHALL BE LAST

A Novel of Love and War

★ ★ ★

Joe C. Ellis

Also by Joe C. Ellis

The Healing Place
Murder at Whalehead

Praise for *Murder at Whalehead*

"An atmospheric and thoroughly engrossing mystery, *Murder at Whalehead* will absorb the reader from its first tantalizing page to its last satisfying conclusion. It's a true page-turner filled with fully realized characters who understand both faith and doubt"

—Michele Rubin, Writers House, NY

"Joe Ellis weaves engaging characters, suspense, and triumph of Spirit together in a great read!"

—Nancy Haddock, author of *La Vida Vampire*, Berkley Books

"Mr. Ellis does a great job of setting a sense of place on the Northern Outer Banks. The plot twists and turns like the two lane roads, and the story is convincing. The characters keep you guessing until the very end."

—Gee Gee Rosell, reviewer for *Island Breeze*

"I've read 37 novels so far this year. *Murder at Whalehead* is at the top of the list. I loved it."

—Gretchen Snodgrass, avid reader and editor

THE FIRST SHALL BE LAST

A Novel of Love and War

★   ★   ★

Joe C. Ellis

Upper Ohio Valley Books
Martins Ferry, Ohio

The First Shall Be Last

A Novel of Love and War

First Edition

Upper Ohio Valley Books

71299 Skyview Drive

Martins Ferry, Ohio 43935

Phone: 1-740-633-0423

ISBN: 978-0-9796655-2-3

AUTHOR'S NOTE

Although this novel, *The First Shall Be Last*, is set in an actual place, Martins Ferry, Ohio, it is a work of fiction. The characters, names, and plot are the products of the author's imagination. Any resemblance of these characters to real people is entirely coincidental. Many of the places mentioned in the novel—Scotch Ridge Presbyterian Church, the Bob Evans Restaurant, Wheeling Medical Park, the Pittsburgh Airport—are wonderful places to visit in the Ohio Valley; however, their involvement in the plot of the story is purely fictional. Much of this story was based on my father's World War II memoirs. James Edward Ellis served as part of a Marine detachment on the *U.S.S. WASP*. After the *WASP* was sunk at Guadal Canal, he was assigned to the First Marine Division and fought in three major battles in the Pacific, including the Battle of Peleliu. He received the Purple Heart for wounds received in battle on Okinawa.

Joe C. Ellis

CATALOGUING INFORMATION

Ellis, Joe C., 1956—

The First Shall Be Last

IBSN 978-0-9796655-2-3

1. World War II—Fiction 2. Mystery—Fiction

2. Martins Ferry, Ohio—Fiction 4. Ohio Valley—Fiction

Author's Email: joecellis@comcast.net

Author's Website: www.joecellis.com

Acknowledgements

The author would like to thank the following people for their help: Terry, Tony, Steve, and Karla from Novel Alchemy, an online critique group. Many great catches, suggestions, and incisive comments issued from their collective and creative minds. Another member of the group, Nancy Haddock, who is also a Berkley Books author, spent many hours doing a reread of the novel for me and offered excellent advice to improve the final draft. A special thanks goes out to Nancy. Gretchen Snodgrass, a great lady and fellow teacher at MFHS, has been generous in providing her line editing talents for my last three novels. Although I'm sure we didn't catch every mistake, Gretchen sees the glitches that sneak past most other eyes.

My wife deserves a hearty "thanks, Hon" for blessing my life all these years and making it possible for me to spend hours in front of my computer without complaining too much. For some reason she puts up with my obsessions. I also want to mention my son, Joseph, and two daughters, Rebekah and Sarah. Although they've flown the nest, we talk often and give each other a ton of support. An extra helping of thanks goes to Rebekah for doing a final read-over for me. Last but not least, to all my readers who enjoyed the first two novels and insisted I write another.

Dedication

About ten years ago I sat down with my father, James Edward Ellis, and asked him to record everything he could remember about his World War II experiences. He was hesitant but agreed to do it. Dealing with difficult memories, Dad told his story. With six hours of recorded testimony, I sat down at the computer and typed out his memoirs. Early in the war my father served with a Marine detachment aboard the *U.S.S. Wasp*. In the Atlantic the Wasp delivered two shipments of Spitfires to the island of Malta, which provided enough air protection to save them from the obliteration of German bombing. The *Wasp* was called to the Pacific Theater to provide air support for the Battle of Guadal Canal. On September 15, 1942 three Japanese torpedoes sank the *Wasp*. My father survived and went on to serve as a scout with the First Marine Division on New Britain, Peleliu, and Okinawa. He received the Purple Heart for wounds received in battle on Okinawa. He died on January 21, 2007. I am dedicating this book to him. He was a courageous man, willing to put his life on the line for our freedom. I tip my hat to all veterans and the price they paid so that I could live freely. My father's memoirs can be found at http://www.joecellis.com/James_Ellis_WWII_Memoirs.htm.

CHAPTER 1

The bodies rotted for two days in the tropical heat. Judd Stone swiped sweat from his eyes. From the top of his shell hole he gazed across Horseshoe Valley. Coral ridges and mesas loomed on all sides. The stench sickened him. He could never get used to the smell of death. Twenty Marines lay scattered across the field, swarms of fat blowflies buzzing above the bloated corpses. The wild palms that once covered the hillsides were now splintered stumps, peels of white bark drooping from their trunks.

Stone's good buddy, Private Emery Snowfield, lay between two black stretcher-bearers, his exposed viscera crawling with maggots. *Sonovabitch.* Stone shook his head. *Thievin' sonovabitch.*

Glancing down, Stone spotted his canteen next to three empty ammunition cans. He snatched the container and shook it. *Not even a gulp left.* After screwing off the top, he drained the last drops into his mouth, tried to swallow, gagged, and coughed.

A slight movement to his left startled him and he dropped the canteen. In an instant he whipped his M-1 to his shoulder and panned the barrel across the draw.

Eyes wide and ears attuned, he inspected the carnage for an infiltrating Jap. His heart thumped in his throat. When Josiah Jackson, one of the black stretcher-bearers, rolled over, Stone almost fired. Jackson opened his eyes and lifted his chin.

"What the hell?" Stone whispered.

The lanky Negro reached his hand toward him, his large brown eyes pleading.

"You're dead!" Stone yelled. "You thievin' sonovabitch. You're dead!"

Jackson stumbled to his feet, but before he could take a step, small arms fire erupted from the hillsides, the bullets snapping and popping into the coral around him. He staggered towards Stone, hands outstretched. Bullets ripped through his already tattered dungarees. One caught the side of his helmet, flipping it off his head. It clanked on the ground in front of Jackson, and he kicked it toward Stone.

Stone's eyes narrowed as he watched the bullets ripping through Jackson, tearing off chunks of flesh. "Go down," Stone said. "Go down, you bastard."

Five feet away Jackson tripped and crumpled onto the sharp coral. The firing stopped. He lay motionless. Stone took a deep breath and exhaled slowly. Jackson raised his head. "Help me, Stone," he groaned.

The dead can't talk. You can't be alive. No way.

Half of Jackson's left ear had been shot off. When the black man lifted his hand, Stone could see two fingers missing. Stone surveyed the hillsides, expecting more enemy fire to finish Jackson off. Instead he heard the agonizing scuffling of the wounded man inching across razor-edged coral. Their gazes met—Jackson' eyes glistening. Maggots infested the open wounds on his face.

"I'm going crazy," Stone said. "This can't be happening."

Jackson's words were barely audible: "I's got . . ." He crawled closer. " . . . a three-year-old son." His shoulders rose as he thrust with his legs and edged forward on his flayed forearms. "Why did you . . . why did . . ." Within two feet of Stone, Jackson collapsed, air hissing from his lungs like a tire going flat.

Stone swallowed and released his breath, his ribcage quivering. He dropped his rifle and leaned on the side of the crater. "Jackson," he whispered. "Jackson." He reached over the rim of the shell hole and touched Jackson's hand—the one with the gold watch. "Why'd you do it, Jackson?" Stone slid his fingers around the face of the watch and tugged until the band slid over the bloody hand. Stone drew it near his mouth and blew the coral dust from the glass cover. He turned the watch over and read the inscription: *First Marine Division Middle Weight Champion.*

Jackson's hands shot toward Stone as if propelled by rockets. They clamped around Stone's neck. His airway shut off, Stone dropped the watch and gripped Jackson's wrists but couldn't dislodge the chokehold. Blackness swallowed Stone's vision of Jackson's grimace. Twitching and jerking, Stone gave one last yank, ripping the hands away. He gulped air. Something to his right beeped rapidly. When he opened his eyes, he saw the heart monitor next to his bed, the digital readout flashing 155 bpm.

CHAPTER 2

Byron Butler glanced above the elevator doors as the numbers lit in succession—2-3-4. When the doors parted, he nodded and deferred to a blue-haired lady in a faded pink dress patterned with daisies. Her smile wrinkled her face like a crumpled paper bag, and she hobbled into the hallway and turned right. He entered the fluorescent brightness and inspected the walls for room direction signs.

"Can I help you?" asked a bespectacled brunette from behind the nurse's station.

Byron pointed both ways. "Room 411?"

"That way." She waved to his left. "Turn left at the corner and go down the hall. Room's on the right."

"Thanks," Byron said but the woman had already shifted her attention to a computer screen. He'd been in that hospital hundreds of times visiting sick or injured members of his flock, but always felt disoriented when finding the rooms. Striding down the corridor, he breathed a repugnant odor—body wastes dulled by strong disinfectant. He almost gagged.

General Judd Stone. It'd been a long time since he spoke to that man. What on God's green orb did that old coot want to see a clergyman about? How long ago was it? Twenty years? No, it had to be twenty-five years ago when Byron was a senior in high school. He glanced up and noticed the 411 sign to the right of the door. *Maybe the General's about to expire and needs some spiritual counsel. If Saint Peter opens the pearly gates for that Marine then just about anyone gets in.* Byron forced a smile and entered the room

The sight of Stone froze Byron just inside the door. On the raised bed next to the window, Stone rested with his eyes closed. The vertical blinds had been pulled back and sunlight doused his emaciated body. His arms, thin and covered with age spots, lay over his stomach. *My God, the years have taken their toll.* Byron stepped closer. The gray butch-cut hair was gone, leaving sparse strands across the pale-purplish dome. Even his craggy eyebrows had thinned to a few white hairs. An oxygen tube clung to his nostrils and snaked across the railing to a unit stationed beside the bed. *Cancer. Has to be cancer.* As Byron drew nearer, he saw discoloration around Stone's neck. *What in God's name? Did someone try to choke him?*

Byron reached and brushed his shoulder. "General. General Stone?" he said, keeping his voice gentle.

The old man's eyes blinked, face muscles twitching, hands lifting as if to fend off an attacker. "Who . . . who the hell are you?"

Byron stepped back. "Relax. I won't hurt you. No needles. No pills. No enema bottles."

Stone's voice rumbled through phlegm: "Do I know you?"

"Annie Mulligan, the head nurse, called me. I'm her pastor. She said you wanted to talk to a member of the clergy."

"She tell you I was a General? I'm not, ya know. Never was. Too gaddamn stubborn to make that rank."

"No. She never told me that. I just knew that's what people call you."

Stone nodded, lifted his skeletal arm and rubbed his eyes. After blinking several times, he studied Byron and said, "You look familiar." His eyes, slightly clouded by cataracts, narrowed. "How'd you know my nickname?"

Byron leaned on the railing to give Stone a better look at his face. "We met many years ago. My name's Byron Butler."

The corners of Stone's mouth drooped, scoring the thin skin on the sides of his face with myriad wrinkles. He pointed to his temple. "Everything's cloudy up here most of the time."

Byron searched his mind to find a point of recall. "Do you remember Stanley Wright?"

"Course I remember Stanley. We fought side by side on Peleliu and Okinawa. He was tops. My best pal."

"His son, William, and I were good friends in high school. Will and I visited you about twenty-five years ago."

Stone rubbed the sparse white stubble on his jaws and closed his eyes. "Someone tried to rob me, and you . . .you . . ." A cough interrupted his words and triggered hacking that wracked his frail body. The seconds passed interminably as Byron watched and wondered if he should summon a nurse. Finally the old man gained control, swallowed, and breathed deeply several times before saying, "You warned me."

"That's right. Will and I overheard some dopeheads plotting to break into your house so we told you about it."

Stone cleared his throat, gathered the phlegm, reached for a plastic bowl on the over-bed tray, and spat into it. After setting the bowl back, he wiped his chin with the corner of the sheet. "People think I'm a gaddamn fool for not putting my wampum in the bank."

Byron shrugged and tapped his hand on the bed railing. "Keeping that much money at home is a risk if the wrong people find out about it."

"That's true. Thieves have broken in a few times. Never have found my stash of cash though. Never will. It's well hidden."

Byron sensed Stone was lonely and wanted to talk. From experience, he knew small talk could lead to more important spiritual issues. "Just curious. Why don't you trust banks?"

"Gaddamn bankers. My old man brought back a small fortune from Europe after the First War. During the depression he lost every cent he'd ever put into that vault. Bastard bankers stole it." Stone averted his eyes to his lap for several seconds then looked up again. "Sorry 'bout the language. Bad habit. Forgot you were a preacher." He pointed to his temple. "Gets kinda cloudy up here most of the time."

"No offense taken. I've heard every word in the book and said a few myself."

Stone grinned, a slight flush coloring his face. "An old dog like me has a hard time changing his ways . . ." He swiveled his head back and forth and peered out the window into the brilliant day. " . . . but I need to change my ways . . . you know . . . make a confession."

"I'm not a priest, just a Presbyterian minister. But I'll gladly listen to anything you want to get off your chest." Byron inhaled, tensing slightly, and felt heat rise to his face. He always battled embarrassment whenever someone expressed shame or humility in front of him. Helping people work through the mistakes of their lives was part of the job, but he felt unworthy—he'd made too many himself and still backslid occasionally. He swallowed the knot that had formed in his throat and said, "Is that why you asked to see a clergyman?"

Stone looked down at his hands folded in his lap and bobbed his head. "I'm dying of cancer. Lung cancer. Too many years smokin' cheap cigars."

Byron raked his fingers through his thick gray hair. "Thought maybe it was cancer."

"Yeah. Lost my flattop to the chemo treatments. Now it's a gaddamn white bowling ball."

"Sorry to hear that."

"Well . . ." Stone sucked air through his nostrils, clearing his sinuses, and swallowed. "There's something I'm sorry about too, and I need to tell someone."

Byron leaned on the bed railing and waited. Stone raised his head and closed his eyes as if he was viewing his sins on the screen of his eyelids. Not knowing what to say, Byron decided just to keep silent, and give the man time to ruminate. Confessions had to be handled delicately. To do it right, a person needed to enter the dark recesses of his being and confront the truth. That could be ugly, painful, ego-shattering—an effective chemo treatment of the soul.

What did this man do to bring on this deathbed confession? Certainly he killed the enemy in battle. But he had to kill or be killed. Something else must have rattled his soul. Byron wondered what it was like to take a human life—what effect killing a man had on his psyche. *Did it create a monster within?* The seconds slipped into minutes as Byron regarded the old Marine. He lay perfectly still in the sunlight, mottled by age and disease. The black and blue marks around his neck kept drawing Byron's eyes. The question of their origin began to overpower his contemplation of Stone's sin. *Who would want to choke an old man on his deathbed?*

Byron checked his watch. He knew at least five minutes had passed. Was Stone sleeping? Those bruises on his neck were so unusual. Why? Byron's patience ran out. He didn't know exactly what to say but couldn't contain his curiosity.

"General," he said softly. He nudged the old man's shoulder. "General Stone."

Stone opened his eyes and gawked at Byron, mouth agape, as if he'd never seen him before.

"General, I'm curious. How did you get those bruises on your neck?"

"Huh?" Stone grunted.

Byron reached his hands across Stone's chest to within inches of his neck. "Those bruises?"

Stone's hands clamped around Byron's wrists and pushed them back. He felt Stone's fingernails digging in and the incredible pressure of the grip. Stone gritted his teeth, his eyes narrow slits. He growled, "You thievin' sonovabitch. You're dead!"

Byron stepped back and jerked his hands away. His heart hammered against his ribcage and sweat trickled down the sides of his torso. He looked to inspect the scratches on his arms and noticed the white band of skin on his wrist. Glancing up, he saw his watch clasped tightly in Stone's bony hand.

CHAPTER 3

When Byron entered the kitchen, Lila asked, "How's the patient?" She wore capri jeans and an old smiley-face t-shirt. A bottle of furniture polish and dust rag sat next to a can of Maxwell House on the counter. She had just brewed a pot of coffee, and the aroma triggered Byron's caffeine craving.

"While you're pouring, I'll take a cup, Hon. My big mug if it's clean." Byron slid a chair out from the table and plopped down.

Lila stepped away from the counter, crossed her arms, and tapped her foot. The thick lenses in her red-framed glasses made her green eyes huge. "Geesh, By, how many cups does that make for you today?"

"Too many, but I need another. Weirdest hospital visit I've ever went on."

She pivoted and opened the cabinet above the coffee maker. "You won't sleep tonight."

"Don't care. Plan on staying up late anyway to do some research."

"Sermon research?" she asked, pouring the coffee.

"No. World War II research."

Lila delivered the cups to the table and sat across from him. "Here we go again, another Byron Butler obsession. Must have been that book Will Wright gave you by Tom what's-his-name."

"Brokaw. I enjoyed the book, but that's not it."

"Was it the hospital visit? Did that old guy give you a history assignment?"

"Indirectly, yes. Judd Stone was a Marine who fought in the Pacific theater. He must have done something terrible on the battlefield. He wanted to speak to a clergyman, make some kind of confession."

"But he didn't?"

Byron tilted his head. "Not quite. During our conversation he drifted into another world. When I tried to get his attention, he became extremely agitated."

Lila leaned forward. "What do you mean, agitated?"

After a long sip of coffee, Byron said, "He thought I was attacking him. Can't blame him though. By the looks of the bruises on his neck, someone recently choked him."

"Great Grandma's molasses. Choked a helpless old man? What happened next?"

"A nurse rushed into the room and told me I had to leave. Oddest thing." Byron rubbed his golden watchband. "Stone ripped my watch from me and didn't want to give it back."

Lila's eyes tensed, deepening her crow's feet. She twirled a lock of auburn hair around her finger, released it and twirled again. "That *is* odd. Maybe you should stay away from him. Is he senile?"

Byron shook his head. "I don't think so. He's in the latter stages of lung cancer. Chemo's been tough on him—physically and mentally. He just . . . went into another world."

"Hmmmm. If he wanted to talk to a minister, he must be worried about the afterlife," Lila said.

Byron stroked his mustache with his thumb and forefinger, his eyes losing their focus. "Perhaps . . ."

"Before I forget, Harvey Hershaw called with the estimates for the church roof repairs. He wants you to call him back."

"Uh huh."

"And Grace MacIntosh wants prayer for her grandson, Jamie. He flipped his Mustang during that cloudburst yesterday. The car's demolished, but Jamie's okay, just a little banged up."

Byron nodded, still unfocused. "I need to talk to Helen Kinloch."

"Helen Kinloch? Didn't you stop by the nursing home just last week?"

"More like two weeks ago. I mentioned to her that I'd read that book—*The Greatest Generation*. We talked about her husband and some of the local boys who served with him in the Pacific. Judd Stone and Stanley Wright, Will's dad, belonged to the same company."

"Small world," Lila said, her eyebrows rising above the red frames. "Do you think she might know some background on Mr. Stone?"

"She knows something about him. She called him a horse's ass."

"Helen said that?"

Byron grinned and nodded. "She told me she had a box of letters and memorabilia from the war years. Said I could look through it if I wanted to. The way she complained about Stone, I'm guessing her husband had some nasty things to write about him."

Lila crossed her arms. "And I'm guessing you're heading over there now to get that box of letters."

Byron met her gaze, seeking a sympathetic smile. "You know me too well."

The smile didn't appear. "I wish *that* were true."

A twinge of guilt needled through him as he rose from his chair and bent to kiss her on the cheek. A quiet voice within whispered to sit back down and talk awhile. *Relax. Those letters can wait. This isn't an emergency.* He almost did, but the anticipation of the investigation wouldn't let him. They could talk later that evening. He needed to get over to the nursing home before dinner.

"I won't be long," Byron said as he headed to the door. "Promise."

"You going to call Harvey back about the roof?"

"That can wait."

* * *

Byron steered into an empty space in the McGraw Nursing Home parking lot, put the van in park, and glanced at his watch. Almost four-thirty. He intended to be home by six, but limiting a visit with Helen to one hour wouldn't be easy. Over the years Helen had become a close friend. Before her accident, she had served on countless committees and put in hundreds of volunteer hours—decorating the sanctuary for holidays, cleaning up after covered-dish dinners, hauling bags of groceries to the community food cupboard—always willing to help in any capacity. She and Byron had spent a lot of time together in meetings and on work projects.

Three years ago she had fallen down the stairs at home and had broken her hip and both legs. Byron had hoped and prayed she'd recover and return soon. He considered her one of the pillars of the church's ministry. But infections set in, followed by surgical complications. The doctors offered no hope that she'd walk again. Confined to a wheelchair, she couldn't handle taking care of herself. Alonna Green, her great niece and only relative living in the Ohio Valley, had helped sell her house and had made arrangements for the nursing home.

As Byron exited the vehicle and headed to the front entrance, he took in the beauty of the country setting. The facility, a redbrick, ranch-style building, was situated on a hilltop about five miles west of Martins Ferry. From their windows the residents had beautiful views of the Appalachian foothills, which were blooming with the pinks, lavenders, and light greens of spring.

Byron swung open the glass door, stepped into the entrance hall, and pressed the button to gain access to the residents' quarters. The lock mechanism buzzed, and he threw open the door and waved to the familiar face at the nurses station, a chubby brunette with an ornery smile.

"Hey, Pastor Byron. Come to flirt with the old ladies again?" she said with a husky voice.

"Would you rather me flirt with you, Rita?" Byron winked.

She planted her hand behind her ear, ala Mae West. "You couldn't *handle* the temptation, Pastor."

"You're probably right. I better get moving before the devil knows I'm here," he said over his shoulder as he paced down the long hallway. Rita's gleeful laughter echoed through the corridor.

Halfway down, he turned left into Helen's room. She sat at the small window in her wheelchair, watching the late-afternoon sun dip toward a crimson horizon. Her white hair, cut short but thick and wavy for a woman of seventy-eight, gleamed in the window's light. A lustrous alabaster sweater and blue quilt across her lap and legs helped to conceal her thin frame.

Her profile reminded him of Katherine Hepburn, dignified and intelligent. Byron cleared his throat. "Hey, good buddy."

When she swiveled her head, a smile lit her face. "Hi, Pastor Byron. Didn't expect to see you for another week or two. Come here. Give me a hug."

Byron crossed the room, bent, and embraced her as she kissed him on the cheek. He whiffed her familiar perfume, a pleasant fragrance of spring flowers. Stepping back, he asked, "You behaving yourself?"

"Can't get into too much trouble 'round here. There's a couple old farts down the hall who try to put the moves on me every once in a while." She tapped her spokes with her palms. "But I'm a lot faster than those geezers. Just call me Hell-on Wheels."

Byron chuckled. "Okay, Ms. Wheels. Don't have to worry about you holding your own, do I?"

"I can take care of myself."

Byron paused, eying the feisty lady, admiring her inner strength that surfaced in the glow of her smile and the brightness of her eyes. "I've come to borrow your box of war memorabilia."

"Thought maybe you were here for a reason. You becoming a World War II buff?"

Byron told her he'd developed an interest but explained how his visit with Stone spurred him to investigate possible motives for Stone's confession. "You know me—like a kid with a new toy when I get focused on a project."

Helen braced her elbow on the armrest and rubbed her chin. "Stone wanted to confess something, eh? Hmmmm. Makes me wonder if it has to do with Howie's death."

"Do you have reason to suspect Stone might have been involved?"

Helen shrugged. "Nothing concrete. Howie mentioned several incidents in the letters—made me want to hate the man. Down through the years I'd run into him at the gas station or grocery store in Martins Ferry. He always looked the other way. Pretended like he didn't know me."

"Maybe he feels guilty?"

"Maybe." She pointed to a tall closet on the other side of the room. "The box is on the top shelf, left side. Now I'm curious."

Byron walked to the closet, slid the door open, reached up, shimmied the box off the shelf, and lowered it. The cardboard felt brittle and smelled of old newspapers. On the side, barely visible, was an A&P logo.

Helen stared wistfully at it, her voice becoming unsteady. "When I moved here, I didn't want to just toss this stuff out like so many other things. You live for decades on this earth collecting memories . . . and they end up in some landfill. There's a lot of personal things in that box."

Byron carried it to her. About the size of a small television, it wasn't heavy. Helen blinked several times, eyes watering. "Brings back some difficult memories, doesn't it?" Byron asked.

"Howie and I were just kids. Fell in love our sophomore year of high school. Got married in June of '43 after we graduated. Six months later he boarded a Greyhound bus to Parris Island." She glanced down, her eyes darkening. "Then Uncle Sam hauled him to the other side of the world to fight the Japanese." She placed her hand on top of the box. "You take these letters home and read them. See what you think."

"Thanks, Helen. I appreciate it."

"One thing, though, before I forget. Let me see the box."

Byron placed it on her lap, and she opened the flaps. After rummaging through its contents, she held up a blue velvet case resembling one that would hold an expensive necklace. "I need to have this close by."

"What is it, Helen?"

"I'll show you later, after you've read the letters. Then you'll understand why I want to keep it with me." She slid the case into a leather satchel attached to the side of her wheelchair. "Now, go home and investigate. This Judd Stone confession has raised some old questions."

"I'll do my best."

She lifted the box. "And Byron . . ."

He reached to take it from her, but she wouldn't let go. "Yes?"

"Some of these letters are hot and heavy. We were two young lovers on fire for one another, ya know," she said, smiling as she released her grip.

Byron whistled. "Now I'm really ready to get started."

* * *

Byron arrived home earlier than expected and rushed up the stairs with the box to his study. He opened the flaps and surveyed the contents. A stack of yellowed envelopes bound by a thick rubber band sat on top. He lifted the letters and saw old newspaper articles, certificates, dog tags, black and white photographs, ribbons, and a plastic bag containing a red and white cloth.

Carefully he inched the rubber band off the stack and inspected the first envelope. The postmark date was still visible in the right corner—October 21, 1943. He filed through the envelopes, noticing they had been ordered chronologically, about twenty of them. He opened the first one, gently sliding the flap out, then extracting and unfolding the faded paper. Helen's script was elegant with wonderful loops and finishing flourishes. Byron had no problem reading her writing.

My Darling Howie,

It has only been three days but I miss you terribly. I feel like one of those teenagers who goes bonkers over Frank Sinatra. What's going to happen in a week? Two weeks? The attendants from the sixth floor of Wheeling Hospital may show up at my door with a straight jacket. At night I imagine you lying beside me in the darkness. I hug the pillow and pretend your arms are around me, but it's a poor substitute.

I'm living on the memories of these last six months together—our married months. It doesn't seem fair they went by so fast, but oh, what memories. How many times did I wake up before you and enjoy watching you sleep? Your sandy blond hair, dimples and cleft chin always reminded me of Kirk Douglas. I couldn't stand it for long. I had to kiss you awake. Those kisses were the sweetest. They still linger in my memory. But what happened after you opened your eyes was even better than the kisses.

Last night Shirley Frazier and I went over to the Victoria to see Bogart and Bergman in Casablanca. A navy man and his girl were in line in front of us. They couldn't take their eyes off each other (or keep their hands off each other for that matter). A heaviness formed in my chest and swallowing didn't make it go away—I miss you so much. And it's only been three days. The movie was great, but the ending left me hollow. I wanted Bogie and Ingrid to fly off in that plane together. He told her they would always have Paris, but for me, Paris wouldn't have been enough.

Tonight, for some reason, this missing-you feeling is even worse. I want to see your cute bare bum. I want to run my hands over your strong arms. I want to feel your warm body against mine. I want to experience the tingling touch of your wonderful hands (and I do mean wonderful) on all of my secret places. My darling, Howie, I am aching for you tonight and this pillow isn't enough.

I pray to God this war ends soon. You are the only one who can satisfy this wanting deep within me. I don't think time will dull it. Somehow I'll have to learn to live with you so far away. God help me. Please write soon. I love you more than life itself.

Your devoted wife,

Helen

The letter felt electric in Byron's hand. He reread the last two paragraphs and pictured Helen at nineteen years old with long raven hair and a firm, attractive body. Memories of the first few months of his own marriage and the intensity of desire between Lila and him blazed like the flames that leap from a well-fed campfire. On his honeymoon night in a cabin in Canaan Valley, West Virginia, he could barely steady his hands as he untied the string of Lila's lavender nighty. He shouldn't have been the nervous one—she was the virgin and he, the experienced Casanova. He wasn't proud of it, but in high school he'd been sexually active. In college, after he'd become serious about his faith, his promiscuity stopped. Perhaps the span of years since last making love to a woman and the deep love he felt for Lila intensified his excitement, making him feel like a kid on Christmas morning finally permitted to open that special gift. His trembling hands had fumbled with the ends of strings as Lila smiled, red-faced.

"Byron! Byron! Supper's ready! Get down here before the food gets cold!"

Lila's hollering snapped him out of his memory. It was almost six and his stomach growled violently. "I'll be right down in a minute," he said. He turned the letter over and noticed writing on the back. The style was very different—clumsy and childlike. Glancing at the bottom he saw Howard's signature. *That's odd. Why would he write on the back of Helen's letter?*

"Byron! Come on! The potatoes are getting cold!"

"I'm coming," Byron said. He placed the letter on the desk and headed to the stairs.

CHAPTER 4

Byron made poor company for his wife and twin sons, Matt and Mark, at the dinner table. Helen's ardent words flickered in his mind like fireflies lighting a trail in darkened woods. He gulped down the roast beef, mashed potatoes, and green beans, barely uttering a sentence or two. Matt and Mark kept any silent intervals at bay by bantering about baseball practice and their chances of regularly providing the battery for the Purple Riders' varsity—Matt pitching and Mark catching. Byron nodded and grunted approval and occasionally gestured while Lila prated about the Baseball Mom's fundraiser she had organized.

His boys took after their mother, but he didn't mind. His daughter, Christine, a senior at Ohio University, turned out to be a female version of him. Like her father, she loved distance running and earned high school All-Ohio honors in cross country and track. She wanted to become a doctor and possibly a medical missionary. At baseball games Byron would relax and enjoy his sons' performance, but at track meets he'd get fired up—yelling, pacing the perimeter of the outside lane, pumping his arms—as if he were running the race.

Byron shoveled the last bite of roast beef into his mouth and snagged his coffee mug. "Gotta get back to my research. Lot's of things in that box to check out before I talk to Judd Stone again."

"Heaven forbid we keep you from your research," Lila said, eyebrows raised. The boys looked up from their plates.

The weight of Lila's words made it difficult for him to stand, but he rose slowly. He glanced at each of their faces, thinking he should sit back down and make a better effort to join in.

After several seconds of awkward silence, Lila said, "Go. You're anxious to get to those letters. The boys have homework to do, and I need to make some phone calls." She waved her hand toward him. "Go, By."

Too late. He'd blown it. With a quick peek he registered her expression to see if she was mad. In the depth of her eyes he did not detect anger. More like resignation. Was that worse? "I guess there's no hurry. I can sit awhile."

Lila shook her head and smiled. "Go, By." The smile was enough to release him.

On the way upstairs he heard her complaining to the boys about his tunnel vision. Maybe she was right. Had his obsessions detracted from the quality of their relationship? But all men have their faults. His was minor compared to a lot of the husbands he counseled in his ministry—drinking problems, gambling addictions, even abusive behaviors. Lila should be thankful he was a faithful, hardworking man. Yet her words gnawed at his conscience; but the discomfort dissipated when he entered his study and saw the letter on the table.

He picked it up and began to read.

My Dearest Helen,

Your letter arrived today and I read it ten times. I'll probably read it at least ten more times before lights out tonight. I decided to write my response on the back of your letter. Paper is scarce around here. Someone stole all my stationery. My friend, Ernie Myers, told me it happens all the time. So much for honorable Marines. He suggested writing on the back of your letters and that made sense. By doing it this way, we can keep a record of our correspondence. Overseas we're supposed to destroy letters from home so the enemy won't get hold of any important information. I'll just send them back to you. Anyway, it would hurt too much to destroy your precious words.

Well, I'm an official boot and I hate it. I know you think I'm a rock, but I don't know how much of this I can handle. The physical conditioning doesn't bother me. Working on the farm since I was a kid helped get me in shape. What I can't stand is the yelling. Boy does Drill Sergeant Powell yell at us a lot. We can't do nothing right. My body can take it, but I don't know if my nerves will. Pray the good Lord will give me calm through the storm.

Funny thing. I'm with a bunch of guys from morning till night, but I still feel lonely. Like I'm lost. Without seeing you every day, a hole has formed in me. I hate this empty feeling. I wish you were here right now. I think about you all the time even when I'm supposed to be learning something important. Today we received an introduction to various weapons—rifles, machineguns, anti-tank guns, mortars. My mind got jumbled. I kept remembering our last night together. How soft your lips were. The feel of your hair through my fingers. The curve of your back as I held you close.

I want you to know, Helen, that I love you more than anybody else in the world. I know I've told you this, but I'm telling you again. I'll love you until my dying day. You are bright and beautiful and all that is good.

If I can't be with you physically, I'll try my best to focus my love spiritually on you. Please write again soon. You are my lifeline.

Your one and only,

Howie

Byron carefully held the letter up to his desk light and examined both sides again. The handwriting styles contrasted so much, yet the intensity of love between Helen and Howard gave the document such unity of purpose and soul. He noticed how the bulb shone through the yellowed paper like the sun rising on a hazy morning and how Howard's clumsy characters through the translucence united with Helen's flowing script to create a unique and undecipherable language. *Why did their love burn so brightly? Did most couples separated by war communicate like this or did they have something special?*

He picked up the next envelope dated October 30, 1943, and eased out the triangular flap, removed a three-page letter and read it. Helen's confessions of longing and loneliness echoed much of the first letter's contents. But then she went on a tirade about the atrocity of the Marines taking "a good-natured, kindhearted, tolerant person" like Howie and trying to turn him into a hateful killer. She claimed their special love and oneness as a couple should not be placed at risk because the government needed violent men. She insisted he apply for rear echelon duty—become a cook, learn to type, fix engines. According to Helen, someone as "bright, super-fine, and mechanically inclined" as Howie should not be used as cannon fodder.

In the last paragraph she wrote: *I'm staring out the window at the moon tonight. That same moon is shining above Parris Island, South Carolina. It wouldn't surprise me if you were looking at it too at this very moment. We're like that, you and I. We think and say and do the same things out of habit. God made us that way. Listen to me, Darling. Please don't put our future in jeopardy by trying to be a hero. Just do your duty. If at all possible, get assigned to something important but safe. You're not a killer, Howie. I know that for a fact. And at night, whenever you see the moon, think of me, for I will be thinking of you.*

In Howard's response, he told her the higher-ups placed him in the infantry and he couldn't do much about it—when you were drafted, your options were few. And as his luck would have it, the Marines reeled him in: *Sergeant Powell says we're always the first to fight—the Marines get all the tough jobs—but the last thing I want to do is kill an enemy soldier. He's a man, just like me. Maybe he has a wife he loves dearly and three or four kids. How can I kill someone who loves other human beings? My buddy, Ernie, told me I would have to learn to kill or else be killed. That's war, he says. Some of the guys in my company are warped inside, saying they can't wait to kill a Nip. They use the foulest language and curse God continuously. Sometimes I catch myself using the same language, and it scares me. I don't want to become like them. Thinking of you, Helen, brings me back to sanity. Tonight I am looking at the moon and thinking of you. It's full—a pale yellow globe against a black-velvet sky. Tonight I am at peace.*

Byron read through letter after letter, intrigued by the intimacy of the separated lovers but anxious to get to ones mentioning Judd Stone. Howard bragged that he now knew how to toss hand grenades without blowing himself up and earned his rifle marksman badge at the shooting range. Helen wrote about the death of her Grandma Della and the birth of her sister Harriet's baby boy. After basic training, trains transported Howard's class of "boots" across the country to the Marine Base in San Diego where they underwent simulated combat maneuvers. Helen worried about "those hot-to-trot hussies" on the west coast.

On February 28, 1944, Howard's battalion, the 46th Replacement Battalion, boarded the *President Polk*, an old troop ship, and sailed into the Pacific Ocean. In a letter dated March 18th he mentioned looking out across the bow as they neared the harbor at Noumea and seeing old ships stranded and abandoned on the Great Barrier Reef. To Howard, the decrepit wooden hulks, held high by the reef, loomed like buzzards on a dead tree. They induced such an ominous feeling that he descended into the bowels of the ship, trading fresh sea air for the foul odor of sweat, grease and tobacco.

At 11:30 Lila, wearing her terrycloth pink robe, leaned into the room and asked if Byron was coming to bed. He peered over his reading glasses and said, "I'll be there in a few minutes, Hon. Just want to read one more." She shook her head and shuffled down the hall.

In the next letter Helen talked about getting a job at the can factory across the river in Warwood, West Virginia. Because of a shortage of men, the company offered good-paying jobs to capable females. Daily a ferry docked at the Martins Ferry Marina and transported nearly a hundred women to the factory. Every morning as she sauntered across the deck, Helen would eavesdrop on the spattering of conversations around her. What shocked her most was the number of women who cheated on their husbands: *I can't believe these girls. Their men are spilling blood on the battlefields of Europe or some God-forsaken Pacific island while they jump in bed with the mailman or milkman or encyclopedia salesman. It's disgusting. Most of them claim the war changes things—their husbands will leap at the chance to visit a French brothel or hop in the bushes with some native girl, so why can't they have their fun? I don't buy it. When I stood before that preacher and God Almighty and said, "I do," I meant it. Don't worry about me, Howie. I'm true blue. You're the only one who has ever tickled my fancy, and believe me, the only one who ever will. Please tell me I don't have to worry about you.*

On the back of Helen's letter, "June 1, 1944" was scrawled on the top right corner. Howard assured her she had nothing to worry about: *Back on Parris Island I had my chances to go drinking and whorehouse hopping with the boys on weekend passes up to Beaufort. All I had to do was pull out my wallet and look at your picture. The temptation skedaddled. Nothing could compare with what we have—especially a roll in the hay with some two-bit floozy. Don't get me wrong, Helen. I'm a man and have strong desires in that department. I don't have to tell you that. But I'm not like most guys around here. They have a one-track mind—the track created whenever a willing woman spreads her legs. A lot of these fellows are sex fiends. That's all they talk about, and the more perverted the better. I've actually seen several fights break out over soldiers stealing dirty pictures out of each other's lockers. At boot camp I'd leave the barracks and take a walk around the training grounds just to get away from them.*

We sailed from New Caledonia a few days ago aboard this new transport ship, the USS General Howze. It's much better than the President Polk. We're not packed in like sardines. But I still need to get away sometimes so I go up top. Earlier this evening I was the only one on deck. The sun had just gone down, and the golden glow on the horizon faded to pink and violet. Then as the sky darkened, one by one stars appeared. They seemed so close I thought I could reach up and pick them just like the apples in Ma's orchard. Once things got real dark I saw flying silver fish, tons of them, jumping out of the water in long, graceful arcs. I thought to myself what an incredibly beautiful scene. But then it hit me. We're heading to an island called Pavuvu—a place where the First Marine Division prepares for battle.

Byron glanced at his watch. It was almost midnight, but he figured Howard would meet up with Judd Stone on that island. The name of the island was crossed out, probably the work of a censor. But Helen had penciled in the word above the black mark. She must have wanted to preserve every word they'd written to each other. He had read about half of the letters, ten or so. Yawning, he reached across his desk and opened his appointment calendar to check on Wednesday's activities. Prayer breakfast—7:00 a.m. in the Scotch Ridge Fellowship

Hall. *Oh no. I forgot about that.* He ran his finger down the page. *And a full slate of meetings, not to mention the time I need for sermon preparation.* He glanced at the letter in his hand. *I'll finish this one and head to bed. Just a couple pages to go.*

By the time he finished, it was several minutes past midnight. After sliding the pages back in the envelope and placing it on the "Already-read" pile, he swiveled and shifted on his chair to prepare to rise, but the next letter in the glow of his desk light caught his eye. *Stone has to be mentioned in that letter. Just one more.*

This letter was dated June 10, 1944. On her side of the pages, Helen complained for the last five days she'd rushed out to the mailbox only to find bills, insurance statements and ads. She tried to ease her dejection by talking to Howard's 8 x 10 photo dressed in his green Marine uniform and hat with its globe, eagle and anchor symbol. But the more she stared at his face, the lonelier she became and the madder she got at the incompetents who managed the mail delivery system—*Don't they know how important these letters are to us war wives? They're all we've got.* Then she confessed she was at that time of month when her craving for him was at its peak. Memories of picnics by the pond, hayrides on Uncle Paul's farm, long walks in the woods, and sweet nights in each other's arms swept over her until she thought she'd go absolutely nuts. She ended by begging him to "play it safe and never take chances" so that one day he'd come home and make up for all these lonely nights.

Howard began his response with the words: *It's a small world, Helen. As soon as I stepped off the gangplank I looked up and saw Stanley Wright. Remember Stanley? He should have graduated with us but he quit school his junior year to join the Marines. He was seeing off some veterans who were leaving on the same ship we came in on. The old boys looked thin and tired. A couple of them thanked me for getting here so they could go home. I must say, I felt a little jealous knowing they were headed back to the good ol' USA.*

I was assigned to Stanley's platoon. Officially I'm in Easy Company, Second Battalion, Fifth Marine Regiment, First Marine Division. This First Marine Division is the famous one. In the fall of '42 they kicked the Japanese off Guadal Canal—our first American offensive victory. After Pearl Harbor and Wake Island nobody thought they could do it, especially when the Jap navy sunk a lot of our ships in a couple of ferocious sea battles near the island. Recently they returned from kicking Tojo's troops out of New Britain. I guess you can tell, I'm in awe. What worries me is that these guys get all the dirty jobs—the battles nobody else wants. Makes me wonder what's in store for you know who.

Let me tell you a little about this island, Pavuvu. If you look on the map, it's a part of the Solomon chain like Guadal Canal. As we approached it from sea, I thought we were headed to some tropical resort. A big plantation house sat high on posts back from the shore. It was surrounded by a coconut grove. Along the coast the breeze stirred the fronds of a long row of palm trees just like you see in the movies. A bunch of piers ran into the water from the docking area. I thought I was arriving in paradise.

It didn't take me long to come to my senses. The first thing I noticed was the horrible smell—rotting coconuts. They're all over the place. It's not safe to walk around without your helmet on because the darn things fall out of the trees without warning. Since the war started they haven't been harvested. A couple soldiers have actually been killed by falling coconuts. Our chow lines are outside so if it rains we eat slop. And it rains all the time. I'm always tromping through ankle-deep mud. Then there's the crabs—slimy repulsive demons that invade our camp in droves. They get into everything. This morning I dumped six of them out of my boondockers. It's the creepiest thing to slide your foot into a shoe full of crabs.

Worse than the crabs, though, are the rats. You know how I hate rats. We sleep in eight-man pyramidal tents. Three nights ago I forgot to tuck in my mosquito net. In the middle of the night I felt a tickling on my chin. I opened my eyes, reached up and touched something big and hairy—a foot-long rat. I'm ashamed to say I lost control of myself. Like a little girl I jumped off my cot screaming. There must have been ten or twelve rats scurrying around my feet. I jumped onto the nearest cot belonging to a fellow by the name of Judd Stone. Big mistake. Stone is the First Marine Division Middle Weight Champion. He has the gold watch to prove it. He hit me with a left hook in the chest. About caved in my ribcage. I landed on the ground with the rats. By then I was shaking like a wet alley cat in a snowstorm. Somehow I managed to climb back onto my cot. Stone hollered, "Who the hell jumped on me?" Someone lit a match and shoved it towards me. Stanley Wright said, "It's Howard Kinloch. What's the matter Howard?" I tried to explain about the rat, but my teeth were chattering too much. Finally they figured it out when they heard the buggers running across the ground. Judd Stone gave me a new nickname that night—Howard the Coward.

I hate to say this, Helen, but I don't believe anybody in my tent likes me. Maybe they do think I am a coward. Being a replacement doesn't help. I'm sleeping on the same cot one of their buddies occupied, a guy that got his head blown off in the battle for Cape Gloucester. The veterans don't get too friendly with replacements. Because we lack experience, we're the first likely to get killed in action. Maybe there's a double whammy on me—they think I'm a coward and that I'm going to get killed as soon as I step on the battlefield. I hope and pray they're wrong.

I've resorted to making friends with the Negro cooks and laborers. They don't care if I'm a replacement. The other evening after dinner I wandered over to their side of the encampment. We had a good time laughing and singing spirituals—Swing Low, Sweet Chariot and Go Tell It On the Mountain. I told them about the incident with the rat, and they rolled on the ground laughing so hard. No one blamed me for being scared. Then I found out something interesting. Big Bill Robinson told me that Judd Stone isn't the best middleweight on the island. That title should go to a fellow by the name of Josiah Jackson. Bill introduced me to him. He's a dark-skinned colored man, but handsome and muscular with piercing eyes. He put on quite a shadowboxing demonstration for me. According to

Marine regulations Josiah can't enter in the official tournament. They won't even allow black Marines to fight in the infantry. On the battlefield they have to be cooks, ammunition carriers, and litter bearers. Don't seem fair to me. These guys are willing to die for their country just like anyone else on this island. I told Josiah about Stone's championship gold watch. He just looked at me, smiled, and said, "That watch belongs to me."

CHAPTER 5

Bryon asked, "How's the wife?" He hadn't talked to Will Wright since the families got together over the Christmas holidays. Inseparable in junior high and high school, they had renewed their friendship seven years ago when Will moved back to the Ohio Valley. Now they met about once a month for coffee or called each other occasionally when one needed a listening ear.

Will sat across from him in a booth at Bob Evans, sipping coffee, the delicious smell of fresh baked rolls in the air. The collar on Will's blue polo shirt was off kilter and wrinkled. His hair, thick, wavy, and sandy during their high school days, had thinned, receded, and turned a medium brown. After swallowing he said, "Jo Ann's doing great, considering."

"Considering what?"

"Two teenagers and a five year old, plus a full time teaching job. We've joined the forty-something crowd. The energy level's not what it used to be."

"Obviously she doesn't have time to iron your shirts."

Will tugged at both corners of his collar in an attempt for symmetry. "My wife's a liberated woman. She didn't attend the

June Cleaver School of Homemaking like Lila. I'd do it myself, but I'm sure I'd scorch the damn thing."

Byron reached for the folder beside him, opened it and extracted a yellowed envelope. He slid his salad bowl out of the way and placed the envelope in front of him.

"What's that?" Will asked.

"Something you might be interested in. How's your novel coming along?"

Will sat up straight and expanded his chest, a smile broadening his narrow face. "Finally finished it. I'll be sending out queries to agents soon."

"Did you ever settle on a title?"

"I thought about calling it *One Season of Our Lives*, but instead I went with *Shadows on the River*—sounds more literary."

Byron nodded and patted the envelope. "I might have inspiration here for your next one."

"Really. Let me see."

Byron raised his palm. "Hold on a second. Let me give you some background info. Do you remember Judd Stone?"

"How could I forget the General? If it weren't for him I wouldn't be here. He saved my father's life. In fact, he moved to Martins Ferry after his military career just because he wanted to live near his best buddy."

"If I recall correctly, Stone killed a Japanese soldier who was about to slice your father's head off with a samurai sword."

"Right. Shot him right between the eyes."

Byron rubbed his silver mustache and nodded. "Stone's in the hospital . . . dying of lung cancer. I plan on seeing him this afternoon."

"Sorry to hear that. Tell him Stanley's boy said hi. Just don't offer my crime fighting services."

Byron smiled and nodded, remembering the night they helped foil the robbery at Stone's house. "I stopped in yesterday to visit him. He wanted to see a clergyman. Wanted to make a confession, actually."

Will leaned forward, spreading his hands on the table. "The man killed hundreds of Japanese soldiers. Remember what he told us? He volunteered to torch the caves using a flame cannon from the top of a tank. Probably enjoyed doing it. No wonder he wanted to make sure his sins were covered before he checked out. Figured Satan was throwing a few extra coals on the barbeque for him."

Byron shook his head. "I don't think so. To Stone, killing the enemy wasn't necessarily a bad thing. He did something much worse. Something he's not proud of." Byron tapped the envelope. "This letter holds a clue."

"Who wrote it?"

"Howard Kinloch."

"That name sounds familiar."

"Howard's wife, Helen, is a member at Scotch Ridge Church. She gave me a box of World War II memorabilia. She and her husband exchanged about twenty letters before he got killed on the battlefield. Howard belonged to the same platoon as your dad and Judd Stone."

Will reached for the letter, but Byron pulled it away. "Not so fast."

"Howard the Coward, right?" Will said, pointing at the letter. "Dad mentioned him on the tapes. Dammit, Byron, let me take a look."

"Tapes?"

"My father recorded his war memories before he died. Mom's had them down Florida all these years. She finally sent them up a couple of weeks ago when I told her I wanted to begin work on a war novel."

"There's something you need to know before you look at this."

"What?"

"Last night I was up till one in the morning reading these things. I made it through more than half of them. This is the last one I read before hitting the sack."

"And . . .?"

"The confession Stone wants to make . . . the act he considers worse than torching hundreds of Japanese holed up in a cave . . ."

"What about it?"

"Your father may have been an accomplice."

Will's questioning look froze for several seconds until Byron handed him the envelope. He extracted and unfolded the pages. After glancing at the top of the letter, he eyed Byron and said, "This is *to* Howard, not *from* him. It says, 'My Darling, Howie.'"

"They wrote on both sides—Helen on the front and Howard on the back. Go ahead and read Helen's first. I think you'll find it interesting. Read it aloud if you don't mind. I want to hear it again."

Will shrugged. "Whatever you say . . . *My Darling Howie, Rarely do I get mad when I read your letters, but that last one got to me. Who does Judd Stone think he is calling you a coward? He sounds like a bully, the kind that picks on the new kid on the playground just to impress his buddies. And remember this—bullies are cowards at heart. I'd like to see a rat crawl on top of on him some night just to see how he'd react. I'm sure he'd be jumping and yelping and squealing like one of those sissy dogs that gets its paw stepped on. I hate him. And why didn't Stanley Wright come to your defense? We grew up with Stanley. I remember watching you two play baseball down at the Stop Four Field. Martins Ferry boys should back each other up. I'm mad at him, and you can tell him I said so.*

"Howard, you are a U.S. Marine, a member of the First Marine Division, part of the toughest fighting outfit of America's entire military might. You are a super-strong, super-brave, super-nice, super-smart, super-incredible, super-guy. You are head and shoulders above Judd Stone and Stanley Wright. I'm proud of you.

"I also think it's wonderful that you made friends with the Negro soldiers. When I was a little girl I often stayed with my grandmother who lived six miles down the river in Bellaire. A colored family rented the house next to her. I played with their two little girls all the time. Grandma May often welcomed my new friends into her house and fed us lunch. Once some neighborhood kids walked by and called me 'nigger-lover.' I felt ashamed. I ran into the house and told Grandma May what they said and that I wasn't going to play with Diana and Donna anymore. She grabbed me by the shoulders and her face turned red. I thought she was going to slap me. She said, 'I don't want to hear you ever use that N-word again. You hear me? I don't care what other children in the neighborhood say. You are to treat colored people with respect. They are human beings just like you and me.' I'll never forget her words. They became a part of me. I'm happy to say I'm still friends with Diana and Donna. I see them occasionally at the A & P and Five and Ten. And I'm proud of you, Howie. You are a compassionate person. Don't let jerks like Judd Stone steal that away from you

"Crossing the river the other morning on the way to work, I leaned on the railing and watched the departing shore as the ferry moved out. The sun had just peeked over the eastern hills, burning off a light mist that hung just above the water. Along the shoreline tall maples and oaks spread leafy branches. When a flock of wrens flew over, I listened to the melody of birds—nature's sweet music. In those few moments the beauty of God's creation overwhelmed me. It made me think: How could there be so much evil in this world? Why do human beings hate each other? Right now around this earth on some of the prettiest lands and tropical islands you could imagine, bombs and bullets are showering death and destruction. Why has sin got such a hold on this planet? I don't have any answers. I wish I did.

40

"I do know this. Despite all the hate, Love will endure. Love will win. I believe that because of my love for you, Howie. Our love is something that we will share forever. It is bigger than us. Bombs and bullets can't destroy it. Hitler, Mussolini, and Tojo Can't wipe it out. Tonight I will lie in bed and think of you. I will imagine you next to me, your arms around me. Although you are not here physically, your love is with me. It sustains me. Somehow I will go on. Tomorrow I'll cross that river again and put in ten hours at the can factory, and then I'll cross back over again. When I see the trees and birds and sunlight sparkling on the water, I'll think of how much you love me and how much I love you. Do the same, Howie. When things get tough, remember—our love will endure.

Yours forever,
Helen"

Will stared at the bottom of the page for several seconds and then looked up. "Sounds like a sensitive person. Didn't have a very high opinion of my father, though, did she?"

Byron shook his head. "No, but your father and Judd Stone didn't have a high opinion of Howard Kinloch either. Howard replaced one of their buddies who got killed on New Britain. Replacements weren't held in high esteem by the vets. Turn it over. Read the other side and see what you think about this next incident."

Will flipped the pages and began to read: *"Dearest Helen, I'm worried about the negro I told you about in an earlier letter—Josiah Jackson. Over the last couple of weeks we've become good friends. Somehow word got back to Judd Stone that Josiah claimed to be the best middleweight on the island. That burned Judd up. He challenged Josiah to a boxing match—sort of a backyard brawl. Josiah refused to fight him unless Stone was willing to put up his gold championship watch. Stone said no way unless Jackson could come up with a lot of money--$500. Later that afternoon Josiah and about twenty of the colored cooks and laborers showed up with the money. They must have tossed in every cent they had to give Josiah a chance to prove himself.*

"The boys in our platoon got excited. Word spread. Before long, close to a hundred men had gathered on the north beach to watch. They wanted to stage the fight as far away from the officers' quarters as possible. Guys were taking bets—the odds rose to three to one against Josiah. I'm ashamed to say it, but I took those odds. I put twenty-five bucks on my new friend.

"Big Bill Robinson stepped up and got everybody's attention. He's one of the biggest colored men I've ever seen—six feet six inches and about 300 pounds, but believe me, he's a gentle giant. With his deep voice he announced they needed someone they could trust to hold the watch and money. None of the white guys would approve of a colored man, so guess what? Big Bill requested that I do it. None of the Negroes complained at all. Judd Stone took off his watch and handed it to me. That surprised me. So there I stood with $500 in one hand and a golden watch in the other.

"All the spectators made a big circle around the two fighters. I know you hate violence, so I won't describe the action to you. Let's just say it was one terrific battle. After about ten minutes Josiah got the upper hand. He knocked Stone down three times. The third time Stone staggered to his feet, his face all bloody, he could barely raise his fists. Then it happened. Right before Josiah was going to pop him good, a white towel came flying into the middle. I have no idea who threw that towel. Of course, anyone could see Stone was whipped. Josiah could have hurt him bad at that point. I handed the money and watch to Big Bill. That's when Stone realized what had happened. "What the hell!" he shouted. "Who threw the damn towel? I can still fight." Nobody believed him, though.

"Josiah's friends lifted him up and carried him back to their camp on their shoulders. Stone came up to me and said, 'Why did you hand over my watch? He didn't win it fair and square. Some nigger must have thrown that towel in.' I told him I reckoned someone from his corner threw it in. He raised his fist to hit me, but by then the pain had set it—he winced like someone just jabbed him in the side with a spear. Stanley Wright stepped up and ushered him off towards our tent.

"Later that night while we were lying on our cots, I heard Stanley and Judd whispering. Judd swore he'd get his watch back. Stanley said he had an idea. I couldn't make out Stanley's plan, but I heard a few words—something about tying Josiah up some place where they practice tossing hand grenades. Then Judd said, 'The only good nigger is a dead nigger.' Helen, I don't know if they were just blowing off steam or what. I wouldn't put anything past Judd Stone. I've decided to keep my eye on them. The next time I get a chance to talk to Josiah, I'll tell him to be careful.

"You sure are right about this world, Helen. It's full of evil. But what's a man to do? Sometimes I feel like I'm smack in the middle. A part of me says stand up and do something. Another part of me says mind your own business. The only thing is when I mind my own business I feel the devil patting me on the back. There's nothing I hate worse than that. Please pray that I do the right thing.

Your loving husband,

Howard

Will looked up, the pages dangling from his fingers, eyes anxious. "What are you doing after lunch?"

"I've got a ministerial association meeting in the conference room at the public library," Byron said.

"Can you blow it off?"

Byron shrugged. He hadn't missed any yet this year. Some of his colleagues rarely came. "I guess so. Why?"

"My father's war tapes. There's one labeled Pavuvu—the island they recovered and trained on between battles. I'll meet you at my house."

CHAPTER 6

On the way out to Will Wright's house, Byron brimmed with an energy and curiosity he hadn't felt for a long time. Talking with Will had re-ignited his adventurous instincts. He smiled and shook his head. Now he had become a rebel again, skipping a ministerial association meeting. He laughed out loud. *Yeah, I'm a real bad dude.*

The time Byron and Will shared during their teen years was filled with escapades, shenanigans, and mishaps. For the past eighteen years Byron had settled into the conservative lifestyle of a Presbyterian pastor. Meeting the needs of his flock and family left little time for adventure. He enjoyed his work, but lately the patterns of life and emotional demands of ministry had become tiresome, a chain that limited him to familiar paths. The visit with Judd Stone and Helen's letters caused a break in the chain or at least an extension. Adding the contribution of Will and his father's tapes reconnected him to those vibrant times when friends were all-important, responsibilities few, and new discoveries around every corner.

Byron pulled his Caravan into the driveway behind Will's little red Chevy. Will lived about five miles from town in an aluminum-sided, ranch-style house perched with a spattering of similar houses on a hillside just above a small man-made lake. About six years ago he'd married Jo Ann Faulkner, a divorcée with two kids, a gal he'd longed to be with since high school. A year later with the couple in their late thirties, Jo Ann gave birth to Olivia, a high-energy blonde fireball.

For Will, a discontented bachelor all of his adult life, the union resulted in rebirth. His ready-made family gave him a sense of responsibility and purpose. He took a job at the local newspaper as a sports writer and in his spare time began penning that novel he'd always told Byron he'd write.

Byron entered the house and heard commotion coming from the kitchen. A brown collie-shepherd charged into the entry and sprang at him, barking and licking.

"Get down, Bowser," Byron said. "I don't want your hair and slobber all over my good clothes."

The dog didn't comply, so Byron pushed him aside with his forearm and strode to the kitchen, Bowser on his heels.

"Control your beast," Byron said as he pulled out a chair and sat down.

"He's just happy to see you." Will fumbled with the contents of a Nike shoebox as Bowser found a spot on the floor and licked himself. A cassette recorder sat on the table in front of Will, its cord stretching to an outlet above the counter near the sink. "Ahhh. Here it is. *Pavuvu*."

"How many of these tapes have you listened to?"

"Three. Haven't got to his one yet. The ones I've heard were great, though. I didn't realize my father was such good a storyteller—all about basic training at Parris Island, the Battle of Guadal Canal. New Britain. He kept me on the edge of my seat."

"You probably inherited some of his talent—his was oral and yours more literary."

Will paused, staring at Byron and nodding. "Yes. You're right." His voice sounded surprised, as if he'd found something he'd lost. "That's an ability the old man sent my way. He and I were a lot alike." Seconds later he punched the eject button and inserted the tape.

"Do you think he'll tell the story accurately? I don't mean to cast doubt, but good storytellers sometimes exaggerate," Byron said.

"Dad had a lot of faults but dishonesty wasn't one of them. The good, the bad and the dirty-dog ugly, he told it like it was. In a previous tape he even confessed to using pliers to yank gold teeth from dead Japanese soldiers on New Britain."

"Disgusting! Why'd they do that? Couldn't have been much money in it."

"No. It was just something they did. War changed people. Brought out the worst. Dad wanted to tell everything on these tapes. I guess it was . . . what's the word . . . cathartic . . . sort of his way to confess."

"But would he confess . . . a felony? Do you think he'd incriminate himself on tape?"

Will tightened his lips and pressed the play button. "We'll see."

Stanley Wright's voice, medium in pitch, surprised Byron at first because it sounded so much like Will's, except a little livelier. "They called us the Raggedy-Ass Marines, the First Marine Division. Not like the Second Division. We called them the Hollywood Marines. Whenever they needed men for movie productions, do you think they'd come to us? In a pig's eye they would. Hell no. We were too busy fighting the battles—too beat up and scarred up and screwed up. No. If they wanted handsome, clean-shaven Marines, they'd call on the Second Division. When they needed a tough job done, that's when we'd get the call. Got used to it after a while. Just expected it.

"One of the worst things they did to us was send us to that piss-poor-excuse-for-a-rest-camp—Pavuvu. Rest? Hell! After chasing the Japs across the tropical jungles of New Britain they dumped us onto this rat-infested clump of mud and coconut trees. There *was* no camp. No roads. No housing. No recreation facilities. We had to build it ourselves. Can you imagine that? And three-quarters of us had malaria and jungle rot to boot. Day after day we'd clean up rotten coconuts, haul coral up from the quarries to pave the roads, and work construction details to build decent facilities. At night we served guard duty.

"It's no wonder some of the guys went Asiatic. I remember one boy, PFC Popavitch, only nineteen or twenty years old. He got in trouble with the Top and had to serve guard duty five nights in a row—four hours worth of marching back and forth in ankle deep mud. At the end of the fifth night, he plopped down in front of his tent and stuck his M-1 in his mouth. Before anyone could get to him, he reached down, pressed the trigger and blew the back of his head off. What a mess. Damn shame too. He was a good boy. Just went crazy.

"That's why we started making jungle juice. It was either get drunk or go nuts and sometimes both. I found a five-gallon paint can and cleaned it out as best I could. Then we stole sugar, raisins, and cans of peaches from the mess tent. It didn't take a college degree to figure out how to make booze—fill the can up with water, dump in the raisins, sugar and peaches and let it ferment. Only problem were the damn flies. I didn't have my batch covered just right and a bunch got into the mix.

Emery Snowfield, my buddy and a damn good Marine, says, 'Stanley, this is what you got to do. Go see Mess Sergeant

Ford and borrow a couple loaves of bread. We'll take the jungle juice and strain it through the bread to get rid of the flies.' Made sense to me. I headed over to the mess tent.

"Now the mess tent was erected on a platform supported by four by fours with a screen all around it. I was already half drunk from a batch of juice my best friend, Judd Stone, had made. When I entered the tent, Mess Sergeant Ford gave me that what-the-hell-you-want look.

"I says, 'Hey, Mess Sergeant Ford, I need a couple loaves of bread.'

"He says, 'Now you just about face and get the hell out of here, Wright. You're drunk.'

"'I'm only half drunk,' I says. 'That's why I need two loaves of bread.'

"'I ain't gonna give you no two loaves of bread,' he says. 'Get out!'

"That made me mad. I grabbed a meat cleaver from off the table, tapped it in my hand a couple of times and says, 'Mess Sergeant Ford, we need those loaves of bread to strain jungle juice. Hand 'em over.'

"He pointed his finger at me and says, 'You ain't getting' no loaves of bread to strain no jungle juice. Now get the hell outta here.'

"I marched outside with that meat cleaver and started chopping on those four by four posts. By the time I chopped through two of them, a Top Sergeant showed up with about eight Marines. They put me down pretty fast. The next thing I remember was waking up surrounded by barbed wire. They'd knocked me out, dropped me in the middle of four coconut trees, and wrapped barbed wire around the trees. That's what you call an impromptu brig.

"My head ached like somebody had cracked me with a baseball bat, but I could hear some southerners talking not far away. Somehow I managed to get to my feet and peek through the barbed wire. I saw about five coloreds on coconut detail, laughing and jawing about their boy who could whip any white Marine on the island. I listened in, getting madder by the second because I knew none of them could take Judd Stone. In a tournament just a few days before, Judd had knocked out every middleweight contender. I saw one of those jigs take a boxing stance, bobbing and weaving, punching the air. He looked like he knew what he was doing. All at once I got an idea.

"I says, 'Hey, come over here!' They took their good old time but finally got there. "What's this bullshit you're shoveling? You think you could whip the First Marine Division Middleweight Champ?'

"The tall one, thin and muscular, says 'Hell yeah I can whup him. 'Cept they ain't gonna let me in the ring.'

"'That's right,' the others say.

"'Now you let me worry about that. What's your name, boy?"

"He raised his fists and circled them. 'Jackson. Josiah Jackson. The Georgia Nightmare.'

"'You as black as night,' I says, but they didn't think that was too funny. I was glad the barbed wire was between us. 'Tell you what. We're always trying to keep ourselves entertained on this island. How about if I set up an unofficial bout between you and the champ?'

"He nodded. 'I'll think about it,' he says. His buddies got all excited.

"'You think good and hard,' I says. 'Lot's of money could be made. You boys camp out on the other side of the chow lines, don't you?'

"The one that looked like a black mountain, Big Bill they called him, says, 'Yeah, we be over there.'

"'Well,' I says. 'I'll send word if I can get something going.'

"It took some dickering, but I set the fight up. Judd had to hand over his watch and Jackson passed the hat around the colored camp to collect five hundred smackers. Winner take all. Figured that was quite generous of them. Judd's gold watch couldn't have been worth more than two hundred and fifty bucks. Course it had sentimental value to him with the championship inscription on the back. To cover my end of handling the proceedings, I worked it out to take twenty-five percent of the pot—that's assuming Judd won. But I had no doubt. I also planned on betting my entire paycheck on the champ. Guess my eyes were filled with dollar signs.

"Couple of days later a crowd gathered on the north beach. Howard the Coward was elected to hold the money and watch—the coloreds didn't trust me to do it. Once the fight started it didn't take long for me to see I misjudged Josiah Jackson. He fought like a Hellcat in a firestorm. Judd held his own for about ten minutes, but then my get-rich dream turned into a Georgia Nightmare. Jackson hit him with a straight right that broke his nose. Man did the blood splatter. Then a left hook caught Judd on the temple, knocking him to the ground. I didn't think he'd get up, but he did. It got real ugly after that. Within three minutes, Jackson put him down two more times. My best friend was in trouble. Big trouble. I didn't know what to do. Then I looked and saw a dishtowel hanging out of one of the colored cooks' back pockets. I reached behind and grabbed it. The guy was cheering so loud he didn't notice. When Judd staggered to his feet for the third time I tossed it in before Jackson could hit him again. I don't think anyone saw me.

"The coloreds all started celebrating. I squeezed through the crowd and rushed in to help Judd stay on his feet. He had this strange look in his eyes. When they lifted Jackson to their shoulders, Judd understood—he just lost his watch. Once he got his bearings, he wanted to punch out poor Howard

Kinloch for handing it over to Big Bill. Wasn't Howard's fault. I never did tell Judd I threw in the towel. He'd a killed me.

"That night, lying on our cots, Judd kept complaining what a crock that fight was. I just wanted to go to sleep. He swore he'd a come back and won the thing if some asshole hadn't thrown in the towel. Man, he wanted that watch back bad. The guilt was killing me. All at once I got an idea. I says, 'Listen, that Jackson's a reasonable man. He's not gonna hand over the watch just because you thought the fight was unfair . . .but. . .'"

"'But what . . . ' Judd says.

"'But if we sweeten the deal, I believe he'll hand it over.'

"'Sweeten the deal. Whadaya mean?' Judd says.

"I reached under my cot and pulled out my samurai sword.

"'You're not gonna give that up are ya? Major Gayle gave that to you on New Britain after you captured that Jap officer.'

"'I know. I know,' I says. 'I'll just capture another officer on the next island.'

"'Shit. We'll just kill a few on the next island. But what if Jackson won't trade a sword for a watch?' he says.

"'How much money you got?' I asks him.

"'Couple hundred bucks. I won that big poker game last week,' he says.

"'We'll bring that with us too, just in case,' I says. 'If he still won't trade, we'll tie him up in a cave and practice tossing hand grenades into it.'

"'' You're kidding, right?' Judd says.

"'Nope,' I says. 'I wouldn't kid over something as serious as your damn golden watch. Now go to sleep.'

"The next day we recruited a native by the name of Bouza, one of those wooly-booly bushmen, to take a fifth of Johnnie Walker's best over to Josiah Jackson. Sent a note with Bouza for Jackson to come alone and bring some of his platoon's winnings if they wanted more of the good stuff. We knew that would get him. J.W.'s rare on the island. Bout a mile into the jungle, Judd and I waited in a cave.

"When they got there, Jackson says, 'What's goin' on? I comes to trade for whiskey, not talk about a rematch.'

"He had the watch on like we figured, showing it off to everyone. We gave Bouza a couple cans of peaches and sent him on his way. 'We're not here about a rematch,' I says. 'We're here to trade.' Jackson had that what-the-hell-you-talkin'-about look in his eyes.

"Judd pulled the towel out of his back pocket and nailed Jackson in the chest with it. 'One of your cooks threw that in,' he says, 'to stop the fight.'

"'The hell,' Jackson says. 'Yo corner threw it in.'

"'Look at it,' Judd says. 'It's just like the ones your boys use on K.P. duty.'

"'So what?' Jackson says.

"'So what? So what *is*—the fight wasn't fair,' Judd says. 'Your man stopped it, not mine. You gotta beat me to take my watch.'

"'Beat you?,' Jackson says. 'I 'bout killed you.'

"I stepped between them and says, 'Now listen. We know you fought one hell of a fight. We're not gonna send you away empty handed. Look there,' I pointed to a rock a few yards into the cave. 'Check that sword out.'

"Jackson picked up the sword, pulled it out of the sheath and inspected it. 'That's a fine sword,' he says. Then he laid it back on the rock. 'But I ain't givin' up my watch.'

"I looked at Judd, and he pulled the cash out of his pocket and tossed it onto the rock. 'That's two hundred buckaroos,' he says. That'd buy you all the Johnny Walker whiskey you can drink, if that's what you want. And we know where to get it. Just hand over the watch.'

"Jackson looked at the watch and rubbed the band. Then he says, 'No suh. I ain't tradin' this watch for money or swords or whiskey. I'm the champion on this island. Not you.'

"That's when Judd pulled out his pistol and told Jackson to stand against the wall. We'd already rigged up the ropes using some of the gaps in the rock formations. I spread him out and tied his hands and feet good and tight.

"'We're gonna give you some time to reconsider,' Judd says. He picked the towel off the ground and draped it over Jackson's shoulder. 'Remember what I told you about this towel. And think hard about that money and sword lying there.'

"We walked out of the cave and sat down under some palm trees thirty paces or so down the hill. Sitting there, we could hear him cussing. After about ten minutes the cussing turned in to crying out for help. That's when we went back up and peeked in.

"'Change your mind yet?' Judd says.

"Jackson settled down when he saw us, took a few deep breaths and says, "No suh, you can leave me here as long as you want. I ain't givin' up the watch.'

"Judd picked a grenade off his belt and says, 'Well then, I guess it's time for some grenade practice.'

"Jackson's eyes got real big then. We sauntered back down to the palm trees. Judd pulled the pin on his grenade and tossed it to the right of the opening. We ducked. Boom! Debris and smoke blew everywhere. That's when Josiah Jackson started screaming—'Hey! What're ya doin'? Get me outta here!' We couldn't help but laugh. I tossed mine to the left side of the opening. Kablam! More screaming. That poor black sonovabitch had to be shitting himself. Judd pulled the third one out of his pocket, took aim and tossed it right into the mouth of the cave. 'I'll give the watch back! I'll give it back!' Jackson hollered just before . . ."

The cassette player made a funny noise and Byron looked at Will. The words became jumbled.

"Oh no," Will gasped. "It's eating the tape" He punched the stop button and hit eject. The plastic cartridge popped out but the thin tape snarled and tangled in the mechanism. "Dammit!" Will lifted the cartridge, and a long brown string hung down to a jumbled pile. Will shook his head, and their eyes met. "I can't believe it. My father helped murder a black man."

CHAPTER 7

Not breaking the speed limit proved difficult for Byron as he drove from Will's house to Wheeling Medical Park. After the cassette player had chewed up a critical section of tape, he didn't have the patience to see if Will could flatten and splice the pieces, rewind it and try again. Besides, Byron wanted to hear the story from Judd Stone's mouth. He hoped the old Marine would be coherent today, able to proceed with the confession that stalled out yesterday. Byron decided not to tell Stone about the tape unless he had to, anxious to compare Stanley Wright's version with Stone's. *What will I do if he confesses murder—killing a man with a hand grenade over a watch? Report it to the authorities? Or just let him get it off his chest and die in peace?*

As Byron pulled into the hospital parking lot, he murmured a prayer for guidance. The elevator ride to the fourth floor intensified an uncertain quavering in the pit of his stomach. The doors parted, and he retraced the path to 411 and entered the room. The back of Stone's bed was elevated.

He sat there, alert, some color tinting his complexion. The bruises on his neck had faded.

"Good afternoon, General. You look better today."

Stone smiled. "Not ready for a twenty-mile hike but feeling better. Some days I almost think I can whip this cancer. Must be the Marine in me. Not looking forward to this afternoon though."

"Why?"

"Another chemo treatment. They 'bout kill me."

"Do you feel like talking today? Yesterday the nurse made me leave before you could . . . you know . . . tell me what was on your mind."

"You mean confess my sins."

"Yes. Your confession."

Stone didn't fade off into the Twilight Zone this time. He began the story when he first met Josiah Jackson on Pavuvu. Surprisingly, his tale matched Stanley's closely with the exception of the infamous towel—Stone believed one of the black cooks tossed it in. When he talked about tying Jackson up in the cave and tossing the grenades, he didn't fudge any of the details to appear justified in his actions.

His voice was steadier today, more resolute. "When we walked back up the hill to the cave, I could hear Jackson whimpering." He turned from Byron and stared at the dry-erase board hanging on the wall opposite his bed. The on-duty nurse's name, Nurse Hinsey, was neatly printed there in blue marker along with several instructions, but Stone focused as if it was a movie screen flickering through the frames of a haunting scene. He swallowed. "We entered the cave, and I bent down and picked up the dud. 'Gaddammit,' I said and tossed the grenade to the side. It clattered on the rocks near Jackson's feet. 'Just my luck,' I said. 'A fizzler. You bring any pineapples, Stanley?'

"Then Stanley reached into his pocket, pulled one out and said, 'I *know* this will blow.'

"Jackson started blubbering like a baby. 'Don't kill me. Please don't kill me. I's got a three-year-old boy at home and a young wife. You can have the damn watch back.' Tears were running down his cheeks. I actually felt sorry for him.

"Then Stanley asked him if he wanted to trade for the cash and the sword.

"Jackson said, 'You can keep yo money and sword. Just let me go'.

"I wouldn't tolerate that. 'No deal,' I said. 'You don't get what's happening here. That watch is mine. One of your buddies stopped the fight. I could've kept going. I'm not saying I would've won, but who knows? The fight didn't end fairly. Do you understand what I'm saying, boy?

"Jackson nodded. I can still see those big whites of his eyes as he blinked away the tears. 'Whateva you say,' he said.

"'No,' I said. 'It's not what I say. It's what's right.' I looked at him to make sure he got what I was telling him, and he nodded again.

"Then Stanley said, 'The money and sword is what's called compensation. We know you're a helluva boxer. You deserve something.'

"Jackson kept nodding like one of those bobble-head dolls you get at the ballpark nowadays. I said, 'When those bastards back at camp ask you what happened to the watch, just show them the sword and money and say what's fair is fair and what's right is right. That's what I'm telling the boys in my platoon. You decided to do what's right.'

"Jackson took a deep breath, got control of himself and said, 'Okay. I'll do that. Just let me go and I'll give you the watch.'

" I told Stanley to untie him, and he undid his feet first.

"As soon as his hands were free, Jackson stuck out his wrist and said, 'Here, take it.'

"I shook my head and said, 'No. You've got to give it to me.' He slid it off and dropped it into my hand and headed out the cave.

"'Jackson!' Stanley hollered. 'You forgot something.'

"Jackson turned and looked at the sword and money.

"'You ain't leaving here without these,' I said. He looked at me like a dog that wants to bite you but knows better. Then he got down on his hands and knees and picked up the bills and samurai sword. While he did that I wiped off my watch and put it back on. Jackson stood and walked out of the cave without looking back."

Stone closed his eyes. The scene had ended. *Was that the confession?* He didn't seem repentant. Byron had detected no tone of regret in his voice as he told the story. What a proud, bigoted, self-righteous old son of a bitch lay before him. *Byron felt like choking him. Surely this can't be all.*

"So, are you saying," Byron asked, "you're sorry you took the watch back?"

Stone quickly glanced up. "Hell no. The watch was mine. I guess I feel bad about the way I went about it."

Feel bad? That's it? That's not quite repentance in my book. Byron decided to shake his cage a little. "You know, General, that *your* corner did throw in the towel."

"Huh?"

"Stanley Wright threw in the towel."

"Like hell he did."

"It's true. I heard him say it himself."

"How could you?"

"Stanley made recordings of his war memoirs. His son, Will, played the tape about Pavuvu for me. He told about the fight and admitted he threw in the towel."

Stone's eyes drifted to the ceiling. He balled his hands into fists. "Gaddamn you, Stanley. Why'd you do that?"

Byron stepped closer and leaned on the bed railing. "Because Jackson would have clobbered you. You were beat, General. Stanley just wanted to protect you."

The corners of Stone's mouth dropped like a bulldog's; his facial muscles tightened, slashing wrinkles across his cheeks resembling deep scars. His breathing quickened. "I don't need protection. I would've rather fought to the death than lose like that."

Byron shook his head, thinking how pride drives a man to cold, hard, lonely places. "Can I ask you a question, General?"

The ice on Stone's face crinkled as he peered up at Byron, his features softening. "Shoot."

"What was so important about that watch that you were willing to totally humiliate another human being to get it back?"

Stone opened his hands in his lap and studied his palms as if the answer could be found in the deep lines that merged and diverged like a weathered roadmap. "You see . . . I . . . I wanted to give that watch to my father."

"To your father?"

He nodded. "I had an older brother who planned on becoming a doctor. He got the brains and I got the brawn. Pop admired how quickly Danny picked things up. Smart as a pistol he was. Could read something once and then quote it word for word a week later. Hell, I'd read something and forget it two minutes later. You don't know how many times I heard my father say to everybody that came through the front door: 'This is my boy, Danny. He wants to be a doctor.' I got sick of it. He barely noticed me.

"One Christmas when I was fourteen years old I asked for boxing gloves. I was a half decent athlete and fighting didn't bother me a bit. After I pulled them out of the box, I begged

Danny to spar with me. He was four years older than me. Said he didn't want to hurt me. I pestered him all day and finally that night we strapped on the gloves. Pop decided to referee so no one would get hurt. At that time Danny must have outweighed me by twenty-five pounds, but I didn't care. I'd fought bigger guys on the playground at school. It wasn't long before I caught him with a good uppercut in the stomach. He bent forward and I plowed his eye with a left hook. Down he went. He was all right. Shook up a little. But Pop looked at me like I was some kind of Greek god. He wouldn't let us spar any more—thought maybe Danny'd get hurt. 'You could be a pro, like Jim Braddock,' he told me. It was the first time he ever admired me for anything.

"Three years later Danny graduated from the University of Colorado with a Bachelor of Science Degree. That put Pop on Cloud Nine. Not only did his boy graduate a year early but also took top honors. That was just before the war started. When Danny declared he was joining the Navy to become a corpsman, Pop just about busted. Like his old man, Danny was serving his country—but as a healer and not a fighter. Pop thought it'd be great experience for a young man who wanted to be a doctor.

"In the meantime I was stumbling my way through high school. My grades were piss poor. I was a decent football and basketball player but nothing to brag about. Then it hit me— Dad served with the Marines in the First War. The day after Danny joined the Navy, I quit school and signed with the Marines. Figured Pop would be more pleased than a monkey in a banana tree. Boy, did I get that wrong. When I got home, he blew his stack. 'What the hell you thinking, Judd?' he said. 'You haven't even graduated yet. Your brother's got a college degree and you quit high school. And my God, if this war breaks out like they say it will, the Marines will go in first. I guarantee you'll be thrown into the fire.' It didn't take me long to find that out—the hard way.

"After basic training when I took up boxing, I made a name for myself in the regiment. People respected me. I felt like that fourteen-year-old boy again with his big brother at his feet, and Dad saying I could be another Jim Braddock.

"Once we got to Pavuvu and I won the First Division Middleweight Championship, I knew Pop would be proud again. I could picture his face when I'd return home from the war and hand him that watch." Stone stared at the dry-erase board again, as if watching another scene from his past.

"Well," Byron said, "did you ever give your dad the watch?"

When Stone looked up, his expression stunned Byron, reminding him of people who just lost a loved one in a tragic accident. It exposed something deep inside Byron, like a harsh light revealing his shortcomings in providing answers to those who were hurting.

"Yeah, I gave it to him." Stone's eyes blinked, dark orbs set deeply into his skull. "But he barely looked at it. Never even said, 'Way to go, champ.'"

"Why?"

"By the end of the war Pop was a changed man. My brother served on Iwo Jima. He was awarded the Navy Cross for giving aid to wounded soldiers while directly exposed to enemy fire. After saving six men he was blown to smithereens by a mortar shell. Pop framed that Navy Cross and hung it next to the picture of Jesus on the living room wall."

"What did he do with your watch?"

Stone chuckled, but his eyes remained mirthless. "I found it in the back of his sock drawer. Took it with me when I headed east. He probably didn't notice it was gone. Pop was never the same after Danny died. Just a shell of a man."

A nurse poked her head in the door and said, "Mr. Stone, I'll be back in about five minutes to take you to your treatment."

Stone lifted his hand and said, "I'll be here."

Byron wrestled with that inadequacy, the one he often battled after hospital visits and funeral services, the one that shouted: *You haven't helped much here! Say something! Do something!* He searched for words. "Mr. Stone, do you want me to come back again? Have you told me everything you wanted to tell me?"

"Huh?"

"The confession you mentioned on my last visit. Was this it—what you did to Josiah Jackson in that cave? Do you want me to pray with you for forgiveness?"

"Hell no. That wasn't it. I admit we scared the boy into giving me back my watch, but that's the least of my sins." He glanced out the window and back to Byron. "There's something much worse."

Byron waited, but Stone just stared at him. Byron finally asked, "Do you want me to come back tomorrow?"

Stone reached and grabbed Byron's hand. His grip was cold, claw-like. He gulped. "Jackson had a son. He must be in his late fifties by now. Do you think you can find him?"

"Find him? Where would I look? What was his name?"

Stone shook his head. "I don't know his name. Maybe Josiah, like his father. Jackson was a Georgia boy—Atlanta, I think."

Byron stepped back from the bed. "That's like finding a twenty dollar bill in a Wal-Mart parking lot. It's possible but not likely."

Stone's eyes widened. "Could you try? I've got to talk to his boy."

"Is this about the confession you wanted to make?"

Stone nodded as the nurse entered the room pushing a wheelchair. "We've got to go now, Mr. Stone," she said.

Byron promised he'd come back tomorrow and headed out the door. Halfway down the hall he ran into Annie Mulligan, the head nurse.

The middle-aged brunette held a clipboard, a stethoscope dangling from her neck. "Pastor Byron, did you get a chance to talk to Mr. Stone? This morning he asked me if you were coming today."

The familiar face of one of Scotch Ridge Church's faithful members brought sudden warmth to Byron. "Hi, Annie. Yes, we've talked a couple times. I'm coming back tomorrow. He has some heavy baggage he wants to get rid of."

"Come to me all ye who are heavy laden, huh?"

"Yes," Byron chuckled. "And I will give you rest, or at least a shoulder to lean on. Hey, I've got a question for you."

"Lay it on me, Pastor," she said and smiled.

"When I stopped in yesterday to see Mr. Stone, I noticed bruising around his neck. Do you know anything about that?"

Annie shook her head. "We're not sure. A nurse found him that way yesterday morning. He didn't want to talk about it."

"Could someone have entered his room and choked him?"

Annie shook her head. "It's not likely, but who knows?"

"Judd Stone does," Byron said.

CHAPTER 8

After a full day of ministry responsibilities, Byron swung by McDonald's drive-thru for a quarter pounder, fries and coffee. He devoured his meal as he drove up Seabright's Lane toward Memorial Park to watch his boys' baseball game. Lila had arrived before him, saving a spot in the bleachers. For late afternoon in April, it was hot, probably high seventies, and slate-gray cumulus clouds hovered over the western hills. Byron hoped they could get the required five innings in before a storm came thundering through. Matt straddled the mound, striving for his fourth victory, and Mark was catching.

Lila handed him a diet Coke she'd pulled out of a small cooler beside her. "Did you stop by and see Mr. Stone again today?"

Byron nodded then swigged.

"Still alive and kicking?" she asked as she glanced from Byron back to the mound. Matt nodded to his brother and raised his glove and ball to his chest.

"Back from the dead, almost. He looked much better today."

"And his confession?"

"We're making progress. He wants me to find someone, the son of a black Marine."

Matt went into his windup and fired a fastball past a gangly hitter for a strikeout.

Lila jumped to her feet, clapping and shouting, "Way to go Matt!" Byron stood and applauded as the Purple Riders, clad in purple and gray, trotted off the field. "The son of a black Marine? Interesting. Was the Marine a friend of his?" Lila asked as they sat down.

Bryon shook his head. "No. More like a rival than a friend. It's not going to be easy finding the guy. Don't know his first name, but Stone thinks he's from Atlanta. I'll do an internet search tonight. Any important messages for me today?"

"Yes. Earl Waller called. He wants you to stop by the house and talk to Eric tomorrow if you have time."

Byron hung his head and closed his eyes. "Poor Eric. I just don't know what to say to the kid."

"You'll think of something, I'm sure."

Six weeks before, Eric Waller had sped down a country road on an ATV with Johnny Owens hanging on the back. When he came to a crossroads, he didn't slow down, just blazed through the stop sign as if they were untouchable. Speeding down the main road, an old pickup clipped the back end of the ATV, tossing the seventeen-year-old boys like rag dolls onto the bank. The ATV landed on top of Johnny. Eric got tangled between two trees, breaking both legs and an arm, but he remained conscious, forced to listen to his best friend's final agonizing minutes. Johnny died before the emergency squad got there.

At first, Byron faithfully visited Eric at the hospital but soon discovered the boy didn't want to communicate about the accident. Their interactions consisted of Byron's small talk—things teenagers couldn't care less about—and Eric's nods and grunts. Earl hoped Byron could break through the citadel of his son's withdrawal. But Byron floundered, tacking it up to his lackluster skills in dealing with emotional crises and family tragedies. His stops by Eric's hospital room became less frequent.

To get his mind off the impending visit, Byron focused on the game, but as usual baseball bored him, especially when his sons sat in the dugout, waiting for their turn at bat. His thoughts drifted to Helen and Howard's letters. In the last one, Howard seemed convinced Judd Stone and Stanley Wright had concocted a wicked plan that threatened Josiah Jackson's life. Now that Byron knew the outcome, he wondered about Howard's thoughts concerning the incident—his reaction to Josiah giving up the championship watch. Byron tried to formulate possibilities for the real motivation of Stone's confession and hoped the remaining letters would provide some clues. Twenty minutes later the thunderstorm blew in and the umpire postponed the game.

* * *

When Byron got to his study that evening, he squelched the urge to delve into the letters, remembering his promise to Judd Stone. At the computer he did an internet search through the white pages of the Atlanta phonebook. There were hundreds of Jackson's but no Josiahs. Satisfied he'd made a decent effort, he turned to Helen's box of war relics.

He lifted the top letter off the not-yet-read pile, extracted the pages, and turned to Helen's side first. It was dated August 6th, 1944.

My Darling, Howie,

Today in church during Pastor Simpson's sermon, my mind wandered. I sat in the pew next to the stained-glass window, the one with the Good Shepherd carrying the lamb. Spots of colored light dotted my lap and the wood grain of the pew next to me. I touched the empty space and thought of you. The splatters of light reminded me of our fifth date when you took me to Patterson Pond for a picnic. Remember how the sunbeams through the trees danced on the surface of the water?

I couldn't help thinking about what happened that day. After we finished off the fried chicken and potato salad, we became hungry for something else—each other. Nobody was around. The blanket, spread across the grass in the shade, was soft and cool. Things started slow enough, but then we turned into a couple of animals. Before that day, the most I'd let you do is kiss my neck. What got into me? Your hands were very bold, and I didn't have the willpower to stop their exploration. You started a fire in me, and there was only one way to put it out.

As I replayed the scene in my mind, I suddenly realized I was sitting in church. Pastor Simpson paused in the middle of his sermon and glanced in my direction. I wondered if my face was bright red. When he resumed he spoke about the weakness of the flesh. I knew exactly what he was talking about. I remembered lying on that blanket beside you, completely satisfied, thinking, 'So this is what heaven is like.' Or hell. I spent the next two weeks a nervous wreck until I got my period. My parents would have killed me if they'd found out.

Somehow we managed not to do it again until our wedding night. Now I'm wishing I would have gotten pregnant at Patterson Pond. I know that sounds silly, but at least I would have had a part of you with me right now—a baby boy or girl. I could hold it, care for it and love it— a little someone we created together. As soon as you get back from the war I want to start a family. Let's have five or six kids. I know you'd make a wonderful father, and I'd do my best to make a good mom.

Howie, you could never guess where I am right now. I'm sitting in that old rowboat on Patterson Pond, the one we used to borrow without asking. I don't think Old Man Patterson will mind. After remembering the first time we made love, I had to come out here this afternoon. Right now a sunbeam has trickled through a hole in the canopy of leaves and alighted on my page, fluttering there like a fairy. Can you see it, Howie, in your mind? A long-legged, white crane is wading in the shallows. There are dragonflies hovering above the cattails along the shore. Can you create these images in your imagination and be here with me? Can you feel the hardness of this seat and the gentle drifting of the boat? Are you with me now? I want to paddle to shore, spread out the blanket, and lie there till I fall asleep. And then I want you to visit me in a dream and show me how much you love me—satisfy me.

I'm sorry if this letter seems strange to you, but something happened that made me miss you so. Jane Harbaugh, the young gal that works on the conveyor belt next to me, received a letter earlier this week from the war department. It stated her husband, Tommy, is Missing In Action in France. He's in the infantry like you. All day Wednesday tears trickled down her cheeks. She said she wasn't going to give up hope and showed up the rest of the week, working those ten-hour shifts. On Friday evening when we stepped off the ferry, I gave her a good hug, and she wept, shaking like a little lost bird.

I don't ever want to feel that way, Howie. I'm worried about this battle coming up. Be brave, but please, please, please don't take any chances. I've prayed that God would watch over you. He knows how much we love each other. Sitting here right now it seems like you are so close I could touch you—like you and God and me are all bound up together into a beautiful ball of light. Everything we have ever done together has been so special whether it was sharing an ice cream cone or watching a falling star. God would never take you away from me. I have to believe that. There are five or six unborn children anxiously waiting for you to come home to me, my love. God will watch over you so that one day he can send them our way. I must believe that.

Yours always
Helen

Byron paused and thought about Helen Kinloch, confined to a wheelchair, childless, a widow for so many years. Alone yet not really lonely. Until her accident she was one of those rare people who overflowed life, who had the knack to bring anyone who spent time with her up from the doldrums. Even in her current state, tucked away in that nursing home, she remained positive, thoughtful, encouraging.

Then his mind drifted to the early days of his marriage, the days when he and Lila couldn't get enough of each other. *Why does the intensity of love's passion have to fade? Or does it? Maybe it's me.* He glanced at the words on the page. *Lila loves me like Helen loved Howard. It's not her fault. She's a wonderful person, a great mom, and a caring wife.* The possibility that he had been negligent in tending the fire of their love pressed on him like a beam placed on his shoulders—all those things that so easily drew him away. He never had thought that much about it until he had started reading . . . these letters.

He turned over page one and read Howie's response. It was dated two weeks later—August 20th, 1944

Dearest Helen,

Your letter was a lifesaver on an ocean of misery. I've read it so many times in the last two days I've lost count. It inspired me to attend worship services this morning at our outdoor chapel. Surprisingly our homemade benches were packed full of hardened Marines. Knowing we'll be boarding LSTs in the near future to sail to some Japanese infested island has got everyone thinking about eternal destinies. I guess facing the real possibility of death does that to a man.

I sat and listened to Chaplain Rooker's sermon but didn't get much out of it. Maybe it's because of all the training we've been through to get us ready for the hell that's coming our way. It's not easy listening to twenty minutes worth of speechifying about faith, hope, compassion and love when you've been bombarded with six days of Marine doctrine. I can sum up the U.S.M.C. Creed with three words: *Kill. Kill. Kill.* And the highest honor that can be bestowed upon a Marine is to die gloriously on the battlefield.

I don't buy it, Helen. There's got to be more. I want to know the why of it all. Life itself is an amazing gift. The sunrise is a marvel. The birth of a baby is a miracle. If I could only fly, escape this island where men are trained to destroy life, I'd come back to you on a westerly wind. And do you know what we'd do? We'd make love and we'd make life—beautiful, innocent babies that laughed and cried and crawled and slobbered and slept peacefully in our loving arms.

This war is not for me. What am I going to do when bullets buzz by my ears and bombs explode all around? I know I'm not cut out for this, Helen. The guys in my squad were right. I am a coward.

The other day Judd Stone and Stanley Wright left the tent with Stanley's precious samurai sword and some rope. That made me suspicious. Ten minutes later I saw Bouza, a native who hangs out around here, and Josiah Jackson pass by, heading in the same direction. Remember, I wrote you about the fight and how Josiah walloped Stone good and won the watch. I decided to follow them.

They walked a long ways into the jungle to an area where we practiced maneuvers for attacking a fortified cave position a few days earlier. I kept my distance, staying out of sight. Bouza and Josiah climbed the hill to the mouth of the cave. Then Stone and Wright stepped out. Hiding in the undergrowth fifty yards back, I couldn't make out what they were saying. Stone handed Bouza a couple large cans, probably peaches or beans, and he took off. Then the three of them went into the cave. I wondered what on earth Stone and Wright were cooking up. Suddenly it hit me—the rope. They wanted to take Josiah's watch, tie him up and leave him in the cave to rot. Then I thought about the samurai sword. That made me really nervous. I almost went running up the hill into the cave, but something inside told me to wait.

About five minutes later Stone and Wright came out, walked to the bottom of the hill, and sat down in the shade of some palm trees. I heard Josiah cursing them, his shouts echoing in that cave. Then he began to cry, and I felt sorry for him. But I figured I'd wait it out to see what those two mean bastards would do. Excuse my language, Helen, but those two bums are bastards. They walked back up the hill and into the cave. It got quiet. A few minutes later they came out and walked down the hill. 'Here we go again,' I thought. But this time Stone pulled a grenade off his belt and tossed it toward the cave. It landed near the opening and blew up. I couldn't believe it. Josiah started screaming. Right then, if I had any guts, I should have charged out of the jungle and stopped them. But like a coward I thought about my own life. If they were going to kill him, why not kill me too? That's when Wright tossed his grenade and it exploded on the other side of the entrance.

I was trembling like a shanty in an earthquake. Stone tossed the third grenade—bull's-eye—right through the opening. I shut my eyes and listened for the explosion to end Josiah's screams. Instead I heard the poor guy hollering that he'd give back the watch. When I opened my eyes, Wright was shaking Stone's hand as if they just sealed the deal on a piece of property. He purposely threw the dud into the cave.

They went back up, and a few minutes later, Josiah came marching down, carrying Wright's sword and a handful of cash. 'What the devil?' I thought. Josiah walked right toward me. When he glanced up and saw me, he jumped. "What're you doing here, Howie?" he asked. I tried to explain as best I could, but I felt so ashamed. I confessed I didn't have the courage to stop them. We walked back to the encampment together. He didn't blame me at all and said they would have killed me just like they were going to kill him. I didn't have the heart to tell him it was a prank. When I asked him why he had the sword and the money, he said, "I'm supposed to say, 'What's right is right and what's fair is fair.'" I got the message. Stone wanted to make sure everybody knew Josiah traded him for the watch.

Josiah told me when the first hand grenade went off, all he could think about was his three-year-old boy, Jeremiah, growing up without a father . . .

"Jeremiah!" Byron gasped. "Jeremiah Jackson." He swiveled his chair to face the computer, grasped the mouse, and directed the cursor to drop down the history menu and retrieve the White Pages website. Quickly he typed the name and city into the entry boxes. The search returned eleven "Jeremiah Jackson"'s and twenty more "Jeremy Jackson"'s in Atlanta. He scanned the list and saw one "Jeremiah J. Jackson." *J as in Josiah, maybe.* He printed out the pages and circled the name and number. Tomorrow he'd do some detective work. He spun back to the letter and read the last few lines.

Josiah said he knew what it was like to grow up without a dad. The watch wasn't worth taking that chance. The only way he'd ever get that watch back would be to peel it off Stone's corpse on some battlefield. I told him that's possible. The scuttlebutt around camp is we're heading to another island like Tarawa. Half of us might not make it back alive.

Pray for me, Helen. Pray God will give me courage to face this battle. And pray that I survive.

Your loving husband,
Howie

CHAPTER 9

Byron decided to stop off at Will Wright's house and borrow the war tapes first thing in the morning. In between destinations throughout the day he could pop them into the Caravan's tape player and glean as much information as possible about what happened during the battle from Stanley Wright's perspective. For the morning he'd scheduled two counseling sessions at the church and some time for sermon preparation. After lunch he intended to start calling the Jeremiah Jacksons of Atlanta, Georgia until he reached *the* Jeremiah Jackson, son of Josiah. Then came the visit he most dreaded, the one with Earl Waller and his son Eric. At least Eric was home from the hospital, and perhaps the comfort of familiar surroundings would prompt him to talk about the accident. From there Byron would head to Wheeling Medical Park to get Stone's side of the story.

At Will's kitchen table, Byron sat down to his third cup of coffee of the morning. He filled Will in on the details about the cave incident and assured him his father wasn't a murderer—a prankster, yes; a bigoted jerk, maybe; but a murderer, no.

"Did you ever repair the Pavuvu tape?" Byron asked.

Will reached into the box and lifted the cassette with the thin, crumpled strips dangling from its feed window. "Figured I'd just make it worse. I'm going to take it to someone who knows what he's doing. Maybe it can be salvaged."

"Have you listened to the rest of them?"

"Not with *my* damn cassette player. Don't trust it. I'll stop by K-mart and pick up a new one sometime this week." He slid the box across the table to Byron. "You'll get to hear the rest of Dad's memoirs before I do. By the way, they're numbered. The next one is tape number five—*The Battle of Peleliu.*"

* * *

Byron started his van, extracted tape number five from the box and inserted it into the player. As he backed out of Will's driveway, Stanley Wright's lively voice piped from the speakers.

"They told us Peleliu would be another Tarawa. Three or four days of pure hell but then over and done. Where'd they get that hogwash? Multiply Tarawa times ten. We went through forty-five days of pure hell.

"The evening before D-day, Judd Stone and me were standing on the deck of the troop ship watching the sun set. Those orange and yellow rays stretched out across the sky and shimmered on the water just like a picture postcard. Sunsets on the Pacific could dazzle you.

"We were leaning on the rail taking it all in when Judd says to me, 'Stanley, how many Marines are in the First Division?'

"I told him about sixteen thousand.

"He gave me the strangest look and says, 'That gives us about a 50/50 chance of making it through this battle.'

"'Why do you say that?' I asks him.

"He says, 'I was down in the hold of the ship earlier this afternoon talking to Supply Sergeant Tanner. He showed me a compartment stacked with tons of white crosses. I asked him how many, and he said about eight thousand. If my math is right, that means one out of two of us won't survive.'

"Just then the sun disappeared below the horizon and the sky darkened. A voice blared over the squawk box: 'Now hear this. Now hear this. All troops lay below. All troops lay below.' We headed across the deck and went down into the bowels of the ship. I wasn't looking forward to the sunrise.

"I didn't sleep good that night, and the steak and eggs they fed us for breakfast grumbled in my stomach like a hand mixer in a bowl of gravel. At the break of dawn I got my gear together and went out on the main deck. The sky was clear blue, the ocean smooth as a satin sheet, and a nice breeze flapped the flags on the main mast. An NCO ordered my platoon to head down the ladder to the tank deck and board the amtrac—that's an amphibious tractor. Not long after that the bow doors opened, and they lowered a ramp into the ocean. Wave after wave of amtracs rumbled down the ramp into the water and bobbed like fat ducks floating towards a hunter's paradise.

"Finally the coxswain started the engine of our amtrac and down we went. "Oh hell," I said, "here we go." Out in the sunshine it got hot real fast. The naval artillery sent 500-pound bombs roaring above us like freight trains. Seemed like the whole island had caught fire. Black smoke rose up behind the flames messing up that beautiful blue sky. Howard Kinloch started puking his guts out. Had to be nerves because the waves weren't bad at all. Sweat poured down my face. I looked at all the equipment I had to lug and thought, 'Oh shit. I'm gonna die of a heatstroke before we even get to shore.' I un-strapped my helmet and took it off. Course I was wearing my campaign cap underneath.

"Lieutenant Baker shouted, 'What the hell you doing, Wright? Put that helmet back on.'

"'What difference does it make?' I says. 'If I get hit in the head, I'm dead anyway.'

"'Put the damn helmet back on,' he says.

"I took the helmet and tossed it over the side of the amtrac. I didn't care. Felt a lot cooler without it. 'I like to kill Japs in comfort,' I says. Couple of the ol' timers laughed.

"Baker just shook his head and says, 'You're gonna get hell for that.'

"Then I reached down and grabbed my gas mask container. 'Don't need this either. It's against the Geneva Convention for the Japs to gas us.' I tossed it over too. The replacements looked at me like I was nuts. Then Judd Stone threw his gas mask overboard. We laughed like hell until an amtrac fifty yards ahead of us took a direct hit. Blood sprayed everywhere and body parts went flying. Didn't seem too funny after that.

"The closer we got to shore the more bullets and shell fragments came whizzing over our heads. For the Japs, it was a shooting gallery. They had nine-inch cannons they'd roll out of their caves in the hills and shoot down on us. I'm talking nine inches in diameter. Those ain't peashooters. Shells hit all around us sending up geysers of water. You'd think we were in the middle of a school of whales if you didn't know better.

"By the time our amtrac rolled up onto the beach all hell had broken loose. Dead bodies were scattered everywhere—floating in the water, tumbling in the waves, scattered along the beach. A dozen or more amtracs, all twisted up and battered, were on fire, charred bodies scattered all around them. I grabbed my gear and jumped over the side. When I landed in the surf, I noticed the water was pink—tinted by all the blood. I took a deep breath and almost choked because of the damn phosphorous smoke that clouded the shoreline. My lungs felt like they were on fire.

"Lieutenant Baker yelled, 'Follow me!' and ran in the direction of the airfield. The brass had assigned my regiment, the Fifth Marines, the task of capturing that air strip on the first day so our fighter planes could land and take off there. After about fifty yards, Baker jumped into a long rut just beyond the beach and waited for everyone to catch up. Two guys had been hit. Smitty, a Texas boy, received a flesh wound on the neck. He'd be fine. But Wally Sinclair caught a bullet in the quad. Emery Snowfield, a hell of a soldier, backtracked to where Wally went down, grabbed him around the shoulders and dragged him over to us. Wally's leg bled like a busted pipe. Baker put a tourniquet on it and called for a corpsman. Poor Wally. He asked me to hold his hand. Over a hundred degrees in the shade and his hand felt cold as ice. I kept thinking, 'Hurry up, corpsman. Get here before Wally's a goner.' By the time medical aid arrived Wally had passed out.

"We thought we were safe, lying in that ditch about 150 yards from the airfield. Baker told us to spread out and wait until he got word to move forward. I couldn't see the enemy. They hid up in the hills in their caves and camouflaged positions. One of their mortar men must have got a good read on us. I heard that eerie whhssshhh uushhhh. Fast as I could I pressed myself flat on the ground and covered my head with my elbows. Kablam! It hit about ten yards away as pieces of shrapnel whistled right by my ears. Then came a terrible scream. The damn thing had landed right between the legs of Private Cornsilk, a Cherokee Indian from Oklahoma. Blew his lower half right off. Terrible thing to witness. He died within the minute.

"Lieutenant Baker hollered, 'They've got us pegged, boys. We've gotta move out.' I grabbed my gear and took off after Baker just as another whhssssshhh—uushhhh came sailing over our heads and then Kablam! Behind me I heard screaming. One of the replacements, I forget his name, caught some shrapnel in the back of his legs, but he still managed to hobble along. A couple of his buddies, Howard Kinloch and Ernie Myers, I think, went back to help him. Up ahead Baker jumped into this huge shell hole. It had to be thirty feet wide and twelve feet deep—perfectly symmetrical. Must have been made by a 1000-pound bomb dropped from one of our planes during the pre-invasion bombardment. Myers, Kinloch, and the injured soldier came tumbling down into the crater, and Baker called for another corpsman. Fifteen minutes into the battle and we already had four casualties—three wounded and one dead.

"We hunkered down for about an hour in that shell hole waiting for the enemy fire to subside. Just when it got quiet I heard whhssssshhh—uushhhh —three or four times. 'Oh hell,' I thought, 'Jap mortars coming our way again, ' and flattened myself against the ground. But the shells exploded on the other side of the airfield. Another round went off, and I realized a company of our mortar men had set up somewhere behind us, slinging those 81 millimeter rounds over our heads. I decided to crawl to the top of the crater and watch the fireworks. They were blowing the hell out of the hillside above the aeronautical building. Just then one of our boys fired a short round. The concussion knocked me clear down to the bottom of the shell hole. Three Judd Stones came scrambling down to see if I was okay. I shook my head and blinked him down to two, then one.

"Lieutenant Baker shouted, 'See, Wright! I told you to wear your damn helmet. You're lucky you still have that hard head of yours!' Then he laughed like hell. Everybody joined in, even me. I guess we were laughing in the face of death.

"With our mortar boys tossing rounds over our heads, keeping the Japs in their holes, Baker decided to move us to a small ridge that would provide a defilade just on this side of the airfield. Figured that'd be a great spot to prepare for a counter-attack later in the afternoon. He checked to make sure everyone was ready and gave us a minute to collect our gear.

"Baker ordered Stone and me to bring up the rear—to keep the stragglers moving and help any wounded. 'Stay low and move fast!' he hollered and then took off over the rim of the crater. Getting to his feet, Howard Kinloch trembled like a newborn colt trying to stand for the first time. The constant explosions had jolted his internal wiring. Judd and I grabbed him by the elbows and helped him to the top. Once there, he got his bearings and started to run. The kid was in big trouble. Our time in hell had just begun.

"Surprisingly, we all made it to the ridge without any casualties. From there, if you were brave enough to stick your head up, you could see the landing strips, barracks and aeronautical building on the other side. Beyond the buildings I could see the Umurbrogol Mountain, flaming and smoking like an old man's birthday cake. Being a rifle platoon, 'bout all we could do at that point was bide our time and try to stay alive. We couldn't see the enemy, so it didn't make sense to waste bullets. Sooner or later some officer would find an objective for us—taking out a machine gun nest or blowing up a well-protected bunker.

"About a half hour later we kept hearing explosions coming from the direction of Umurbrogol. Judd stuck his head up to watch the action. 'Oh shit,' he says, 'Lieutenant Baker, there's a lot of green and yellow smoke at the base of the mountain. It looks like it's drifting this way.''

"Baker stuck his head up, and his eyes got big as pies. He says, 'What the hell? That's gas. The Nips are using gas on us. Get your masks on, boys. Fast!' Everybody scrambled to find his container.

"Judd looked at me and says, 'Stanley, we tossed our masks into the ocean. You said we didn't need 'em.'

"I raised up and peeked over the ridge. Sure enough, that yellow cloud was drifting our way. 'I'll go find us a couple on the beach,' I said.

I must have been crazy. No way the Japs would use gas on us. Had to be one of those picric acid shells I'd heard about—they let off a greenish yellow smoke when they exploded. I took off zigzagging toward the beach, thinking any second I could step on a mine and be blown to kingdom come. Not only that, the Japs had declared an open season on crazy Marines, and there I was dodging bullets, shrapnel and bombs like some wild turkey fluttering through the woods the day before Thanksgiving.

When I got to the water's edge, I had no trouble finding mask containers—'bout every dead man had one. I turned over one Marine to get to the mask. All his intestines spilled out onto the sand. I gagged as I pulled the container out of the muck and decided to give that one to Judd. A few yards away I saw another hooked onto a dead Marine's belt. As I was unhooking it, a shower of machine gun bullets swept across the sand and out into the surf, sending up a long whip of splashes in the water. I dove beside the corpse and listened to the bullets whumping into it. 'Oh hell,' I thought. 'This was a big mistake.'

When the machinegun finally stopped, I jumped up and hightailed it back to my platoon. As I neared the ridge, I could see the yellow fog just about on us. I came sliding in against the ridge and tossed Judd the container. Everyone had his mask on except Howard Kinloch. His hands shook so violently he couldn't get the container open. He started to hyperventilate. Lieutenant Baker rushed over to him. By then I had popped open my container. 'What the hell?' I says. It was filled with yellow apples. The dead Marine I'd snatched it from didn't think the Japs would use gas either. Lieutenant Baker was having a hell of a time because Howie had passed out and rolled over. Just then that greenish-yellow fog blew over us. I waited for my eyes to burn and my sinuses to catch fire, but nothing happened. Just smoke from a picric acid shell like I figured.

"I glanced around at my buddies. They looked like giant insects from some Boris Karloff matinee. I reached into my container, pulled out a big yellow apple and took a bite. Damn it tasted good.

"Judd pulled his mask off and says, 'Give me one of them.' He reached over and grabbed a couple out of the container. Lieutenant Baker turned Howard over and slapped him a couple times until he came to. When Howard sat up, Judd threw an apple at him and says, 'A yellow apple for a yellow belly.'

"Lieutenant Baker gave Judd that you-just-keep-your-mouth-shut stare.

"Thinking back, that apple was the best thing I tasted on Peleliu."

Byron hit the stop button on the cassette player as he pulled into his parking place at the church. Stanley's description of the battle made Byron wonder if he could have handled the firestorm of that day's invasion. Would he have turned to jelly when the Japanese shells exploded all around the amtrac in the water? Could he have kept his head together on the beach surrounded by blood and gore? How would he have reacted when the yellow smoke drifted his way? He concluded he might never know. In order to answer those questions he'd have to step onto a battlefield. At forty-three, he'd never have to face that possibility.

Glancing across the lot he saw Mrs. Shaffer's blue Malibu. Her husband had died two months ago and she'd taken it very hard. To Byron, grief counseling was just as difficult as preaching a funeral. He felt he lacked the emotional depth and connection with people that an effective pastor needed. Perhaps growing up without a father had conditioned him to be more aloof, more clinical in his approach in dealing with the pain of others. For a doctor that would be acceptable, but for a pastor, he knew it was a weakness he had to improve on.

In his mind he reviewed the stages of grief Mrs. Shaffer was working through—denial, anger, bargaining, depression, and acceptance. She had entered the depression stage several weeks ago, and everything Byron had shared with her failed to help. Now he was at a loss. As he sat there, trying to think of a new approach, his chest tightened and his breathing became difficult. Byron wished he could take off on a seven-mile run and leave Mrs. Shaffer behind. He reached over to the passenger seat and grabbed the brown paper bag lunch Lila had prepared for him. When he opened the car door, the bag slipped from his fingers and plopped onto the floor of the car. He looked down and noticed a yellow apple had rolled out. *A yellow apple for a yellow belly.*

CHAPTER 10

The counseling session with Mrs. Shaffer went better than expected. Unable to think of a new angle to help her deal with depression, Byron offered very little advice. Instead, he opened by asking how she was doing and then sat back and listened for an hour. On the way out she thanked him for being so understanding. All he did was listen. Sometimes the simplest approaches were better than the seven-step plans. Mrs. Shaffer just wanted someone who cared to sit down with her and allow her to talk through her pain. If only all counseling sessions could go so smoothly.

The engaged couple canceled their hour session, which gave him more time for sermon preparation. Now that was his specialty—words, ideas, the discovering of higher truth. He spent two hours in the church library going over Bible commentary on the scriptures listed in this week's lectionary. Then came lunch—the usual turkey sandwich, carrots, Cheetos, and that yellow apple, which he ate last, remembering Stanley's gas mask story and Howard's humiliation.

After lunch he brought out the list of phone numbers for the Jeremiah Jacksons of Atlanta. He said a prayer for God's guidance, and started halfway down the list with Jeremiah J. Jackson—the one whose potential middle name was Josiah. After dialing the area code and number, he listened through five rings.

"Hello." It was a woman's voice, rich and mellow.

"Yes, my name's Byron Butler. I'm looking for a Jeremiah Jackson who is the son of Josiah Jackson."

"Son of Josiah Jackson?"

"Yes, ma'am."

"What's the purpose of this call?"

"Well, . . ." Byron cleared his throat as he considered his wording. " . . . I'm a Presbyterian minister in the Ohio Valley. Recently I've counseled a World War II veteran who knew Josiah. The veteran wanted to talk to Mr. Jackson about his father."

The mellow voice raised and octave. "Is that a fact?"

"Yes it is. Am I correct in assuming I've reached the right number?"

"Indeed you have, but you'll want to talk to my husband, J.J. I bet he'll be quite interested if you have some information about his father."

"Wonderful. Could I speak to him?"

"He's at the center, but you could call him there."

"The center?"

"Yes. J.J.'s the executive director of Atlanta's Center for Fatherless Teens."

After getting the contact information, Byron hung up, thinking miracles still happen. He'd found the right Jeremiah Jackson on the first try.

Byron called the Center, but J.J. was out at a fund-raising luncheon. Byron left his home phone number, the reason for the call, and asked for J.J. to call him that evening if at all possible. Now, he had to focus on preparing for a most unpleasant duty—his visit with the Wallers. He knew the sit-back-and-listen technique wouldn't work with Eric. Talking about the incident only reminded Eric of his irresponsible behavior which resulted in his friend's death. As Byron headed to the car, he started a mental review of the last book he'd read on dealing with loss and guilt, but his brain drew a blank. Eric's face kept appearing on the screen of his mind, a young face looking sullen and haggard.

Earl and Eric lived by themselves on a farm about fifteen minutes from the church along a dusty country road. Instead of listening to Stanley Wright's battle narrative, Byron scoured his memory for a personal illustration or anecdote or life trial that could bridge the gap between Eric and him. The closer he got to the Wallers, the tighter his chest became, as if a masochistic nurse had velcroed a huge blood pressure wrap around his torso and kept squeezing that hand pump.

Driving the final few hundred yards down County Road 16, the one Eric and Johnny had traveled on the day of the accident, he remembered a phone call. It had come during the middle of July before his junior year in college. At the time Byron had just gotten home from work, cutting grass on the athletic fields for the Martins Ferry Recreation Department.

He immediately recognized the voice, the captain of Pitt University's cross country team, Bruce Coglan. At first he assumed Bruce had called to check on his summer training—the coach insisted on ten or more miles a day. But Bruce's voice lacked its usual mettle. "Byron, I've got terrible news."

"What's wrong?"

"We've lost a teammate." Bruce's breathing sounded controlled—long, tense breaths between sentences. "Joel

Duncan wrecked his motorcycle . . . head on collision with a car."

"No." The word escaped Byron's mouth without forethought. It's departure left an aching void. "Joel's dead?"

As Bruce explained the circumstances of the accident, myriad images of Joel Duncan splashed across Byron's mind like a haphazard photo collage on a bulletin board. Joel playing cards. Joel scarfing down fries in the cafeteria. Joel shooting pool at the student union. Joel running, his lanky strides and that elbow that jutted slightly. Byron's legs became weak and he had to sit down. A young man he loved, a good kid with incredible potential was instantly gone. The funeral was scheduled for that Saturday in Joel's hometown of Nitro, West Virginia, but Byron couldn't raise the courage to face that finality. He spent the day by himself at the river with a cooler full of Budweiser, fishing, grieving, drinking.

The memory of Joel's death triggered a melancholy aching within. Perhaps sharing this story would establish common ground between him and Eric.

Byron pulled into the Waller's driveway and noticed a beat up Camero parked in front of the barn. Stepping out of the van, he glanced over his shoulder and watched the dust settle on the dirt road. Beyond he saw fence rails and the rolling field, newly plowed and planted, waiting for life to sprout.

Earl met him at the front door. "Glad you could make it, Pastor Byron. He's in an upbeat mood today."

Byron placed his hand on Earl's shoulder. "Great. Maybe we can get some talking done. Who does the Camero belong to?"

"Couple of Eric's buddies are here. Wouldn't hurt them a bit to listen to what you have to say."

When Byron entered the family room, Eric glanced up from the adjustable bed and smiled. Two teenage boys sat beside him, sharing an ottoman that sat in front of a big leather chair. Casts marked with colorful graffiti encompassed three of Eric's limbs. His right leg hung from a cable threaded through a pulley suspended above the bed. Propped on pillows, his left leg was covered in plaster from toe to knee. A support rod extended from the elbow of his arm cast to a brace strapped around his ribcage. Byron nodded and smiled.

One friend, tall and thin with long blond hair, wore a tank top and threadbare blue jeans. The other boy, shorter with bushy black sideburns and thick eyebrows, sported a tan cowboy hat.

Earl pulled a wooden chair next to the bed and motioned Byron to sit down. "Pastor Byron, I'd like you to meet Phillip and Eddie." Byron briefly shook each of the boys' hands.

"We don't call him Phillip," Eric said, lifting his good arm and pointing to the blond boy. "He's Weasel."

"I'll try to remember that," Byron said. "Why do they call you Weasel?"

"He looks like a weasel," Eddie said. He laughed and poked the tall boy's cheek.

"Naw. That's not it," Weasel said. "My last name's Wetsel. My buddies say I weasel out of everything, but that's not true. It's just my last name."

"Don't believe it, Reverend," Eddie said. "He weasels out of homework and chores and anything else he don't want to do."

"That's bullshit. Ooops. S-s-sorry, R-reverend. That just slipped out," Weasel stammered as he raised his hand to his mouth.

"No offense taken," Byron said.

"Hey, Pastor Byron, we been practicing a Charlie Daniel's song. Do you want to hear it?" Eric said, and his smile widened revealing two missing front teeth.

"Sure," Byron said. "I love Charlie Daniels. I didn't know you boys played instruments."

"Oh yeah." Eddie tilted his cowboy hat upward. "We can play any instrument as good as ol' Charlie."

"Me and Eddie are expert fiddlers," Weasel said.

Eric picked up a drumstick from the bed and pointed it at his father. "Hit it, Dad."

Grinning, Earl walked to the shelves near the front wall, reached above the television and selected the correct track on the CD player. Eric began to tap his drumstick on the bed rail and the speakers erupted with squealing fiddles. Bryon turned to see Eddie and Weasel holding invisible instruments, sawing their imaginary bows across the strings. Eric beat out the introductory rhythm as his friends, with perfect synch, executed the string intro.

Then Eric's expression turned solemn, and he raised the drumstick like a microphone to his mouth. With a whiskey-rough voice he spoke the first line of "The Devil Went Down to Georgia."

The music sent Eric into a euphoric state. The boy's eyes widened and nostrils flared. Byron felt the energy of the base and drums pounding through the speakers. As Eric spouted the lyrics, Byron sensed that strange spiritual lift that he sometimes experienced when singing a favorite hymn.

With incredible precision and enthusiasm, the boys orchestrated the song, Eric loudly delivering every word. When the fiddle duel between the devil and hero, Johnny, unfolded, Weasel and Eddie strutted to the middle of the room and clashed like two swashbucklers—Eddie taking the devil's role and Weasel, as Johnny, jabbing his invisible bow with abandon. Byron tapped his foot and clapped through the final crescendo. The two boys bowed, and Eric twirled his drumstick.

Earl rose and cut the power to the CD player as the next song began, and the teenagers booed.

"That's enough, guys. Pastor Byron came over here to do some serious talking, and it wouldn't hurt y'all to stick around and listen to what he has to say," Earl said.

Eddie snickered and winked at Weasel as Eric gazed at the drumstick in his hand.

"I don't mind listening to a preacher," Eddie said. "I go to church every Christmas and Easter."

"And you got a holy t-shirt to prove it," Weasel said as he poked his finger through a hole in Eddie's worn out *Confederate Railroad* shirt.

"You don't have to worry, boys. I didn't come to preach at you," Byron said. "Eric, I'm glad to see you've got a couple of good buddies to help you through these tough times."

"We've been friends since kindergarten," Eddie said. He reached out and tousled Eric's hair "You don't have to worry, Reverend. We'll get him back in the saddle."

"I'm sure he'll be up and around in no time," Byron said. "Eric, I just wanted to share with you that sometimes things like this happen to us in life. We ask God why, but there doesn't seem to be any answers."

Eric lowered his eyes and fingered the drumstick. Weasel and Eddie averted their gaze, and the room became uncomfortably quiet. In the silence Byron struggled to find the right words. "Some things have happened in my life I just don't understand. In college, one of my best friends got killed in a motorcycle accident. He was flying down a country road to see his girlfriend, came around a turn and hit a patch of gravel. The bike slid into the other lane and hit a car head on. Broke his neck and killed him instantly. It just happened. I asked God why, but I never got any answers."

With dark eyes Eric looked up. "But you didn't kill him."

"What?"

"You didn't kill your friend. I killed Johnny."

"Now Eric," Byron said, "you didn't mean to. Have you ever heard of something called survivor's guilt?"

Eric shook his head.

"People experience it when they survive a tragic accident in which others die. That's what you're feeling right now. You're wondering, why me?"

Eric tapped the drumstick against the mattress. He tried to talk, but his voice faltered, and he reached up and smudged a tear across his cheek.

"You didn't know that car would be coming the other way. That's a lonely crossroads. You didn't expect any traffic."

Eric swallowed and regained his voice. "But I went through the stop sign, Pastor Byron. I should have stopped. It's my fault."

"It was a mistake. We all make them," Byron said.

Eric shook his head and blinked.

"God can take the worst things that happen to us and somehow bring good from it. For some reason, God allowed you to live through that accident."

Eric glowered at Byron. "I wish I was dead."

"Don't say that!" his father barked. "I don't ever want to hear you say that again."

"It's true."

"Listen to me, Eric," Byron said. "If you were dead, then you would never discover God's purpose for allowing you to live."

"I don't care. Johnny's dead. What was his purpose? There ain't no purpose."

Byron felt flustered. *I don't know the answers to this kid's question. Why did God take one and not the other? What is the purpose?* Byron swallowed. "There's got to be a reason God allowed you to live. Make it your purpose to find that reason."

Weasel and Eddie sat quietly staring at their hands. Anger crept into Eric's face. He jammed the drumstick between the rail and the mattress and tried to break it.

"Don't do that," his father scolded. "Breaking that stick won't make you feel any better."

"No. That won't help," Byron said. "It's true, Eric. I can't say I know exactly how you feel. We both lost friends. Our circumstances were different. But I was eighteen years old once too. I remember what that feels like. When you're that young you do things without thinking. Sometimes you screw up, but God won't turn his back on you. Maybe I haven't learned all the answers to the tough questions in life, but I know God put me here for a reason. And there's a reason you lived through that accident."

"I still don't get it," muttered Eric. "I should have been the one who died. It was my fault. Why did God take Johnny and let me live? It doesn't make sense."

"Life doesn't always make sense. That doesn't mean you give up. You've got a long life ahead of you. Make the most of it. Maybe one day it will make sense." Byron reached out and touched his shoulder.

With his good arm, Eric pushed himself away from Byron's reach and stared at the wall. "I'm tired," he said. "I want to get some sleep."

"Can I pray with you before I leave?" Byron asked.

Eric shrugged.

Byron glanced at Weasel and Eddie. "Do you boys want to join us?"

They looked at each other and nodded. Byron reached out and grasped Eddie's hand. He sensed Eric's embarrassment over involving his friends in the prayer, but Byron felt compelled to do his duty—offer some kind of spiritual comfort. Reaching out with his other hand, he touched Eric's head as Weasel and Earl joined the circle. Byron's prayer rambled awkwardly with interspersed moments of self-conscious silence. He felt helpless in trying to pray the right words to offer hope to this kid. After the amen, he told Eric to hang in there and thanked the two boys for joining them.

As Earl walked him to the front door, Byron wondered if Earl was disappointed. *I'm only a man, not a miracle worker. Just because I marry, bury, baptize and preach a sermon every Sunday doesn't mean I have all the answers.* Earl lifted Byron's jacket from a row of hooks near the front door and handed it to him.

Bryon took the jacket. "I'm sorry, Earl. I know I didn't help much. I just didn't know what to say."

"You did what you could. The boy has a wild streak. When my wife and I broke up a few years back, we babied him too much and he got worse. He'd spend a couple weeks with Barbara in the summer doing whatever he wanted. When he'd come home, I'd try to keep him happy—she gets him a new trail bike, so I put out the cash for this ATV—a helluva mistake on my part. I blame myself more than anybody else."

Byron looked at Earl's face. He had curly-brown hair, tinged with gray about the ears. In his late forties, his skin was tanned and wrinkled from riding a tractor in the blaze of the afternoon sun, and the dark circles below his eyes sagged, adding greater depth to the sadness of his features.

Byron placed his hand on Earl's shoulder and looked at the floor. "I have to make a confession, Earl," Byron said.

"A confession? What're you talking about?"

Byron kept staring at the floor, not willing to meet Earl's gaze. "I'm not too good at this sort of thing."

"Whadaya mean?"

"You know." Byron finally looked up. "Trying to make sense of all the bad things that happen in life. I'm better at preaching a sermon than talking with people who are hurting."

"You shouldn't feel that way," Earl said. "It's not your fault all this happened. You're just doing your best to help out."

Byron shrugged. "The problem is my best hasn't helped much."

Earl slapped Byron on the shoulder. "Bullshit, preacher. You've helped more than you know."

Byron glanced down, then up again. "Thanks, Earl. If there's anything else I can do, just give a call."

Earl nodded, his eyes glazing over. "I'm just worried about what Eric'll do once he gets out of his casts. I'm gonna hide all my medicines and guns."

"Do you think he's suicidal?"

"I hope he's just spouting off, but he keeps wishing he was dead."

"I'll come out and talk to him again in a few days. You ought to get in touch with a psychologist."

Earl shook his head and stared at the ceiling. "Already have. He came yesterday. Those guys shovel up a load of crap and charge you by the minute."

"It's not an exact science, but some are pretty good at it."

"Maybe I'm just a skeptic, but you did more good in ten minutes than that psycho-snooper did in an hour." Earl held out his hand, and Byron grasped it. "We'll see ya in a few days, Pastor."

"Thanks, Earl. I'll keep you and Eric in my prayers."

* * *

Driving to Wheeling Medical Park, Byron intended to listen to the rest of Stanley Wright's story of the Battle of Peleliu, but Earl's revelation had left him unsettled: *He keeps wishing he was dead.* Was Eric about to give up on life? He was only sixteen years old for God's sake. To what kind of dark and desperate place had the boy sunk? Did Earl expect Byron to go there like some hero and say the magic words, reach down with a strong arm, heave the boy onto his back, and carry him out of danger? Byron doubted his spiritual arms were strong enough. Hell, he didn't even want to go there—to that battleground where Death crooks his bony finger to those he has seduced and says, "Follow me." And if Byron did venture there, would Eric even be willing to take his hand?

Then it occurred to Byron that Judd Stone was reaching out his hand from that dark place. Whether Byron liked it or not, he was a spiritual corpsman, treading on battlefields.

CHAPTER 11

The afternoon sun slanted its rays through the hospital blinds striping the room with light and shadow. Stone, his bed propped at a slight angle, slept, his breaths staggered and irregular. Suspended from the ceiling, a television emitted scenes of a lovers' feud on the *Maury Povich Show*, with Maury in the midst commenting above the accusations and screams. Byron reached up and pressed the power button, and the screen darkened. The silence seemed to trip up Stone's slumber. He snorted twice and opened his eyes.

"Good afternoon, General. Hope I didn't interrupt a pleasant dream."

"Don't have pleasant dreams anymore." His voice sounded raspy and weak. He reached for a plastic cup on the bed stand, raised it to his lips, and gulped water, trickles escaping at the corners of his mouth. With a drenched throat, his words came easier. "Only nightmares. Or I should say 'nightmare.' The same one over and over."

Byron slid a padded chair next to the bed and sat down. "Is the dream . . . I mean the nightmare . . . about the battle? About Josiah Jackson?"

Stone nodded. "Did you get a hold of his boy?"

"I talked to his son's wife. His name is Jeremiah. He's the director of the Center for Fatherless Teens in Atlanta."

Stone shifted his gaze to the window. The ribbing of light and shadow patterned his face and chest. "He helps fatherless teens? That's good. I was hoping he wasn't all screwed up—an alcoholic or jailbird."

"No. Sounds like a good man. I called the Center, but he wasn't there. Out on some kind of fundraising mission. I told his secretary to have him call me tonight."

"When you talk to him, tell him I want to see him. Face to face."

"Why, General? Why should he fly clear up here from Atlanta to talk to you?"

Stone coughed several times and took another drink of water. "I need to tell him something about his father."

"What happened during the Battle of Peleliu? When did you and Josiah Jackson cross paths there?"

Stone took a long, slow breath. "The first time I saw Jackson on Peleliu was during the first day of the battle near the airfield. We expected a counterattack. It came late in the afternoon. I heard someone yell, 'Here they come!' A Nippon tank poked its ugly nose through the dust and crossed the airfield. Talk about piss-poor engineering. The thing looked like a Cracker Jack box with treads. Out from behind a bunker came another. Within a few seconds ten or twelve of them busted loose from their hiding places and made a charge to break through our line around the perimeter of the airfield.

"We let everything fly—small arms, machine guns, bazookas. Lucky for us, several of our Sherman tanks just arrived on the scene. Three of them moved up and started blasting away. Their tanks crisscrossed and circled the field like wind-up toys. One of 'em broke through the line on the right and ran over top a machine gun pit. The Nip tank caught hell then. Everyone took a shot at it. It burst into flames and rolled toward the beach. A Jap dropped out of the trap door on the bottom, but the sonovabitch didn't last long. Everybody in my squad claimed they killed him."

Stone took a labored breath, cleared his throat, grabbed the cup, and took another sip of water. When his breathing slowed, he continued. "One of our Shermans moved right into the middle of the fight. It fired high-explosive shells. You could tell because they didn't pierce through that thin Japanese armor but blew up on impact. The crew was skilled as hell. Must have destroyed six or seven Nip tanks before they took a direct hit. Flames shot up and smoke poured into the sky.

"Then the top of the Sherman popped open and a Marine climbed out. Damnedest thing I ever saw. His foot was a bloody stump. But somehow he ran on it forty or fifty yards to our side of the ridge. You'd be amazed what a man can do to save himself. I asked him his name. He gritted his teeth and said, 'Bobby Lee from Gainesville, Georgia.' Had to be in a lot of pain. I told him to hang in there and we'd get him some help. I yelled for a corpsman and then pulled a handkerchief out of my pocket to try to stop the bleeding. Damn thing was soaked with sweat, but I did my best to apply pressure with it.

"A few minutes later Lieutenant Baker crawled over to check him out. By then the poor guy had went into shock with all the blood loss. Baker called for stretcher-bearers to get him outta there quick. That's when I saw Jackson again. He wasn't on the kitchen crew anymore. Guess he wanted a taste of battle from the front line instead of the chow line. He and another colored boy came running across the sand and carrying their stretcher between them.

"I said, 'Hey, Jackson. Take care of that soldier. He's a Georgia boy just like you.'

"He gave me the dirtiest look. Guess he saw the watch. I was wearing it for good luck. As he and his partner lifted Bobby Lee onto the stretcher, he glanced over his shoulder and said, 'What's right is right and what's fair is fair.'

"I said, 'That's right, Jackson.'

"'Wait and see,' he said. 'Wait and see.'

"Over the years I've thought about those three words— *wait and see.* At the time I thought he figured I'd get killed on that island. You know what I mean? Wait and see. You'll find out what's right and fair. But now that I'm old and weak, now that I've got both feet and one arm in the grave, I know exactly what he meant."

Stone leaned forward, turned his head, and met Byron's stare. In the slatted light his head resembled a skull with eyes. "What do you think he meant, General?" Byron asked.

His voice rumbled low and solemn, "Wait and see, Judd Stone. Your judgment day will come."

Byron's lower back tightened as if someone had splashed a cup of cold water on him. *That day comes for all of us sooner or later.* Stone lay back and stared at the ceiling. "Was that the last time you saw him on Peleliu?" Byron asked.

Stone shook his head sideways. "We met one more time." He coughed again, this time his body wracking convulsively. When he finally stopped, he had difficulty catching his breath. "I'm tired. I need to rest. Yesterday's chemo was tough."

Byron stood and leaned on the bed railing. "I'll stop back soon."

Stone reached and gripped his wrist. "Please . . . bring Jackson's son with you."

* * *

Byron pulled onto Interstate 70 and drove toward the Wheeling Tunnel as Stanley Wright, from the minivan's speakers, narrated his version of the Japanese tank counter attack. "The boy's name was Bobby Edward Lee. That's a hell of an ironic thing, ain't it? Robert E. Lee driving a Sherman tank. That's like Abe Lincoln whistling Dixie. Sherman sure knew what he was talking about, though—'War *is* hell.' We proved it on Peleliu.

"As soon as the stretcher bearers hauled Lee away, the Japanese infantry decided to make a banzai charge. Were they crazy? Didn't they see what we just did to their tanks? Must have been at least four squads appeared like ghosts out of the smoke and dust on the airfield, shooting their rifles and Nambu pistols, swinging their swords, screaming like banshees. It didn't take us long to turn them into real ghosts. In less than two minutes, eighty or ninety of the Emperor's finest bowed down to American bullets. I glanced around the perimeter of the line to see the smoking barrels of hundreds of M1s.

"Then things got quiet. On the airfield, anyway. To our left Chesty Puller's First Regiment was still blasting Umurbrogol. Had to be 110 degrees in the shade—and there wasn't much shade left after the Navy blew the trees all to hell. The smoke slowly drifted east toward the mangrove swamp. On the airstrip the twisted hulks of the Jap tanks smoked and burned between us and the buildings. From a big hole in the tank nearest me, an arm hung down. Dead bodies littered the ground, and the smell of cordite and charred flesh stunk up the air. It was something to see.

"I turned onto my back and grabbed my canteen. Two gulps was all that was left. I'd drained most of it during the heat of the day. Those two gulps did jack squat to ease my thirst. I tried to bum a swig or two, but everyone was dry. Then Judd Stone asked Lieutenant Baker if he could gather up some canteens and head over to the aeronautical buildings to look for water. Said he'd use the burned-out tanks for cover. Baker was impressed and started to gather up canteens for him.

"I pulled Judd aside and says, 'Are you Asiatic? You're gonna cross the airfield just to get us some water?'

"'Listen,' he says. 'We just destroyed the squads assigned to guard the airfield. It'll be a while before they send more troops our way. Now's my chance to look for souvenirs in those buildings before anyone else gets there.'

"Good ol' Judd. The wheels were always turning in that warped mind. So Baker looped the straps of a dozen or so canteens around Judd's neck. Judd handed me his rifle. Said it would just slow him down. Then he slid his watch off his wrist and turned to Ernie Myers. He says, 'Myers, you're from out West like me. If some Jap gets lucky and blows my head off, promise me you'll get this watch to my old man in Jackson Hole, Wyoming.'

"Now Myers was a replacement. Nervous as hell on the first day of battle but still a good man. He'd do anything you'd ask him. He nodded and put Judd's watch on his wrist. 'I'll make sure he gets it,' he says. 'My Uncle Clem lives up that way.' Then off Judd went, running low and crouching from tank to tank. He crossed the field without a hitch and disappeared into the closest building.

"In the meantime, some Italian from Charlie Company, a real hairy son of a bitch named Sabatini, came stumbling by with an armful of canteens and water dripping from them. Lieutenant Baker stopped him and asked where he got the 'acqua'. Sabatini pointed south and told him that a couple hundred yards down the beach the bottom of a huge shell hole filled up with water. 'You better hurry,' Sabitini says, "'Fore anybody else finds it.'

"Baker gathered up the rest of the canteens and told Ernie Myers to head south to see if he could find that shell hole, just in case Stone came up empty. Myers didn't look too happy about it, but like I said, he'd do anything for you.

"'Bout ten minutes later Judd came zigzagging across the field carrying a small box and jumping over those dead Japs like Red Grange returning a kickoff for a touchdown. He hopped over to our side of the ridge with a big smile on his face.

"'Did you find water?' Baker asks.

"'Stone slipped the straps over his head, dumping the canteens onto the ground and says, 'Hell yeah, Lieutenant. All filled up. But look here. I hit the jackpot.' He opened the box and pulled out a Japanese flag about the size of a bank calendar. It had a red ball in the middle against a white field— the kind you find on dead Nip soldiers. You'd think Judd was Santy Claus on Christmas morn' the way he passed them out to everyone in our squad. Then from the bottom of the box he pulled this huge Regimental flag, the kind with red rays extending from the circle. Now those are rare. With everybody admiring that one, he reached into the box and pulled out another one. Two damn Japanese Regimental flags. Lucky bastard. Said he was gonna give one to Major Gayle and keep one for himself.

"Then he asked where the hell Myers was. I told him Baker sent Myers down along the beach to a big shell hole where Charley Company found some water. At the time Judd didn't seem too concerned, just glanced in that direction. More than ten minutes went by and Judd got antsy. He says to Baker, 'I'm gonna go look for Myers.'

"Not much was happening at that time. Just hunkering down along that ridge waiting for further instructions. Baker says, 'Take Wright with you. It's only about two hundred yards from here. Get down there and get back quick as you can.'

"Shit. I didn't want to go traipsing along the beach again, but what the hell. Can't disobey orders. I knew it was all because of that damn watch. We kept low, moving as fast as we could. Since all the Leathernecks were ashore, the Japs weren't lobbing shells at the beach any more. That was all right with me.

"When we got to the shell hole we saw six Marines filling canteens. None of them was Myers. 'Hey you bunch of eight balls,' Judd yells. They all looked up. Didn't recognize any of them. 'We sent a boy this way 'bout twenty minutes ago to fetch water. His name was Myers. You see him?'

"One of them capped his canteen and climbed up the side of the crater about halfway to where we stood. His face was filthy with lighter streaks where sweat dripped down. I remember looking at his expression and thinking, Oh hell. He's got bad news. He says, 'A fellow come from the direction of the airfield just as I was getting' here. Wasn't more than thirty yards ahead of me. Stepped on a mine.' He pulled on the bottom of his blouse and held it up. 'That's his blood. Splattered all over me. Damn mine blew him to smithereens. Couple nigger boys come by here with a stretcher 'bout ten minutes ago, picking up the pieces. Wasn't much left of him.'

"'Gadammit to hell!' Judd says. 'Did anybody find a gold watch?'

"'A watch?' the guy says. 'Hell, they were lucky to find his head.'"

CHAPTER 12

Byron dumped a load of mashed potatoes on his plate. "How was ball practice today, boys?" The aroma of fried pork chops, buttered corn, and fresh-baked bread permeated the kitchen.

Mark and Matt, mouths chomping away, glanced up, grunted and nodded. After taking a long drink of milk, Matt said, "I'll be pitching again on Saturday, Dad. You coming?"

"Sure. Wouldn't miss it." Byron knifed a slab of butter from the end of the stick and shook it onto the mound of potatoes.

"How's Eric Waller doing?" Lila asked.

"Earl's worried about him. You know. He blames himself for everything."

Mark swallowed, swiped his mouth with a napkin and said, "It *was* all his fault, wasn't it?"

Byron eyed Mark, sensing slight hostility in his tone. " The lion's share of the responsibility belongs to Eric, but he's not the only one at fault here."

"Why not?" Mark asked.

"Because it's not that simple, Mark. Life isn't always black and white. His parents raised him, right?"

Mark nodded.

"Well, the decisions you make as a sixteen-year-old boy have been greatly influenced by the kind of job your mom and dad did bringing you up."

"You don't think Mr. Waller did a good job?" Matt asked.

"Now I didn't say that, did I? Earl's a single father doing the best he can. He and Barbara had marital problems for years before they split up. That kind of environment can mess with a kid's mind. Once they divorced, it became a competition for Eric's love. That's never good because all that taught Eric was how to manipulate them. How do you think he ended up with the ATV in the first place? Mom buys him a dirt bike, so Dad buys him a four-wheeler."

"Still, Dad," Mark said, "his parents weren't at the wheel when he went cruising through that stop sign."

"Not directly, maybe, but indirectly, they were. And there's something else to consider. Johnny Owens may be partly to blame."

"Johnny Owens?" Matt said. "How could that be? Johnny Owens got killed."

"Do you guys hang out with Eric?" Byron asked.

The boys swiveled their heads sideways.

"Why not?"

"He's a redneck and we're jocks," Mark said.

"That's not the real reason," Byron said. "You guys have known Eric for years, right?"

"Right," they both said.

"But you never have felt comfortable around him. Why not?"

"Because he's a wild man, a psycho," Mark said. "You never know what a guy like that is gonna do."

"Exactly. But Johnny knew what Eric was like. In fact, Johnny and Eric were two ears from the same cornstalk. Both of them were a little crazy. When Johnny climbed onto the back of that ATV, he knew that Eric didn't follow the rules."

The boys sat quietly, expressions softening at their father's logic.

"But there's another person to blame too," Byron continued.

"Who?" Matt asked.

Byron poked himself in the chest with his forefinger. "I'm Eric's pastor. I should have been a better spiritual influence. Somewhere along the line I dropped the ball."

At that statement, Lila dropped her fork. "Don't be ridiculous, Byron. You surely can't be blaming yourself for what happened to Johnny Owens? As a pastor you can only do so much."

"That's my problem, Lila. Sometimes I only do so much."

"What happened, happened," Lila said. "Now all you can do is help Eric and Earl pick up the pieces. Just make sure you're there for them. Maybe stop by tomorrow and see him again."

Byron took a deep breath, let it out, and then nodded. "Good idea. I think I will."

The conversation returned to baseball as Byron toyed with his food. When he stood to get a second cup of coffee, the phone rang. Matt sprang from his seat and cut in front of Byron to answer it. Byron glanced at Mark, raising his eyebrows, and Mark said, "Tabitha Russell—Matt's new flame."

Byron grinned and winked, but Matt announced, "It's for you, Dad."

"Who is it?" Byron asked.

"J.J. Jackson, from Atlanta."

"I'll take it in my study," Byron said and rushed toward the stairs.

* * *

Byron lifted the receiver off the phone on his desk and said, "I've got it, Mark. You can hang up." Upon hearing the click Byron introduced himself.

He expected a strong accent but the man's deep voice carried only a slight Southern flavor. "J.J. Jackson, here. Just returning your call—something about my father, right?"

"Yes, Mr. Jackson. I've been counseling a man who knew your father. An old Marine."

The pace of Jackson's words accelerated slightly. "Someone who knew my father. Yes. That's great. I'm very interested. Did you say an old Marine? My father was in the First Marine Division."

"Yes, I know. This man who knew him, Judd Stone, wanted me to contact you. He believes he has something important to tell you about your father."

"Really? That's great. I'm all ears. Over the last few years I've become interested in learning more about my father's war experiences. Been reading a lot of World War II history, especially the Pacific Theater. How do I contact him?"

"Well . . ." Byron cleared his throat and swallowed. "Mr. Stone would really like to see you in person."

"In person . . .ummm. You're up in Ohio, right?"

"Yes. I told Mr. Stone that's a long way to travel—clear from Atlanta, but he insisted he had something important to tell you."

"Can you give me some background? What has Mr. Stone said to you about my father?"

Byron considered how much he should reveal. This was Judd Stone's confession, not his. Should he hit Jackson with the shocker that Stone may have caused his father serious harm? How could he say something like that when he wasn't one hundred percent sure? Because he wasn't certain, Byron decided to play it conservatively. "Your father and Judd Stone first met as opponents in a boxing match."

"Oh yes!" Jackson's voice soared. "That was in one of his letters. I've read all the war letters my father sent to Momma. She's got them in a shoebox at home. My father claimed he won the First Marine Division Championship and had a watch to give me when he returned from the war. Do you know anything about that?"

Byron hesitated, quickly assessing what he knew to be true to that point. "From what I understand your father won that watch fair and square."

"I knew it! Momma said the watch never arrived with the rest of his belongings after he got killed, but I knew he was telling the truth. Did this man, Stone, and my father become friends?"

"Not exactly, but I would rather Mr. Stone tell you in his own words about his relationship with your father. He hasn't told me everything. I don't want to start a story I can't finish."

"Well, you've got my curiosity stirred up. I'm fairly busy right now with fundraising projects, but by early summer, I should be able to find some free time to fly up there."

"That may be too late, Mr. Jackson. Mr. Stone is dying of cancer."

"Oh, I see. Well . . . maybe I can schedule a flight for Saturday morning. Is there an airport nearby?"

"Pittsburgh is about an hour away. I'll pick you up if you can swing it." After saying the words, Byron remembered the boys' baseball game and cringed.

"I'll get back to you tomorrow on this and let you know for sure," J.J. said.

After exchanging a few parting words and hanging up, Byron questioned his priorities. Even before tying the knot with Lila, he had determined he'd be there for his kids. No father had tossed baseball in the backyard with Byron or signed him up for Little League. His mother never married and refused to reveal the identity of his father until it was too late, after the man had died. Byron pledged to himself that his family would be different. He hadn't missed a baseball game all season. Would just one matter? He inhaled deeply and blew the air out through pursed lips. *Just take it one day at a time. Don't get so stressed about something that may not even happen.*

He turned to Helen's box and lifted it from the desk onto his lap. As he withdrew the next letter from the yet-to-read pile he noticed a Ziplock bag containing a white cloth at the bottom of the box underneath old newspaper clippings and a few ribbons and medals. Remembering Judd's quest to find souvenirs in the buildings on the other side of the airfield, he pinched the corner of the bag and extracted it. After setting the box on the desk, he held it to the light on his desk and noticed splotches of red beneath the folds. *The Japanese flag. Judd even gave one to Howard.* He peeled open the plastic seam and pulled out the cloth.

Holding the corners and letting it fall into his lap, Byron estimated it to be about two feet by three feet. As expected, the large red circle dotted the middle, but more faded shades of red, slightly darker, splattered the bottom half. Byron tilted the reading lamp to expose the cloth to direct light. *Blood? It has to be blood. But whose?* He carefully draped it over the file cabinet next to his desk as if it was a revered religious object—something fraught with symbolic meaning. *Someone bled all over this flag for his country. For something bigger than himself.* Byron wondered if there was anything *he* would be willing to die for. His wife? His kids? Yes. But would he die for freedom?

Slowly he turned from the flag and picked up the letter. It was only two pages long. Usually Helen and Howard had exchanged four or five-page letters. He began reading Helen's side.

My Darling Howie,

Life has been unbearable lately. How much longer will this war go on? I feel lower than low. Forgive me, Darling, for the depressing mood of this letter, but I am extremely blue. How did you and I, two people so in love, get caught up in this whirlpool that has swept away so many lives. As the days slip by, I feel like we are being robbed of the most precious thing we can share—time. Time that we can never get back.

The can factory is driving me loopier than a loon. For hours I go through the same motions—lift the same boxes, press the same buttons, hear the same noises, and see the same faces. I try to think about you, but then I worry that you are in danger. My nerves are getting frayed, but how can I complain? You are the one in harm's way. You are the one facing bullets and bombs. Please forgive me, Howie, but there's no other shoulder to cry on. And for the last two hours I have sat in this empty house and boo-hooed. Tears are dripping down my cheeks and staining the stationery as I write this letter.

The worst thought that comes to me is that something bad will happen to you. It sneaks up from behind, grabs me when I least expect it, wraps its scaly arms around me, and squeezes until I think I'm going to die. I know it's just nerves. Perhaps I should see Doc Wiant and get some pills. I've never taken nerve medicine before. Am I becoming unstable? I wish you were here to tell me what to do. But if you were here, I wouldn't be going crazy.

There, I've poured out my heart. Forgive me for putting this burden on you, when I know you are dealing with so many hardships. You are such a good man, Howie, always helping those who are facing difficulties. I have been praying for your friend, Josiah. Please don't feel bad that you did not rush to his rescue. You had every reason to believe that those two bullies meant him great harm and would have gone after you. Anyone in your shoes would have thought the same thing.

By the time this letter reaches Peleliu, you may have faced your first battle. I have asked God to help you be brave, strong, but most of all, careful. I'm including a Bible and some cookies in this package. I hope it makes it halfway around the world before the cookies become stale. Whenever you need spiritual strength, read your Bible. That's what my grandmother always told me. You must be thinking I need to take my own advice after seeing the first few paragraphs of this letter. Well, I have been reading it more often lately. Here's the verse that caught my attention today:

Psalm 23:4 Yea, though I walk through the valley of the shadow of death, I will fear no evil: for Thou art with me; Thy rod and Thy staff, they comfort me.

You and I are both walking through that valley. Although we are on separate sides of the world, we can walk it together. If you'll be brave for me, I'll be brave for you.

Write me as soon as you get the chance, Howie. Reading your words does more for my sad heart than anything in this world.

I love you more than I could ever express,
Helen

Byron held the letter up to the light and detected several small spots, not perfectly round, slightly darker than the shade of the paper. *Helen's teardrops.* The sheets took on a psychological weight, words and tears poured out onto paper from a heavy heart. He carefully turned the pages over and read Howard's reply.

Dearest Helen,

I feel lucky to be alive. I've been through ten straight days of hell. At times it seemed worse than hell. The general in charge of this whole operation finally called in the army to give the Marines some relief. I feel sorry for those dogfaces. They replaced our First Regiment, which suffered unbelievable casualties in their attack on Mount Umurbrogol. Helen, please pray my regiment won't be sent up on those ridges to relieve the army. It's a suicide mission.

This afternoon was the first time since we came ashore that we had a mail call. I got three letters and a package from you. I feel like I died and went to heaven. I'll try to crowd as many words as I can on each of these pages and send them back in three separate envelopes.

The cookies were delicious, even though a little stale. It was like eating gourmet food compared to my usual K-rations. I wish I could have shared them with my two best buddies, Tyler Fredrick and Ernie Myers. On the first day of battle a Japanese mortar shell sent a bunch of shrapnel into the back of Tyler's legs. Yours truly and Ernie Myers helped carry him to the nearest shell hole where a corpsman patched him up as best he could. Not long after that some stretcher-bearers arrived and hauled him away. Last I heard he was transported to a hospital ship. Maybe he got the million-dollar wound—one bad enough to get him out of the war but not make him permanently handicapped.

Ernie wasn't so lucky. Lieutenant Baker sent him down the beach to find water for our squad. On the way he stepped on a mine and was blown to bits. I've known Ernie since boot camp. He was one of my few friends on this island. In the last ten days almost half the men in my platoon have been killed or wounded. I've witnessed so many horrible things. Why have I been spared? I don't deserve to be alive when all these other good men have died. The only thing I can figure is your prayers are getting through. Keep praying for me, Helen, and I'll keep praying for you. Sounds like we are both at the end of our fishing lines. Let's hope they don't snap. You can probably tell that I'm a bundle of nerves if you look closely at my penmanship. It's pretty shaky.

By the way, thanks for the Bible. As soon as I got it I opened it randomly and read a chapter. Sometimes God speaks to me that way. The verse that stood out was Matthew 5:44: "But I say unto you, love your enemies, bless them that curse you, do good to them that hate you, and pray for them which despitefully use you, and persecute you."

I haven't killed my enemy yet, Helen. Does that make me a coward or a saint? Several days into the battle, we got orders to attack pillboxes and machinegun pits on the eastern side of the island. Word got to us that the enemy had organized a counter attack from out of the jungle near the swamp. When a squad of Japanese soldiers crossed an opening in front of us, my platoon opened fire. Judd Stone noticed I purposely shot my rifle too high. After the smoke cleared, he slapped me and cursed me. He said because I wasn't willing to kill the enemy, more Marines would die. He's probably right. What am I going to do? I'm damned if I kill and damned if I don't.

I'm running out of space on this paper, but I'll try to fit in this last story about someone you've been praying for—my friend, Josiah Jackson. Coming back from breakfast this morning, I ran into him. He has survived the battle so far, even though he risks his life daily as a stretcher-bearer. Because of his bravery, many men have been saved. Here's the amazing thing—I noticed he was wearing the golden watch, the one Stone and Wright took from him at the cave. I asked him how he got hold of it. He told me Stone stepped on a mine and got blown to pieces. One of those pieces was an arm. The watch was still on the wrist so he took it just like he said he would if he ever found Stone's corpse on the battlefield.

I had to tell him—Stone gave his watch for safekeeping to Ernie Myers while Stone crossed the airfield to look for souvenirs. Myers stepped on that mine. Josiah just shook his head and said, "Finders keepers. What's right is right and what's fair is fair." I had to agree with him.

I plan on opening your next letter in a few minutes. I'll write more on the back of those pages.

Your loving husband,
Howie

CHAPTER 13

Byron spent most of the morning writing his sermon, but decided to make a brief stop at the Wallers before lunch. Rarely did he pay a ministerial visit to the same person two days in a row, but Eric's mental state warranted an exception. Even if he only stayed ten minutes to say hello, offer a listening ear and encouragement to keep hanging in there, at least he could show the boy he cared. Enough people caring may be the lifeline Eric needed to pull him from the deep waters of self-condemnation.

Byron expected a call from J.J. Jackson sometime that day. He hoped J.J. would be able to fly in on Saturday and meet with Stone. Many questions probably wouldn't be answered unless that meeting took place. Knowing Josiah retrieved the watch spurred Byron's curiosity about the events between the first day of battle and Judd Stone's final encounter with him. Was there a fight over the watch? Did Stone kill him in cold blood? Or was it self-defense? Perhaps Stone didn't have anything to do with Josiah's death. Byron wanted to glean as much information as possible from Stanley Wright's account of the battle before talking to Stone or J.J. again. As he pulled out of the driveway and headed to the Wallers, he hit the play button on the Caravan's tape player.

Wright continued the story. "Shortly after the counter attack, Baker moved our platoon from the ridge in front of the airfield to the edge of the jungle beyond the end of the longest runway. He figured what was left of the undergrowth would provide some cover as we dug in for the night. He knew what was coming—infiltrators. Those Bushido bastards were crazy. They prided themselves in their skill swinging a samurai sword. Like panthers on the prowl, they'd creep down from the hills at night. In each foxhole the man on guard had to listen to every sound and watch for any movement. Fall asleep for a few seconds and you just may hear a "swooooosh." If you do, don't turn your head too fast or it might fall off. That's why the officers always issued passwords with lots of L's like 'Lily liver.' The Japs had a hard time with that letter. They'd say 'Riry River.' Then we'd fire off a clip of 30.06s right through their lily livers.

"During the first night on Peleliu the password was Lollypop Land. Believe me, the place didn't resemble the password. It looked more like the Devil's garbage dump with all the wrecked vehicles and dead bodies. Ships offshore fired flares all night long so we could see the surroundings. The flares floated down on small parachutes, swinging back and forth. Their spooky green lights cast jumpy shadows. It reminded me of walking through the funhouse at the county fair as a kid—every other step something would pop out at you. On my watch I did my best to listen to every sound and watch the shadows. It was the creepiest night of my life. I could have sworn I saw a samurai warrior peeking out behind every bush.

"Not far away, maybe thirty or forty yards, I heard a soldier call for the password. No answer. That made the hair on the back of my neck stand up. He called for it again. Someone yelled, 'Don't shoot! Don't shoot! I'm a Marine.' Lucky for him they recognized his voice. Found out the next day it was Sausage Kirby, some halfwit in Dog Company. He crawled out of the hole to take a crap and forgot the password.

114

The soldier on watch came within a nose hair of blowing Sausage's head off.

"About halfway through the night a replacement in our platoon lost his mind. Started crying for his Mother— 'Mommy, Mommy, Mommy, I want my Mommy!' Lieutenant Baker kept telling him to shut up because he was giving away our position. Finally someone hit him in the back of the head with an entrenching tool. That shut him up.

"With all the calamity going on, I got no sleep that night. When Judd Stone took over the watch, I lay in the bottom of that foxhole and stared at the stars, wide awake. Damn, I thought. I wish I was back in Shutter's field looking up at those same stars. Back when I was sixteen, I stayed with the Shutters several weeks during the summer and helped them harvest strawberries. I was the best damn strawberry picker in Belmont County. Isn't that a helluva thing to think about while you're lying at the bottom of a foxhole? Strawberries. Seeing those stars so far away made me wish I was far away.

"On day two of the battle everyone in my platoon wished they were far away from Peleliu. The brass ordered our regiment to cross that wide-open airfield in broad daylight and establish the front line on the other side at the fringe of the jungle. By mid-morning it felt like a blast furnace. Waves of heat rose up from the field making the buildings and mountain ridges look like they were melting. The Japs knew we were coming. They sat up in the hills with their mortars and cannons concentrated on the airfield, waiting for us to cross. I doubt if the replacements knew what to expect, but we vets did—absolute chaos. Earlier that morning I took a helmet off a dead Marine. Had to admit it—Lieutenant Baker was right. I didn't want to cross that field without one. I was hardheaded, but I wasn't stupid.

"Lying in that ditch, waiting for the command, I felt a knot form in my chest big as a grapefruit. Then some captain down the line yells, 'Let's go!' When I stood up, I swear I couldn't feel my legs. At first we crouched and walked. Small arms fire erupted. Bullets popped and snapped all around me. Tracers went by trailing white smoke as the Nip machine gunners found their targets. To my left and right soldiers got hit and went down. We picked up our pace, bent over, running as best we could.

"About a third of the way across, the mortars and cannons let loose. Facing the small arms fire seemed like a picnic in the park compared to the artillery. When the shells hit, everything shook. I thought the ground would open up and swallow me. The flash and blast of explosions tore through the air. Chunks of coral showered down. Hunks of shrapnel whirled and howled by my ears. Just ahead of me a boy from New Jersey, Tommy Pyles, stopped when his buddy toppled over. A shell landed nearby, and a fragment took the top of his head clean off. I'll never forget it. His body slumped right over his friend, and his brains spilled out. I hesitated for a second and leaned over him, wanting to put his brains back in. But he was dead. What could I do? Just keep going.

"With all the smoke and dust, flashes and blasts, it felt like running through the thick clouds of a lightning storm. The explosions were deafening. I thought, 'What's the use? I'm dead meat.' But then, through the blur I saw the edge of the jungle, so I kept running. I jumped into some bushes, rolled down a slight ridge, and flattened my body."

Byron hit the stop button on the cassette player. Wright's gruesome description of the head wound kept replaying in his mind. He didn't want that image to linger like a bad dream when he talked to Eric. Instead he tried to erase it like chalk from a slate. But a blank slate invited the gore to reappear, like when someone says, *Don't think about a pink elephant.*

A red Firebird cutting into his lane as it came around the turn ahead got his attention. He hit his brakes and horn as a young brunette flew by, giving him the finger. He recognized her—*Heather . . . What's her last name . . . Richards? Eric's girlfriend.* For the last six months whenever Eric attended church, she came with him. Byron shook his head and inhaled deeply, trying to get his heart to slow down. *Birds of a feather. Why are the wild ones so attracted to each other?* With only three miles to the Waller's house, Byron needed to settle his nerves and get focused.

He decided to get Eric talking about something he liked— hunting, fishing, NASCAR. Forget pushing the serious talk. If he could establish good rapport with the boy, perhaps Eric would open up on his own. It was worth trying. The standard fare wasn't working.

As he pulled into the driveway and slowed to a stop, he felt a lump form in his chest. *Big as a grapefruit.* He clamped his eyes shut and gritted his teeth. *Get out of my head, Stanley Wright.* The image of the shimmering airfield and the hundreds of tense Marines anticipating the charge clouded his inner vision. He glanced to his right and saw the beat up Camero. *The reinforcements are here. Weasel and Eddie, or at least one of them. Get a hold of yourself, Butler. It's time to cross the field.*

He crossed the yard, climbed the few steps, knocked on the screen and waited, but no one answered. For an April day it was warm, probably low sixties, and the front door was ajar. He opened the screen and slipped inside. "Earl, you here?" he called out. No response. Glancing through the kitchen and dining room, he listened. The twang of country music filtered in from the family room, the same place Eric's bed had been stationed yesterday. He walked through the darkened rooms toward the music with that grapefruit swelling in his chest.

When he entered the family room he saw Eric lying on his bed, fumbling with something. "Hey, Eric. You need some help." Byron stepped closer. Eric, with his one good hand, slipped a bullet into the cylinder of a pistol. Byron stopped, huffed in a surprised breath and said, "What're you doing?"

Eric flipped the cylinder closed and raised the pistol, aiming it at Byron. "Stop right there. I mean it."

Byron stared at the barrel. His body stiffened. "Eric. No. Don't."

Footsteps pounded down stairs. Byron glanced to his left to see Weasel appear in the doorway holding a camera. "Hi, Reverend," Weasel said as he shook his long blond hair out of his eyes.

"Hold it," Byron said, raising his hand. "Eric's got a gun."

Weasel pointed. "Don't worry. It ain't loaded. That's my Smith and Wesson. Just got it for my birthday."

Eric's face blanched and the gun trembled.

"I just saw him put a bullet in it," Byron blurted.

"Huh?"

Eric raised the gun to his temple and pulled the trigger. Click. Click.

Byron dove. As his hand knocked the pistol, it went off.

CHAPTER 14

When Byron opened his eyes he saw red splattered on the blue wall behind the bed. Eric's head slumped, and blood oozed, a large crimson splotch against the white pillowcase. The bullet had blown off a small portion of the top of Eric's skull. Gray brain matter appeared through strands of his brown hair. Byron instinctively clamped his hand over the wound and felt the warm wetness. He turned his head, feeling nauseated. "My God. Oh God. Help. Help me."

Weasel dropped the camera and rushed to the bed. "I didn't know he had a bullet," he shrieked. "I swear, I didn't know."

Byron glanced at Eric's chest to see it rise and fall. "Call 911!"

Weasel turned, tripped and fell into the coffee table, jumped up, and sprinted through the dining room into the kitchen. Then came the sounds of fumbling with a phone. After a few seconds of silence Weasel hollered, "We need help! My best friend just shot himself!" Weasel's breaths came fast while he listened. "Okay, okay. I'm calming down. But you've got to hurry."

As Weasel gave the operator more information, Byron stared at the floor, not wanting to look at the wound. He kept his hand in place over the bloody mess, not knowing if the effort helped or hindered. The waffles and coffee he'd eaten for breakfast burbled in his stomach causing his midsection to involuntarily clench several times. He hoped he wouldn't throw up all over Eric. When he noticed the disposable camera on the floor he wondered what the boys were planning to do. He closed his eyes. *What's going on? Lord, help this kid. Keep me from losing it.*

Weasel charged back into the room and slid to a stop. "They're on their way." He edged closer. "I'm sorry, Reverend. I didn't know he had a bullet. Is Eric gonna be all right?"

Byron felt his heart pounding as he inhaled to speak. "He's hurt bad, Weasel. It doesn't look good." He was afraid to remove his hand, as if exposing Eric's brain to air would damage it. Confronting the gory scene with a sense of utter helplessness caused Stanley Wright's words to echo: *I hesitated for a second and leaned over him, wanting to put his brains back in. But he was dead.* Byron glanced at Eric's face. The boy's eyes were closed, his mouth agape. "Eric. Eric, can you hear me." He didn't respond. All Byron could think to do was pray.

* * *

The minutes passed interminably before a siren wailed in the distance. Byron ordered Weasel to go out onto the road and flag them down. After the teen left, he noticed Eric still gripped the pistol. It had a brown handle and resembled a larger version of the toy cowboy guns Byron played with as a kid. He reached for Eric's wrist to check his pulse, but Byron's fingers trembled too much. Eric's breathing could no longer be detected by looking at his chest. *Is he dead? God, please don't let him die.*

Poor Earl. This'll devastate him. Where is Earl? Byron tried to think logically. *Out on his tractor? Probably on the other side of the farm.* The siren grew louder, and within a minute, footsteps pounded into the house, and Weasel charged into the room followed by four attendants. A stocky man with a close-cut beard and EMT badge relieved Byron. The blood was thick and sticky as Byron pulled his hand away from Eric's head. A long red smudge stained Byron's forearm from where he'd rested it on the pillow.

The medical crew worked quickly as Byron explained the circumstances. The room became a flurry of activity—they moved furniture; wrapped bandages; brought in a stretcher with collapsible legs; worked on detaching Eric from the pulleys and cords; and connected tubes, bottles and needles.

Byron scurried out of their way. Knowing the sheriff would soon arrive, he ushered Weasel into the kitchen to question him.

He pulled out a chair and told Weasel to sit down at the table.

"How'd this happen?" Byron asked.

Weasel glanced up and shook his head. "My dad bought me that gun for my birthday. Eric called this morning and wanted me to bring it over. Just to take a look at it."

"Didn't Earl tell you he didn't want any guns around Eric?"

"Yeah, but it wasn't loaded. How could an unloaded gun hurt anyone?"

Byron swallowed and tried to relax so his knees wouldn't shake so much. "Somehow Eric got hold of a bullet that matched your gun."

Weasel gasped and said, "Must've been his lucky bullet."

"His *lucky* bullet?"

"He kept a bullet in the seat bag of his mountain bike. He found it last summer when we were out riding trails. Called it his lucky bullet. But the bike's out in the garage. How could he get to it?"

Byron closed his eyes and envisioned a red Firebird sliding around a turn into his lane on the drive over. *Heather—Eric's girlfriend.* "Was Heather here when you got here?"

Weasel glanced at the ceiling, eyes narrowing. "She was pullin' out when I was pullin' in." He met Byron's gaze. "She looked mad, too. Her and Eric must've battled."

"Of course. That's what he wanted."

"What?"

"Eric sent her out to get the bullet and then purposely fought with her."

Weasel forked his fingers through his bangs to clear them from his vision. "Why would he do that?"

"Because he wanted her out of here before you arrived with the gun. When you got here, Eric asked if he could hold the gun, didn't he?"

"Yeah. Said he wanted a picture of himself showing it off." Weasel's mouth dropped open. "That's why he wanted me to go up to his bedroom to get the camera."

Byron nodded. "To give him time to load it and shoot himself. But he wasn't expecting me to barge in on him."

About five minutes later the sheriff arrived and entered the kitchen as the emergency crew navigated the gurney through the house. The sheriff exchanged a few words with one of the EMTs. Byron recognized the square-jawed lawman—the same guy who had helped organize a search party when his daughter, Christine, had disappeared in the woods eight years ago. He wore a black-brimmed hat and dark green sunglasses. A thick, salt-and-pepper mustache covered his upper lip, and sharply squared sideburns edged his tanned face.

When he spoke, Byron caught a whiff of cigarette breath. "Bernard Taylor, Belmont County Sheriff. You two witness the shooting?" He didn't seem to recognize Byron or offer a handshake. Instead, he pulled a notepad from his back pocket.

"Yes, sir," Byron said, and Weasel nodded.

"Your names."

They told him their names. Byron took a deep breath, ordered his thoughts, and gave a brief description of the incident.

"Is that the victim's blood on your arm?" The pitch of Taylor's voice, low and abrupt, varied little.

Byron glanced at his forearm and hand. The blood had dried and cracked in the wrinkles of his palm and wrist. "Yes. I did the best I could to stop the bleeding."

"Uh huh. Can you show me where the incident occurred?"

Byron led them into the family room, and Taylor examined the blood on the wall. He pulled on rubber gloves, lifted the gun from the bed and dropped it into a plastic bag. "Both of you are in agreement then. Simple case of attempted suicide."

They nodded.

Taylor held up the plastic bag containing the Smith and Wesson. "Now the question is why did this young man in his mental state have access to this gun?"

Weasel blabbered about the gun being his birthday present and Eric's lucky bullet, but Byron cut him off and explained his theory of how Eric manipulated both Weasel and Heather. Taylor jotted notes, making sure he had the full names of everyone involved.

"Where's Eric's father?" Taylor asked.

"We're not sure," Byron said. "He might be on the back of the farm plowing or planting."

"Can we get out there in my vehicle?" Taylor asked.

"Yeah. I know the way," Weasel said.

Earl Waller rode a green John Deere, pulling a plow across the top of a hillock, the earth rolling and collapsing through the row of blades like small brown waves. Sheriff Taylor drove the black Crown Victoria along a dirt pathway running parallel to the tractor and gave a short blast on his siren. Earl glanced over his shoulder and the tractor jolted to a stop, the engine sputtering out.

Byron exited the vehicle and gazed at the farmer as he dismounted and tromped through the newly plowed field toward them. Earl's face lost its bright redness as he neared, his mouth tensing as if affected by temporary paralysis. He pulled a blue and white handkerchief from his back pocket and wiped his entire face, breaking the frozen expression. "Did something happen to Eric?" he managed to ask.

Before Byron could formulate words, Sheriff Taylor stepped forward and said, "Mr. Waller, your son has been taken to Wheeling Medical Park with a serious gunshot wound."

"Gunshot wound?" Earl's eyes darted from face to face, wrinkles deepening across his cheeks as his jaw muscles tensed.

"I'm sorry, Earl," Byron said, reaching and grasping his shoulder.

Earl's voice quavered. "W-Was it an a-accident? Who p-pulled the trigger?"

"Self-inflicted," the lawman said.

"Self-inflicted? Impossible. My guns are all locked up."

Byron glanced at Weasel. The teenager shuffled his feet, staring at the ground.

"Young Mr. Wetsel brought a handgun to your house today," the sheriff said.

"Weasel, how could you?" Earl said, his tone incredulous.

Tears streamed down Weasel's cheeks. "I'm sorry, Mr. Waller. I didn't know he had a bullet."

"We think Eric persuaded Heather Richards to get the bullet he had tucked away in his mountain bike bag. She left before Weasel got there," Byron said.

"Oh, hell." Earl closed his eyes, and his head dropped forward as if the muscles in his neck gave out.

"Mr. Waller, I'd rather you not drive yourself to the hospital. This is quite a shock," Taylor said.

"I'll take him," Byron offered as he slipped his arm around Earl's back.

"Thank you," Taylor said. "A couple more of my boys should be here soon to secure the scene. I'll drop you off at the house, finish up my work there, and then meet you at the hospital."

* * *

Byron sat with Earl in the ER waiting room while the doctors worked on Eric. Sheriff Taylor stopped in about a half hour later and confirmed that Heather Richards acquired the bullet for Eric from the bike bag. Eric had told her the gunpowder had been removed, and he had wanted the bullet for good luck. Once he had it, he accused her of cheating on him with another boy. They fought, and he demanded that she leave. Taylor offered his sympathies and asked that he be contacted if any other pertinent information surfaced. Earl mumbled some words of appreciation, and the sheriff departed.

Earl's anger at Heather and Weasel gradually shifted to self-condemnation. Byron did his best to assure him that many factors contributed to this tragedy—the responsibility didn't fall on one person. He encouraged Earl to be strong for Eric's sake and to hope that things would turn around from here. Earl broke down several times, weeping uncontrollably, "What if he doesn't make it, Pastor Byron? What if he doesn't make it?"

"We'll only worry about that if we have to," Byron said. "For now, let's hope and pray he survives."

After a couple of hours, a doctor in blue scrubs showed up and told them Eric was out of danger for now but still unconscious, and they moved him to ICU. The medical staff wasn't sure to what extent Eric's brain had been damaged. It would take several days of observation and testing to gain an accurate assessment. Byron accompanied Earl into the intensive care cubicle and stood next to him at Eric's bedside. White bandages encompassed the top of Eric's head. Tubes and wires, hanging from monitors and bags, snaked to various parts of his body—wrists, mouth, chest, and parts covered by the sheet.

Byron felt numb, emotionally spent. *What now? I need to call Lila. The prayer chain.* After standing silently for many minutes, he decided to ask Earl to pray with him. Byron's words to God were short and to the point, like sentences spoken to a friend with whom one had just had a disagreement. After the amen, Byron informed Earl he would check back later and excused himself. There wasn't much else he could do.

* * *

Byron left the Intensive Care Unit and walked down the corridor feeling like he'd just finished a marathon. He stopped at the nearest pay phone and called Lila, not giving her many details—just that the boy had tried to commit suicide. She promised to initiate the prayer chain. After hanging up, he oriented himself and headed for the elevator.

When the doors parted, he entered, glanced at the numbered buttons, and on impulse pressed four. For some strange reason he wanted to talk to someone and thought of Judd Stone. Perhaps he needed to connect with a person who'd understand what he'd just been through—the horror of seeing a young man violently harmed by a weapon. He needed to talk to someone who knew what it meant to be splattered by another's blood.

The blinds in Stone's room had been pulled shut, and the mid-afternoon sun trickled through occasional thin spaces. Stone sat up in bed watching a baseball game on the suspended television. As Byron's eyes adjusted to the shadows, he noticed the old man appeared more vibrant than yesterday.

Stone cut the power to the television. "I was wonderin' if you'd get a chance to stop in today." His voice was steady, more upbeat.

"Glad to see you're looking better, General."

"Yeah. I've bounced back from the chemo a little. You didn't bring Jackson's boy with you?"

"I'm afraid not. I'm expecting a call from him tonight. He may fly up on Saturday."

Stone nodded. "Good. I hope for his sake and . . . my sake he comes." He squinted up at Byron. "You don't look so hot, Preacher. You all right?"

"It hasn't been a good day. A young man from my congregation tried to commit suicide. I just came from ICU."

"No shit . . ." Stone looked away and shook his head. "That's a damn shame. How'd he do it?"

Byron took a slow breath, remembering the scene. "He shot himself in the head with a pistol. I was there. Tried to stop him but didn't react in time."

"Is he gonna live?"

"I think so. He blew a small portion of his skull away. I did my best to stop the bleeding. It was . . . gruesome."

Stone nodded. "I saw a lot of head wounds in the war. Always buckets of blood when a guy gets it in the noggin'. I got used to it. What'd you do to stop the bleeding?"

"I cupped my hand over top of the . . . opening. Don't think it helped much."

"You do what you gotta do. Now you know what the Navy corpsman on Peleliu went through. We called them 'Docs.' Those boys were something else. In fact, you remind me of one of them."

"Really?"

"Doc Halleran. You look like him. 'Bout forty years old, tall, silver hair. Fearless sonovabitch."

"Did he save any lives?"

"Hell, yeah. All kinds. I remember the seventh or eighth day on Peleliu we were attacking the pillboxes on the eastern slopes of Mount Umurbrogol—the other side of Bloody Nose Ridge. Lieutenant Baker sent me and a young replacement named Keys out on the flank. Well, one of them saw us cutting through a gap in the undergrowth and cut loose with a machine gun. We jumped behind a large outcropping of coral. Those slugs went buzzing over our heads and popping into the mound in front of us. Thought we were safe. Then came this terrible crack—one shot. Keys yelled, 'Oh God. I'm hit. I'm hit.' Blood soaked through the sleeve.

Then came another one—pow! I swear the bullet brushed the tip of my nose and snapped into the coral behind me. 'Shit!' I said. 'Sniper.' I grabbed Keys and dragged him to the other side of the rock—a small defilade where the machine gunner or the sniper couldn't get us." Then I hollered for a corpsman, and guess who showed up within two minutes."

"The guy that looked like me?"

"That's right. Doc Halleran. He came running right through the machinegun and sniper fire. Fearless sonovabitch. Just dove behind the rock at our feet. I took out my K-bar knife and cut the sleeve off Key's blouse. Then, with bullets buzzin' all around us, Doc Halleran patched him up. Within ten minutes a Sherman pulled up and blasted the pillbox and then turned the turret onto the sniper who'd perched himself in a tree. Made short work of him. Then me and Doc Halleran helped get Keys back to the medical station."

Byron rubbed the late-afternoon stubble on his cheeks, envisioning the heroic corpsman's deed. "Halleran was a courageous man. That's not me. When Eric pointed the gun at my chest I about fainted. It wasn't until he stuck the barrel against his own head that I tried stop him."

"How'd you stop him?"

"I dove and knocked the gun."

Stone nodded. "When I called Halleran fearless, I didn't mean *without* fear."

"What did you mean?"

"Willing to *face* fear. I'd say that you were fearless today too."

Byron pointed to his chest. "Me?"

"You dove, didn't you?"

CHAPTER 15

Byron sat at his desk in the study and stared into Helen's box, which he held on his lap.

"Who was on the phone?" Lila asked.

He glanced over his shoulder and saw her standing in the doorway. "That was J.J. Jackson. He's flying in tomorrow afternoon to see Judd Stone. I have to pick him up at the airport."

"Tomorrow afternoon?" Her brows tensed, scoring her forehead with wrinkles. "You'll miss the boys' game."

Byron lowered his eyes. "I know. I'm sorry." He swallowed the lump in his throat and met her gaze. "It's the first one I've missed all season."

"I'll be glad when this business with Mr. Stone is over. You've got enough to worry about now with what happened today."

"Me too. Hopefully their meeting will help put the past behind them and allow me to step aside."

"Didn't you say J.J. Jackson was from Atlanta?"

"Yes."

She walked over and stood behind him. "Wow. He must be more obsessed about old war stories than you—coming that far on a few day's notice."

Byron shrugged.

Lila wrapped her arms around his shoulders, clasping them on his chest, and rubbed her cheek against his. "Are you all right?"

"I'm fine, Hon. It's been a bad day, that's all."

She raised herself and massaged his shoulders. "You barely said two words at the dinner table then ran up here to lose yourself in these war letters."

Byron leaned his head back against the softness of her belly and felt her breasts brush against his hair. "I'm sorry, but I needed to get my mind off of what happened at the Wallers. Besides, I didn't want to say anything in front of the boys."

"I know. But we're alone now. Don't you want to talk about it?"

Byron swiveled the chair around to face his wife. "It would only upset you to hear the details."

"I'm stronger than you give me credit for." Lila dragged a wooden chair from beside the filing cabinet to within a couple feet of Byron and sat down. Her eyes narrowed. "I want to know what happened."

"All right. Believe me, it's not pleasant to talk about."

"I can handle it."

"Well, I told you on the phone that Eric tried to commit suicide."

She nodded. "But you wouldn't tell me how. Did he get hold of a bottle of pills?"

Byron shook his head, remembering Eric's finger squeezing the trigger. "No. He shot himself."

Lila sat straight up, eyes widening. "Great Grandma's molasses."

"I walked in on him when he was loading the gun. Before he put the pistol to his head, he pointed it at me."

Lila gasped. "At you? Why?"

"To keep me from stopping him. He aimed right at my chest."

Color drained from her face. "What if he would have pulled the trigger?"

"I could have died."

She closed her eyes and took several deep breaths.

"I told you the details would upset you. Do you want me to go on?"

She nodded.

"After he stuck the gun to his head he pulled the trigger, but the first chamber was empty. I didn't think fast enough. I should have reacted then. Maybe I would have stopped him, but I didn't dive for the gun until I heard the second click. As he pulled the trigger a third time, I knocked the gun upward. It went off, and the bullet caught the top of his head."

She raised her hand to her mouth.

"I swear, Lila, I felt absolutely helpless. Had no idea what to do. The blood was seeping out so I cupped my hand over the hole."

She swallowed. "Precious Jesus." She took his hand and squeezed it. "What a horrible thing to witness."

"Now can you see why I just want to put my mind somewhere else?"

"I understand. It's just that you've been so . . . so distant lately." She pointed at the box on his lap. "So obsessed with those things."

Byron stared at the contents. "I know. I'm sorry." He took a slow breath and wiped his hand across his face, fingers leaving red lines on his cheeks. "Sometimes I forget what's really important. Lila, you know how much I love you. I don't mean to shut you and the boys out."

"Could you read one of the letters to me?"

Byron glanced up. "Sure," he said, restraining his surprise. Lila rarely showed interest in his obsessions. Their life together, like a big roll-top desk, had drawers and compartments they shared, but others they kept to themselves. Byron liked it that way. Growing up he'd spent many hours alone and learned to appreciate his private spaces—his research and writing, his distance running, his love for classical music, Bach and Mozart, his fascination with Old Testament history. Usually he balked at anyone invading his separate worlds, but the letters contained such ardor and pathos he wanted to share their beauty with someone—why not with *his* lover? He reached into the box and picked up the next letter in the yet-to-be-read pile. "You'll be surprised at the way Helen and Howard expressed themselves so passionately."

"Really?"

"Oh yes. Just imagine. It's 1944—nearing the end of the war—and these two young lovers are now separated after only six months of marriage."

"Married for only six months?" Lila said. "Great Grandma's molasses, they were just learning to enjoy one another. I remember those first few months after we got hitched." Lila smiled, blushing. "We hit the sack early a lot but didn't get much sleep."

Byron chuckled but then sobered. "It's hard for us to understand what happened to these couples. To be pulled apart at a time when a man and woman are learning to share the most intimate experiences together had to be heart wrenching. Add to that the great possibility of never seeing your husband or wife alive again. Can you imagine?"

"I don't know if I could have faced something like that."

Byron met his wife's gaze. "Sometimes we don't have a choice. Life comes at you, ready or not."

Lila glanced at her hands and rubbed her finger across her wedding band. "Please, read the letter."

Byron slid the flap out of the envelope and extracted the yellowed pages.

"My Darling, Howie,

"It's been three long weeks and I still haven't heard from you. I feel like dying. Not knowing is worse than anything. Did you make it through your first battle? Are you wounded? Did a Japanese submarine sink the ship carrying my last letter? Have you grown tired of writing me? These questions feel like knives piercing my soul. Forgive me for being so morbid, but I can't help it."

Byron paused and looked up. "Howard had spent the last ten days in one of the bloodiest battles of the Pacific Theater. Almost half of his platoon had been killed or wounded. When the general sent in replacements to relieve his company, he finally got the chance to collect his mail." He lifted the pages. "This is the second of three letters Helen had sent to him that he hadn't opened yet because of the battle."

"She sounds miserable," Lila said. "Helen has always been such a positive person. It's hard to imagine her so depressed. Please, read on."

Byron continued.

"Yesterday my good friend, Jane Harbaugh, never showed up for work. I found out today from some of the girls that word came from the war department about her husband who was missing in action. They finally identified his remains. Poor Jane. She loved Tommy so much. But at least now she's not in limbo. She's not wondering anymore whether or not he is sitting in some German prison camp. That's how I feel, Howie, when I don't hear from you—like I'm in limbo or purgatory or some in-between place where the seconds tick by slower than a three-legged turtle.

"*The newspapers have barely mentioned the Battle of Peleliu. Just a few paragraphs here or there. Last week I read that the invasion was met with stiff opposition. Other than that, not much at all. Most headlines are about the Allies liberating Europe or General MacArthur returning to the Philippines. Why have they forgotten our Marines? Don't they know thousands of wives and mothers and fathers are waiting for some kind of news?*

"*Am I being selfish, Howie? I hate this war. Does that make me a bad American? I've always been patriotic. I know this is the best country on God's green earth. We enjoy freedom and the pursuit of happiness. But why do we have to be the ones to save the world? Why do we have to stick our noses into the mess that people on the other side of the globe created? They say this is the Land of the Free and the Home of the Brave. Lots of blood has been shed to preserve our freedom. I guess that's all well and good until it hits home. So many young men from the Ohio Valley have died. What a terrible price to pay. I wonder if Jane Harbaugh thinks it's worth it? Lately, whenever someone knocks on the door, I dread answering it. Whenever I go to the mailbox to look for your letters, I hold my breath, hoping I don't get one from the war department.*

"*Forgive me, Howie. I don't mean to bring you down. If only I could be a bright and happy person and write letters that inspire you, instead of ones that put burdens on you. I think I need a good long bath. I'm going to fill the tub to the top with steaming hot water and soak for an hour. Maybe that will raise my spirits.*

"*Do you know what would be wonderful? If, while I am sitting in that tub, you could come and join me. Remember how we used to bathe each other? You'd sit behind me with that big sponge and squeeze it. The warm water would pour down my back and trickle on my neck. Then you would soap it up good and gently rub. After finishing my back, you'd reach around and very slowly and gently lather up my front. Then it was my turn. We'd stand up and face each other, and I would take over the sponge. I'd start at the top and work my way down. We had a lot of good clean fun, didn't we?*

"O, Howie, I miss you so much. Please come back to me. I want to hold you in my arms again. I want to feel your warm skin against mine. I want to kiss you long and lovingly. I want to feel you deeply in me and lose myself in you. Keep your eyes open. Keep your head down. Keep reading your Bible and saying your prayers, but most of all, keep thinking of me, for I will be thinking of you.

I love you. I need you now more than ever,

Helen"

When Byron glanced up, he saw a tear trace a shiny line down Lila's cheek. "Are you all right?" he asked.

Nodding, she blinked and wiped the wet streak away with two fingers.

He placed the letter on the corner of the desk and stood. She rose at the same time. They embraced. He felt her take an unsteady breath. Leaning back, gazing into her blue-green eyes, he sensed the heat of her longing and felt instantly aroused. "Where are the boys?" he asked.

"They went out to the mall to see a movie."

She cupped the back of his neck and pulled him to her. He kissed her softly at first, but the tingling pleasure stirred a hunger that moved him to press hard against her open mouth, seeking her tongue. He was throbbing now, but he couldn't help wonder what sparked these flames after what he had gone through just hours ago—facing the barrel of a gun, seeing a boy shoot himself, confronting death. Was it the letter? Was it remembering those wonderful first few months of marriage?

She broke from the deep kiss and pushed him back.

"What's wrong?" he asked.

"Not a thing." She turned and walked down the hallway.

"Where're you going?"

"To fill up the tub with hot water."

136

"Oh."

"You coming?"

* * *

Byron couldn't remember the last time their lovemaking had been so intense. Every touch of Lila's fingers on all parts of his body sent waves of ecstasy through him. His mind rose to a rare level of focus on physical pleasure, and his being yielded fully to the joy and wonder of their exploration. Every time she peaked, he lost himself in the rapture of her gratification. Lying on top of her, after the final thrust, he felt every muscle slacken, as if his bones, organs, and sinew had turned to jelly. He felt at peace, satisfied, overjoyed, but baffled. Why was it so good? Why now?

"Whew, partner," Lila said as he rolled off. "What got into us?"

"I wish I knew."

She turned toward him and placed her hand over his heart, twirling his chest hair with her forefinger. "For some reason I really wanted you tonight, but it started even before you read the letter. Helen's words just fueled the fire."

"I guess it's something you can't put in a bottle. Sometimes it just happens."

Lila giggled. "Please, Lord, let it happen more often."

* * *

Later that night, Byron sat up in bed reading Matthew Henry's commentary on the Book of Job. Glancing at Lila, he noticed she had nodded off with a romance novel open facedown on her stomach, her hand resting on it. He laid the Henry tome on his nightstand and gently slid the novel from her grasp, pulled the bookmark from the previous spot, and placed it at the current page. Closing the book, he looked at the cover. A young soldier embraced a pretty blonde in front of a train, duffle bags at his feet. Byron read the title—*When We Meet Again*. Immediately his thoughts turned to Howard's response to Helen's last letter. The wonderful interlude with Lila had temporarily suspended his fixation on the war years. He shifted his legs over the side of the bed and rose slowly, careful not to wake his wife.

In the darkness he walked down the hall, entered his study and picked up the pages where he had left them on the corner of his desk. He reached for the switch on the lamp but then decided to take it back to the bedroom in case Lila woke up and wondered where he went. After climbing into bed, he examined the pages to find Howard's sides of the letter and began to read.

My Dearest Helen,

Reading your last letter brought back the best memories of my life. I never realized how precious our times together were until I landed on this horrible island. Now it is so clear. I know we've dreamed of a great life together—a nice house, a good income, an automobile, and lots of kids— but all of these things don't mean much in comparison to loving each other. Right now that's the only important thing to me. I want the chance to hold you again and show you how much I love you.

In the last ten days I've seen so many things that have fouled up my thinking--terrible scenes of death and destruction. I try to put these horrible pictures out of my mind, but they barge in when I least expect it. Thinking of you and writing these letters offers me a chance to escape this world. For now we will be given a couple days to recover, but I'm sure the brass will send us back to the front lines. By then, those who replaced us will have suffered great losses.

I just heard our First Regiment is heading back to Pavuvu. They sustained more than seventy-five percent casualties on Bloody Nose Ridge.

Some rifle companies were completely wiped out. On this island the Japanese are using a new strategy—very few Banzai charges like on Guadal Canal. They've learned a tough lesson: Marines don't drop their weapons and run like the Chinese. Marines mow you down with machineguns, M1s and BARs. The enemy's new plan is to sit up in the caves and fortified positions on the hillsides and wait for us to come get them. It worked. The officers kept sending the First Regiment up the ridges and the Japs kept knocking them down.

I'm afraid that sooner or later it will be our turn on Bloody Nose Ridge. There's not much we can do about it, though. I guess I'll have to face it. The fear of death is an awful thing. A lot of the guys are cracking up. Helen, I'm afraid that if I can't get my thinking straight, I might lose my mind.

Judd Stone told me his secret to overcoming fear of battle—he accepts the fact that he's not going to survive. He considers himself a dead man already. When he faces the enemy he's not afraid to die because he's given up the hope of surviving. If he does make it through, he'll feel like he just won the big pot in a poker game. Icing on the cake, he says.

I can't look at it that way. If I'm dead already, then I've lost you. And If I've lost you, I've lost everything. Somehow I'll have to find my courage elsewhere—reading my Bible, saying my prayers and thinking of you.

Helen, I'm dreaming of you now. We are lying beside each other on that wonderful feather bed at home. We've just made the sweetest love that any couple ever shared. You've drifted off to sleep with a smile on your face, and I'm at peace, next to you—the luckiest man in the world. I know what's important in life now—US. If only I can make it back to you.

Yours always,

Howie

Byron gazed at Lila sleeping on her side and noticed the contour of her body as it sloped to her waist and rose to her rounded hip and slanted down her leg. He folded the two pages of the letter back together and placed them on top of Matthew Henry's commentary. Looking at the faded tear-stained paper, he marveled at how their words on each side of the page captured their spirits. For years the two pages had clung to each other in that envelope hidden away in the box. Somehow, by reopening the letter and reading it, he released the spirit of their love. He turned off the lamp and snuggled next to Lila, draping his hand across her belly, molding his body to hers. She took a deep breath and sighed softly. Her warmth relaxed him. He smelled the sweetness of strawberries on the back of her neck. In those moments before sleep quietly crept over him, he felt at peace—lucky to be alive and in love.

CHAPTER 16

Byron stood on the back porch watching his sons toss the baseball in the yard. His thoughts drifted to Eric and the confusion that tormented the boy's soul and led him to the edge of self-destruction. *I didn't make time to connect with him until it was too late. Figured he was Earl's kid. Earl's responsibility.* Byron shook his head. *There's always something pulling me away. Always something I get stuck on.*

As the ball sailed back and forth he wondered how each of his boys felt inside—the whole self-concept thing so crucial to a healthy mental outlook. Were they happy? Stable? Normal? He assumed they were but realized appearances didn't always hold true. Had he done enough to assure them of his love?

Before climbing into the van, he called them over, wished them good luck, and apologized in advance for missing that afternoon's game. Mark promised to bring home pitching victory number five. Byron rarely hugged the twins since they entered high school, but now he didn't hesitate, wrapping his arms around Mark first and squeezing hard, then Matt. When he stood back and eyed them, their faces reddened slightly with questioning looks and awkward smiles.

"Do your best, guys. You know I love you."

"We will, Dad," Matt said, glancing at the ground then up again.

"Yeah. For sure. W-we love you too, Dad." Mark stammered.

Byron fumbled in his pocket for the keys, opened the van door and slid into the driver's seat. *These days are slipping away from me. They grew up too fast.* His throat tightened and he swallowed, taking a quick peek at his watch. *Time doesn't care, though. Just keeps movin' along. I'll make it up to them. Guys' night out next week. Maybe bowling or a Pirate's game. We'll have a good time then.* He backed out of the driveway and waved, but the boys had already turned to walk to the house. As he headed down the road, Cat Stevens' lyrics infiltrated his mind—*the cat's in the cradle and the silver spoon.*

* * *

The drive to the Pittsburgh Airport would take a little over an hour—plenty of time to listen to the rest of Stanley Wright's account of the Battle of Peleliu. Hopefully Byron could gather some information to prepare J.J. for Stone's confession. If Stone's transgression was egregious, if it involved Josiah's Jackson's death, then Byron wanted to make sure J.J. was ready for the concussion of the shock. During their phone conversation, Byron had never hinted about the possibilities of foul play. Maybe he should have. Instead of pawing around the doghouse, he should have gone right in and made it clear that Stone might be his father's murderer. Why had Stone been so obtuse about it? *Why didn't he just come out and tell me what happened?* Regardless, J.J. came in good faith and deserved as much recon info as possible. Byron hit the play button on the cassette player.

"I woke up early on the third morning of the battle smelling hot Joe. Didn't expect that. When the wind shifted on the island lots of odors came our way—cordite and gunpowder, the rotting stink of death, and human waste. You couldn't dig shit-holes where we hunkered down because of the coral. We just crapped in ammunition cans and tossed them as far from our shell holes as possible. To wake up to the smell of coffee did me good. My best pal, Judd Stone, had heated a couple canteen cups of water over sterno tablets. 'Get up, Buddyboy,' Judd said. 'Lieutenant Baker has a helluva day planned for us.' He wasn't kidding.

"Let me tell you, being members of a rifle company in the Pacific wasn't the romance and adventure I'd hoped for when I admired Marine recruitment posters back in high school. We were the hell catchers. By the third day our regiment had secured the airfield and set its sights on the eastern coast and the backside of Mount Umurbrogol. The officers would decide on an objective—some pillbox or emplacement. Then, from a fairly safe distance, the mortar boys would launch a few rounds. After that the machine gunners would feed a couple belts through the chambers. By then, the Japs were wide-awake and ready. That's when the officers commanded the rifle companies to attack.

"Now I admit, most of us weren't grade-A T-bones, but hell, who decided we deserved the meat grinder? That's what it was—a damn ground beef maker. We'd go rushing forward and the Japs would come out of their holes and start shredding us. We did everything by the book too—zigzagged across open ground, kept five-yard intervals, ran fast and low—didn't matter. Down we went. After a couple hours of attacking the lower ridges, we pulled back to the beach and counted our losses.

"I have to give our officers credit. They weren't as glory happy as the gung ho colonel that commanded the First Regiment—Chesty Puller. Two hours of Bloody Nose Ridge wasn't enough for him. He kept sending his rifle companies up the hill and the Japs kept making ground beef. From the other side of the mountain we listened to the constant rumbles and thought, man are they catching hell. It was bad enough on our side of the mountain. No way I wanted any part of the western slopes of Umurbrogol.

"Judd Stone came up to me and says, 'It'll be our turn sooner or later.'

"'What're you talking about?' I says.

"He pointed at the mountain and says, 'Puller'll make the First Regiment attack 'til there's none left. Then it'll be our turn. That's the word, anyway.'

"'Oh shit,' I says. 'I hope that scuttlebut's phooey.'

"Judd says, 'I got the straight dope. Heard a couple officers yapping.'

"I just shook my head.

"After we downed some K-rations, Lieutenant Baker came along and says, 'Get ready, men, we're heading south.' Suited me fine. The further from the mountain we got the better.

"The south end of the island consisted of thick jungle, a mangrove swamp, and a couple of promontories called the Lobster Claw. At least the jungle was shady. Problem was it had to be 110 degrees in the shade that day. We took our time working our way through the jungle. Damn mangrove trees, each one sproutin' a hundred roots, clogged all the paths. We snaked our way around tidal inlets or tromped through them holding our rifles in the air. Sweat poured off my face, soaked my blouse and dungarees. My boondockers filled with water. Every step—squish, squish, squish.

"Finally, after about an hour, Baker told us to find a dry spot and take five. I plopped my ass down in front of this tree with low branches and long, pointy leaves. My throat was dryer than a sand sandwich, so I drained my canteen. Stupid thing to do because we had a long day ahead of us. 'Course, wasn't the first time I did something stupid. Then I pulled off my boondockers and poured a quart of swamp water out of each one. When I looked up, I saw the most incredible thing. This giant black bird swooped down through an opening in the trees and landed on a low branch right in front of me. It puffed out its red throat like it was showing off then spread its wings. Must have had a seven-foot wingspan. Made me 'bout topple over in amazement. Damn thing had no fear of us whatsoever.

"My good pal, Emery 'Gator' Snowfield, sat next to me. Gator was a Florida boy. Can you imagine living in Florida with a last name like Snowfield? Anyway, he says, 'That's a man-o-war bird.'

"'How the hell do you know that?' I says.

"'Cause I've seen 'em along the coast in Florida,' he says.

"I says, 'The damn thing sure picked a helluva island to visit.'

"'Well,' Gator says, 'must be why they call it a man-o-war bird.'

"All at once a shot rang out, whizzing right by my ear into the trunk of that tree. The damn bird screeched and squawked and took off with those huge wings flappin' right over top of me. Lieutenant Baker hollered, 'Sniper! Everybody down!'

"I flopped over, spread-eagle on the jungle floor and crawled for cover. Behind me, Gator says, 'Lieutenant, I got him.' Snowfield was the bravest man in the platoon and a sharpshooter to boot. He grabbed his M1 and disappeared into the bushes.

"A few minutes later we heard the crack of Gator's rifle then the sound of swishing branches and a thump. We looked at each other and smiled. 'Damn, he's good,' Judd Stone says.

"Before we could pull out our smokes and light 'em up, Gator showed up with a Japanese flag, Nambu pistol, and dagger. 'Chalk one up for the Florida boy,' Baker says. Gator grinned bigger than a king-sized jack-o-lantern. He knew those navy swabbies would pay good dough for those souvenirs once we got sent to the rear.

"For several days we patrolled the southeastern beaches taking out pillboxes and machinegun pits, always keeping our eyes open for counterattacks. Gator Snowfield and Judd Stone volunteered to scout the offshore jungle just in case the enemy got any crazy ideas about ambushing us. Must have been about the sixth day Judd and Gator returned from a morning recon all excited. Judd told Lieutenant Baker the enemy was amassing troops 'bout a half mile inland, probably preparing to attack in our direction. Gator guessed their numbers to be company size, between a hundred and a hundred-and-fifty. In the sand, they sketched out the paths through the jungle, the swamps bordering each side and clearings that had to be crossed between here and there. Baker looked over their artwork and decided to move two platoons of Easy Company into a position three hundred yards deep into the jungle near one of the biggest clearings. If the Japs were coming our way, Baker wanted to catch them in the open.

"We gathered up our equipment and moved fast. When we got there, any fool could see it was the perfect set up. The path spread out into a clearing about forty yards wide and narrowed again as the jungle thickened. On our side we had plenty of places behind undergrowth and trees to hide and wait. Everyone found a spot and made sure ammunition was within easy reach. Baker told us to fire at his command—he'd wait 'til the opening filled up like a pond full of mallards. Kneeling in the bushes with Marlene, my trusty M1, I got that jumpy stomach feeling—the kind athletes get just before the big game.

146

"Bout half an hour went by when we heard this gibberish coming from down the path on the other side. Everybody lifted his rifle. Next to me, Kinloch, shivered like it was twenty degrees out. We called him Howard the Coward. He was either having a malaria attack or was scared shitless. I whispers, 'Come on, Kinloch, steady yourself. They're coming.' Then those yellow bastards filed into the clearing. I swear the ones in front came within ten feet before Baker yelled, 'Fire!'

"Holy hell. What a massacre. They didn't have a chance. Marlene spit bullets like a Roman candle—fifteen shots and all of them connecting. Nip blood splattered everywhere. When I stopped to change the magazine, I glanced over to see Howard the Coward shooting up in the air. Hell, what was he hunting? Man-o-war birds? Damn him.

"Within three minutes the clearing became clogged with dead bodies, and the firing stopped. Bet we killed half of them. The other half hightailed it back into the jungle. I looked over and says, 'What the hell you doing, Kinloch? You ain't gonna kill any Japs shooting into the clouds.' Howard just stared at me, eyes big as pies.

"Judd Stone must have seen him too. He got hotter than Marlene's barrel. 'Gaddamn you, Kinloch,' he says. 'Whose side you on?' He scrambled over and grabbed Howard by the collar and pulled him to his feet. He says, 'Don't you ever let me see you wasting ammo again.' He slapped him hard on the face and says, 'You hear me?' Then slapped him again. Howard tried to say something but couldn't get the words out. Judd shoved him, and he collapsed into a shaking heap. Standing over him, Judd says, 'Don't you know it's us or them? You let them live and we die.'

Howard started bawling and Lieutenant Baker told Judd to lay off. It was true, though. We fought for each other. Every Jap I put in the grave improved my buddies' chances of living another day. I guarantee you the enemy showed us no mercy.

From day one they knew it was a matter of time before we'd root them out of their caves and secure the island. Do you think they'd surrender to spare human life? Hell no. They considered surrender disgraceful. They wanted to die gloriously for their emperor and we obliged. Until that last man fell, they'd deliver as much suffering and death as possible. No quarter. Hell, I didn't feel sorry for the enemy. Not at all.

"Working our way up the east coast a couple of days later, we heard jabbering coming from the edge of the jungle—those high pitched singsong sounds the Nips make when they're having a good time. Judd and Gator crept into the undergrowth to see what they could find. Didn't take long. Maybe three minutes later they came back and told Lieutenant Baker they'd located a pillbox set against the hillside forty yards offshore and camouflaged with palm leaves. It was full of Japs and firing ports.

"Baker says, 'We gotta take it out. Those bastards must be the welcoming committee for any craft approaching shore or troops crossing the beach here.' He asked for a volunteer to sneak up to the damn thing and drop a magnesium grenade down the ventilation shaft. Sounded like a suicide mission to me. Guess whose hand popped up quicker than overdue toast? Gator Snowfield. The guy had King Kong balls. Baker decided to spread the rest of us out. When the Japs poured from the pillbox to escape the blinding effects of the grenade, we'd turn 'em into Swiss cheese.

"Baker sent Judd and a boy by the name of Keys into the jungle on the left flank. Howard Kinloch and an old vet, Razor Hanes, headed to the right flank. The rest of us spread out, crouching and crawling from all angles in front of the damn thing. Before Gator could even work his way safely to the pillbox, we heard machinegun fire and saw flashes spitting out the left firing ports. 'Oh shit,' I thought, 'Judd's in trouble.' A few seconds later Judd yells, 'Corpsman! Corpsman!' Deep in the pit of my stomach I felt a knot tighten. 'Oh, for godsakes,' I thought. 'The shit's gonna hit the fan.'

The commotion alerted the Japs that something was up. But Gator was a pro. Took his time. We lay there, waiting, sweating, wondering what the hell would happen next. Finally, Gator charged out of the jungle from the rear—he'd circled clear around—jumped on top of the pillbox, and slipped that magnesium grenade down the ventilation shaft. All hell broke loose then.

"'Bout half of those Nips couldn't take the smoke and charged out of the doors right towards us. 'Course we ripped 'em in two with small arms fire. The rest, though, stayed at their guns, firing away. We knew their eyes had to be stinging. Lieutenant Baker says to me, 'They're firing blind, Wright. Let's crawl up there and toss grenades into one of the ports. I never claimed to be a hero—not like Snowfield. Just try to do my job and not get killed. But what could I do? Baker asked me to go with him. I ain't no coward. 'Lead the way,' I says.

We crept toward the damn thing, tracers zipping over our heads and bullets popping in the coral all around us. I used dead Jap bodies for protection as much as possible. When we got to within fifteen feet, Baker pulled a grenade off his belt. I followed suit. He pointed to the biggest hole, a machinegun port. Pretty easy to hit that target from fifteen feet. We pulled the pins and let 'em fly. Bull's-eye! Some Nip in the pillbox had quick hands because three seconds later both grenades came flying back at us. I swear they landed within five feet. I jumped up, took three steps and dove. Baker did too, 'cept he dove a second too late. The grenades exploded, peppering his back with shrapnel.

"What could I do? Had to get him out of there or he was a goner. I grabbed him around the back of the shoulders and dragged him toward the nearest bushes. At any second I expected a bullet to part my hair. Didn't happen, though. I had to be one of the luckiest sons of bitches in the Fifth Marines. After I pulled Baker into the undergrowth, I looked for the nearest ridge or sand bank to get him out of harm's way. About forty yards towards the beach I could see a nice slope on the shore down to the water. I says, 'Hang in there, Lieutenant. I'll get you outta here.' He just groaned until I started dragging him again. Then he screamed. Not much I could do about it. Blood poured out of the wounds on his back. Had to get him help fast.

"Baker wasn't a heavy man, maybe five-ten and a hundred and sixty, but it was so damn hot and I was so damn tired, felt like I was dragging a three-hundred-pound buck. Finally, we got to the sand bank, and I plopped down beside him, panting like a scared hound. I'd managed to lay him on his belly. Blood soaked the back of his blouse and pants. His groans came quicker, like he couldn't get air into his lungs. Oh hell, I thought, don't' die on me, Lieutenant.

"Then I peered down the beach 'bout fifty yards and saw a couple stretcher bearers comin' our way. I shouted, "Help! Over here!" and waved. They ran low along the shore to us, and I recognized them—Jackson and his buddy, Parker. 'Well I'll be a cross-eyed jackass,' I says. 'You boys got good timing.'

"They slid into the sand right below us and spread out their stretcher. That's when I saw it, sparkling in the sunshine. 'What the hell?' I says. 'Where'd you get that gaddamn watch?'

Jackson gave me that none-of-your-damn-business look.

"'You thievin' bastard. You sonovabitch. You stole that off a dead body,' I says.

He ignored me and scooted closer to Baker, then mumbled something to Parker 'bout the best way to lift the body.

"'Hey,' I says and pointed at his wrist, 'Gimme that gaddamn watch.'

"He turned on me like a cornered weasel. 'Screw you,' he says. 'You robbed me once. Ain't gonna happen again. Not as long as my heart's still beatin'.'

"That's when I pulled out my pistol and aimed right between his eyes. 'Gimme the gaddamn watch. Now!' I says."

CHAPTER 17

Byron had arranged to pick up J.J. Jackson at the arrivals curb outside the baggage claim. He steered into the proper lane, which curved downhill to the lower level of the terminal, and checked the signs to find Southwestern's release area. From hearing J.J.'s deep voice on the phone, Byron pictured a large man, an ex-football player in his younger days perhaps, but now overweight with the natural spread of middle age and losing his hair. Byron had told J.J. to look for a white Caravan. When he saw the tall, lanky, white-haired, silver-mustached gentleman wearing a stylish blue suit, he almost passed him. The handsome man waved and reached for his suitcase, and Byron hit his brakes. As he slowed to a stop, he thought, 'Whadaya know? J.J.'s a black version of me.'

Byron jumped out of the van and rushed around the front of the vehicle. "J.J.?" he said, extending his hand.

The dapper man nodded, his smile spreading the silver mustache. "You got it. Byron Butler, I presume, and right on time."

The handshake was firm, white against rich copper. J.J.'s eyes quickly met Byron's gaze and twinkled with merriment.

"It's nice to meet you face to face," Byron said before releasing his grip.

"Been looking forward to this for the last couple of days. Had to rearrange some things. But I'm here. Raring to go. Ready to roll."

"Well . . ." Byron lowered his eyes, lips tightening into a frozen smile. Remembering the tape—Stanley Wright's pistol aimed between Josiah's eyes during the firefight on the beach—he wondered how J.J. would handle the revelation of a crime against his father. "I hope what you discover here about your dad's war days will make this trip worth it."

"I have no doubt. Couldn't pass up the chance. Hope to get some questions answered. Maybe learn more about my old man—what kind of soldier he was, how he died—that sort of thing. Do you think Mr. Stone will have answers?"

Byron nodded. *Maybe not the ones you want to hear.* He said, "Yes, J.J, there's a good chance Judd Stone knows what happened to your father."

"Great. If that's the only question that gets answered, then the trip'll be worth it."

Byron opened the side door of the van, and J.J. placed his small suitcase on the nearest seat. "Good, old mini-van," J.J. said as Byron slid the door shut. "My wife and I put a ton of miles on several of these down through the years—hauling kids to baseball and soccer practice, packing it to the gills for trips to Disney World."

Byron chuckled. They climbed into the front seats and Byron pointed to the odometer. "This one's got ninety thousand miles on it. Just broken in. My goal is two hundred thousand."

J.J.'s laugh was hearty and contagious. "Two hundred thousand? That would even break my record—one and eighty-five thousand on a Pontiac Transport. Good luck on that one."

As Byron pulled out of the pickup area, the tension he'd felt in his back and chest on the drive up eased with the conversation. He sensed J.J. was one of those rare people with whom he felt comfortable the first time meeting him, as if he'd known him for years.

"Judd Stone had chemo this morning," Byron said as he moved into the passing lane to get by an old pickup truck. "I'm worried he may need a few hours to recover before talking to us."

"I've got all day. Can even stay the night somewhere if need be, but I definitely have to get back by tomorrow evening. Lot's to do on Monday."

"You hungry, J.J.? There's a King's Restaurant down the road about ten miles. My treat."

"Your treat?"

Byron glanced at him, catching that glint of fun in his eyes. "Well, haaaell yeah," J.J. said, "I'm hungry if you's buying. Specially if they's got fried chicken."

Byron did a double take to make sure J.J. exaggerated the accent to be humorous. On the second look J.J. burst out with another hearty laugh. "That's right, Byron," J.J. said. "I'm fluent in several dialects. You gotta know which one'll be more effective at a particular fundraiser. I practice the psychology of making potential donors feel more comfortable."

"I should be taking notes for my next stewardship sermon."

J.J. laughed again.

On the way to the restaurant they talked about their families. J.J. lamented that his nest emptied five years ago. His oldest boy worked as a district attorney in the Augusta area, and his youngest son had just signed a contract with the Richmond Braves, Atlanta's farm team. Byron related that his twin boys loved baseball and would have lots of questions about making it in the pros. J.J. beamed about his middle child, his daughter, Damika, who taught history at an inner-city school in Charleston, South Carolina. Last spring her peers in the state association voted her Educator of the Year. Byron shared about his daughter Christine's plans to attend medical school at Ohio University in the fall. As he pulled into the restaurant's parking lot, Byron looked forward to the rest of the day, the opportunity to spend time with a kindred spirit.

* * *

Byron pushed aside the remains of his baked scrod and mashed potatoes, centered his recently refilled coffee cup in front of him, and reached for the cream. "Tell me about the teen center," he said. "How long have you been running the place?"

After swallowing the last of his spinach salad, J.J. said, "Almost fifteen years. It started as a dream during my days as a social worker. Back then I dealt with too many broken homes and mixed up kids. Most of the time I arrived on the scene too late—when things had already turned sour."

"Must've been a tough job."

"Definitely frustrating. Kept thinking there's gotta be a better way. Time after time I noticed these families shared a common factor."

"Poverty?"

J.J. shook his head sideways. "Nope. Not always. The common thread was a missing father. The dads were either in jail, dead or had abandoned them."

The word *abandoned* reverberated in Byron's ears like a cracked bell. His father had *abandoned* him. The early years were the worst. Some of the most painful images still rippled in the distant pool of childhood memory—walking through

155

the neighborhood alleys alone; seeing boys with their fathers tossing the football, washing the car, wrestling in the yard, building a snowman. At the age of seven he didn't know what the word abandoned meant, but he felt the pain the act had created within him. It was a gaping wound that could be healed only by a father's love. But Byron's father never stepped forward to tend that wound.

By the time Byron entered the fifth grade he'd found a friend with a dad who showed him some attention. He remembered tagging along with Will Wright during those boyhood years and looking up to Will's father, Stanley Wright. With a bad temper and a penchant to occasionally drink with his buddies, Mr. Wright wasn't the perfect father figure, but at least he welcomed Byron with open arms to come along wherever they went. Perhaps it was Stanley Wright's open-arms policy that kept Byron from becoming a troubled kid—from experimenting with drugs or committing adolescent crimes like shoplifting or vandalism. At least one adult male cared enough to spend time with him. Ironically, the same Stanley Wright may have killed J.J.'s father.

"I know what it's like to grow up in a fatherless home—" Byron said. "Incredibly difficult. Did your mother ever remarry?"

"Nope. Just me and her. Momma was a saint. She worked three jobs to keep a roof over our heads and the repo man two steps behind us. And she never let me forget about Dad: the kind of man he was—a good athlete, a championship boxer in the Marines, and, most importantly, a war hero, dying for freedom."

Byron bobbed his head. "Knowing he was a great man had to comfort you during those years."

"Yeah," J.J. said as he shoved the salad bowl to the side. "But that doesn't replace the man. Did you know your father at all?"

156

"No. Not until it was too late. My mother told me who he was after he died."

"Too bad." J.J. pointed to his chest. "Leaves a hole right here, doesn't it?"

Byron nodded.

"That's why I started the center. Too many kids with holes in their souls. I wanted to offer help before things got out of hand—before a kid started gang-banging or shooting up or robbing Seven-Elevens."

"Has the center made much of a difference?"

"Haaaell yeah." J.J.'s smile returned. "My volunteers and I have been substitute dads for hundreds of kids. It's hard to say how many lives we've touched—how many kids are on the right road today because of the center. That's why I bust my ass all year long to raise money. We don't receive government funding. I knock on a lot of doors and speak at every Rotary luncheon in the greater Atlanta area."

"I hope the trip up here didn't take too many potential contributions from the coffers."

"Actually it did. I had to cancel a couple of fundraisers. But I'll work twice as hard when I get back. We're down about twenty-five thousand for the year." J.J. took a deep breath and blew it out with a slight whistle. "I feel a little guilty, but I couldn't pass up this chance to learn more about what happened to my father."

Byron placed a five-dollar tip next to his coffee cup, lifted the bill from the end of the table, slid out from the booth and stood. "Well then, we better quit flapping our jaws and get on the road again."

J.J. stood and slapped Byron on the back. "Haaaell yeah. Let's not keep Mr. Stone waiting any longer than necessary."

* * *

As they drove down Route 7 through Steubenville, their conversation trailed off. Byron tried to generate the nerve to reveal the darker side of Stone and Wright's dealings with Josiah Jackson. With the effort, the tightness in his chest and back returned. Nevertheless, J.J. had to be prepared for Stone's confession, but how do you tell someone his father may have been murdered on the battlefield by a fellow Marine over something as inconsequential as a wristwatch?

Byron had stopped the tape at the point where Stanley Wright aimed the gun at Josiah and demanded the return of the watch. Maybe he should rewind the tape for a few seconds and replay it. That would be a starting point. But J.J. would have a hundred questions. Byron needed to give a condensed version of the story from his three sources—Stone' narrative, Wright's tapes, and Helen's letters—then play the tape. Now was the time. Waiting until after the hospital visit wouldn't be fair.

"J.J., I need to tell you something," Byron said.

J.J. had been eyeing the acres of rusted metal buildings, train tracks, and smokestacks of the steel plant along the river. He turned and said, "Sounds serious."

"It is. I should have told you over the phone."

After a few seconds of silence, J.J. said, "Well, don't keep me waiting now. Let the snake out of the sack."

"What Judd Stone wants to say to you—it's . . . it's more like a confession."

"A confession?"

"Yes. The first time I visited him in the hospital earlier this week he led me to believe he had something to do with your father's death."

"He killed my father?"

Byron swallowed and searched for the right words. A semi tractor-trailer truck loaded with steel coils thundered by on the left, too close for comfort. He gripped the steering wheel tighter and inched the van toward the right edge line. "I don't think he killed your father, but I'm not sure. He had a friend by the name of Stanley Wright who might have killed him over the watch."

"Over the watch? Do you mean the championship watch? The one my father won?"

"Yes. But your father never won it officially."

"What the haaaell are you talking about? Never won it officially? I've got a letter in my pocket claiming that he did."

"A letter?"

"I'll read it to you."

Byron guessed J.J. brought along one of his father's letters. Of course, Josiah would have claimed to be the First Marine Division Champion. He beat the official champion. He deserved the recognition. But that wasn't the point. Official or unofficial, two bigoted white guys were willing to go to extremes to get the watch back. Byron decided to remain silent and let J.J. try to prove his point.

"Here it is," J.J. said, unfolding the page. "*To my darling wife, Anita,* . . . that's my momma. *I finally got a break. A chance to write. Been thinking about you and J.J. a lot. Give that little man a big hug and kiss for me.*

"*As I write I hear the bombs our planes are dropping on enemy positions. A minute don't go by on this island that I don't hear explosions. Guess I'll never get used to it. I can see a big fire and lots of smoke on the mountain. Glad I'm not there right now. Soon I will be, though. They always send us back up to carry the wounded and dead down the ridges. I know you wanted me to stay a cook. Sorry, but I needed to see real action, and this is the most they'll let me do.*

"*What the hell's wrong with the Marine brass? Don't they know we coloreds can shoot as good as those white boys? Probably better. Give us cats some rifles, and we would whip the Japs in no time flat. No use complaining. What good would it do? Maybe before this battle is over we'll get our chance.*

"Got good news. A while back I wrote to you about winning the middleweight championship. I promised to bring home the golden watch for J.J. Then two white jackasses scared me into giving the watch back. They said I didn't win it fair and square. The hell I didn't. God knows I'm the champion. I proved it in front of everybody. What could I do, though? They threatened to kill me. So I let them have it. Then I just prayed—God, if I am the true champion, bring that watch back to me.

"God answered my prayer. On the first day of the battle me and Parker volunteered to move bodies from the beach. I was kneeling near a dead Marine. Something on the ground glowed in the sunshine like a sign from heaven—it was the watch. I picked it up and read the words on the back—First Marine Division Middleweight Champion. Can you believe it? A true miracle. Right then and there I promised God, Jesus, and the Holy Ghost I wouldn't take it off again until I stepped through our front door and handed it to J.J. You know I'm a man who keeps his word.

"That's all I have for now. Can't wait to get home, baby. We'll make up for lost time. You better be ready for me. Tell my little man I love him and to make a special place on his shelf for the watch. His daddy is the First Division champion. Even God says so.

With all my love,

Josiah"

J.J. folded the letter and lowered it into his lap. "How could he not be the official champion? If the judges declare you the winner, then you're the champ. Sounds like a couple of jackasses disagreed with the decision. What difference does that make? They strong-armed the watch off my father, but somehow he got it back. Just because two good ol' boys swipe the prize doesn't make it unofficial."

Byron cleared his throat and swallowed. "You don't quite understand what happened. Judd Stone was the First Marine Division Middleweight Champion. Blacks weren't allowed to compete in the tournament. Your father claimed to be the best boxer on Pavuvu and challenged Stone to a fight. Josiah and his buddies put up $500 for a chance to win the watch. Your dad pounded the crap out of Stone, but someone threw in the towel—Stanley Wright. A private by the name of Howard Kinloch handed over the watch and money to your father. There were no *official* judges—just a soldier both the blacks and whites trusted to hold the goods. When Stone regained his bearings, he claimed your father's corner threw in the towel. Wright kept his mouth shut, and nobody could prove anything. It's a long story, but Stone and Wright determined to get that watch back at any cost."

For several seconds Byron could hear J.J.'s breathing accelerate like a diver building oxygen for a deep plunge. He tucked the letter into his suit pocket and placed his hands on the dashboard. "Do you mean to tell me my father didn't die on the battlefield? One of these two jackasses murdered him over a damn watch?"

"I want to play a tape for you. Stanley Wright, one of those two jackasses you're talking about, recorded his war memoirs years ago. I was listening to it on the way to the airport. You need to hear this before we visit Judd Stone."

J.J. took a deep breath. "Okay. But you know I wasn't expecting anything like this when I stepped off the plane today. You've rattled me a little, Byron."

"Again, I apologize. I should have told you more on the phone, but I didn't hear this tape until today." Byron hit the button on the player to rewind the tape for about ten seconds. Then he pressed play.

Stanley Wright's voice began midway through a sentence about dragging Lieutenant Baker toward the beach. When he mentioned seeing the stretcher-bearers fifty yards away, J.J. leaned forward, apparently tuned to Wright's every word: "They slid into the sand right below us and spread out their stretcher. That's when I saw it, sparkling in the sunshine. 'What the hell?' I says. 'Where'd you get that gaddamn watch?'

Jackson gave me that none-of-your-damn-business look.

"'You thievin' bastard. You sonovabitch. You stole that off a dead body,' I says.

He ignored me and scooted closer to Baker, then mumbled something to Parker 'bout the best way to lift the body.

"'Hey,' I says and pointed at his wrist, 'Gimme that gaddamn watch.'

"He turned on me like a cornered weasel. 'Screw you,' he says. 'You robbed me once. Ain't gonna happen again. Not as long as long as my heart's still beatin'.'

"That's when I pulled out my pistol and aimed right between his eyes. 'Gimme the gaddamn watch. Now!' I says."

"Can you believe it? He ignored me. I felt like pulling the trigger right then and there. Parker was shaking like I was gonna shoot him too.

"Jackson says, 'Pick up your end, Parker. Let's get movin'.'

"As they walked away, I aimed right at his back. But I couldn't do it. Hell, they were carrying Lieutenant Baker to safety. How could I shoot the stretcher-bearer right out from under my Lieutenant?

"Later that day Judd Stone caught up with the platoon. Guess a sniper shot Keys, and Judd had to help haul him back to the medical station. I told Judd about Lieutenant Baker getting a back full of shrapnel. Then I hit him with the big one—Josiah Jackson stole his watch off a dead man. Whewweee, did the shit hit the fan. To a good Marine there's nothing worse than robbing your own dead.

"Judd looked at me with hell's fire in his eyes and said, 'I'm gonna kill that nigger. I swear on my mother's grave that sonovabitch won't get off this island alive."

Byron reached and hit the stop button.

No one said anything for several minutes. Byron wondered if he made a mistake following up on Stone's strange request. Did J.J. need to know this? The ugly truth seemed to be materializing—Josiah Jackson died a victim rather than a hero. Was it worth giving Stone an opportunity to clear his conscience?

Finally J.J. said, "This is the same Judd Stone we're going to see at the hospital, right? The one that swore he was going to murder my father?"

Byron nodded. "The one and the same."

CHAPTER 18

With his voice trembling slightly, J.J. said, "I want to hear the rest of the tape." He pressed his hands to the dashboard. "I need to know what happened. If Stone's the one who tore this hole in me and crushed my momma, then I have to prepare myself before I talk to him."

Byron nodded. *Oh God, this man's in agony. An old wound just got ripped open.* He reached and pressed the play button.

Stanley Wright's matter-of-fact tone continued, impervious to the palpable emotion in the car. "That black Sambo was in trouble. Believe me, you didn't want to get Judd Stone's hackles up. He'd get even. You could bet a month's wages on it.

"We'd been fighting for ten straight days. I never felt tireder, dirtier, hungrier, or thirstier in my life. Finally, we got orders to head north along the main road. Our commanders figured they'd better give us a couple days' break before we all bit the dust from exhaustion. Hell, nearly half of us were dead or wounded anyway. How you gonna win the battle without rifle squads? Impossible.

"To get to the north end, we climbed into troop trucks and traveled the road along the east beach. I looked to my right and saw the white trails of Japanese machinegun tracers and the flash—BANG of mortars and artillery along Bloody Nose Ridge. Oh shit, I thought, the Japs are smackin' our troops harder than Babe Ruth wallops a changeup. Glad I wasn't there. In the pit of my belly I knew sooner or later I would be.

"On the north end of the island we found some nice shell holes and set up camp in the fringe of the jungle. Time to lay back, catch some Zs, and write a letter or two. We weren't out of harm's way by no means, but I didn't mind an occasional bullet or mortar shell compared to the constant barrage of the first ten days. Despite the stink, the dirt, the heat, the insects and the noise, I must have slept three hours straight. Judd had to wake me up for supper. Our first hot chow since D-day— pork chops, boiled potatoes, and green beans. Tasted like a gourmet meal at the Ritz.

"After supper we took turns sleeping and watching. With all we'd been through, you'd think the Nips would give us a break for one night. Hell no. On my second watch, probably three o'clock in the morning, I heard a terrible racket coming from a hole about twenty yards away. Had to be an infiltrator. I whipped Marlene to my shoulder and aimed but couldn't see much. Heard plenty, though—screams, cursing, and those terrible 'chunnkkk' sounds of a sword chopping into flesh and bone.

"'Judd! Get up! Infiltrator!' I says. Then came the footsteps. I couldn't get a bead on the zigzagging sonovabitch 'til he came right up on me. When he swung that samurai sword over his head, I raised Marlene's barrel to his chest and pulled the trigger. Jammed! Gaddamn tropics—hell on M1s. I closed my eyes, expecting to lose my head in the next second. Boom! Judd squeezed off a shot. Down came the Jap on top of me. His sword went clanging on the coral. I threw him off and checked to make sure he'd bought the whole nine acres. Deader than a bear rug. I'll be damned if Judd didn't put a bullet right between his eyes. Saved my life. That's something you don't soon forget.

"Judd jumped out of the hole and scrambled toward the screams. By the sound of it, I knew those boys had suffered some horrible hacking. A part of me didn't want to look, but I made myself hustle over to help.

"Awful groans and shrieks rose from the pit along with shuffling noises. I peered into the darkness and tried to make out who was who. Judd had jumped into the hole to check their wounds. A few seconds later the new lieutenant, Wallace Preston, showed up. He was an English teacher back in the states, a little green around the gills.

"'What happened, men?' Preston says.

"'Infiltrator,' I says. 'Samurai warrior. Judd put his lights out, but not before he cut these boys up pretty bad.'

Preston pulled out his lighter, flicked a flame, and lowered it into the hole. Sergeant Ed Dunmore looked up at us with blank eyes, his head cocked at an odd angle. The sword had sliced three-quarters of the way through his neck.

"'Oh God,' Hollingsworth says, and then vomited up those pork chops we had for dinner.

"Judd says, 'Drake's got a bad cut on his shoulder. The sword must have glanced off his helmet.'

"I yelled for a corpsman. Within two minutes good ol' Doc Halleran showed up. Doc was a helluva man. Always there when you needed him.

"Lieutenant Preston says, 'We'll take care of Drake. You boys go bury that Jap you killed.'

"'I'll bury him all right,' Judd says.

166

"I thought, Oh hell, what's he gonna do now. Judd hadn't been in a good humor since I told him about Jackson stealing the watch. He and Ed Dunmore had been buddies since boot camp. Seeing Dunmore's head dangling by a few shreds had to set him off. Sometimes a strange mood would come over Judd like a wicked banshee. Whenever that happened, I tried to stay out of his way. He headed toward that dead Jap like a madman about to put a lid on this whole incident.

"The Jap officer's body had slid to the bottom of our hole. Judd jumped in, hoisted him up by the armpits, and leaned him on the side of the crater with his neck arched and head resting on level ground.

"'What the hell you gonna do?' I says.

"Judd leapt out of the hole and grabbed the samurai sword. 'You can have the sword when I'm done,' he says. Then he raised it over his head with both hands and whacked that Nip's noggin off with one chop.

"'Are you nuts?' I says. 'You can't kill a man twice.'

"His voice sounded like a junkyard dog growling at me. 'The sonovabitch killed Ed Dunmore. He can go to hell without a head.' Then he handed me the sword. Knowing that weapon had just ended a Marine's life, wounded another, and decapitated a dead Jap made my stomach do flip flops. I pulled out my handkerchief and wiped blood off the blade. Glad it wasn't mine.

"We carried the body about thirty yards into the jungle and tossed it. Hell, we didn't want to waste time trying to dig a grave in the damn coral. Figured the flies, bugs and buzzards could feast for the next few days. Judd put the head on the floor of our shell hole next to his gear. Gave me the willies. I kept picturing the damn thing smiling at me, saying, 'You Rucky bastard. I Rost my head over you.'

"The next morning Judd built a good fire, borrowed a pot, and filled it with swamp water. I wondered if he was gonna wash his clothes, cook some crabs, or make fish-head soup. When the water started bubbling like a witch's cauldron, he fetched the head out of the bottom of the hole and dropped it into the pot. I didn't say a word to him. Just stayed out of his way. After he boiled all the skin off the skull, he lifted it out with an entrenching tool and started to dig the brains out with a stick. I couldn't watch anymore, so I went for a walk to show off my new sword.

"Making my rounds, I kept hearing scuttlebutt about our regiment's next assignment—Ngesebus Island. Ngesebus was a small island a few hundred yards off the northern shore of Peleliu. Like pesky bumblebees, the few hundred Jap troops that occupied the place stung us occasionally with small arms fire. Because the island had a few bunkers and a landing strip, the brass decided the time had come to send in the exterminators.

"I headed back to camp to give Judd the lowdown. He was still as sour as a constipated crocodile. While he was polishing up his new souvenir, I told him about our latest assignment.

He gave me that don't-bother-me-with-shitty-news look and held up the skull. 'To be or not to be,' he says and then laughed like a loony.

"I says, 'What the *hell's* the matter? Have you gone Asiatic on me?'

He shook his head and says, 'Figures a bumpkin like you has never read Shakespeare.'

"'Shakespeare?' I says. 'What the hell you talking about?'

"He says, 'I can't remember which play, but some king holds up a skull and says, 'To be or not to be, that's the question.' Haven't you ever heard that line before?'

"'Sure,' I says. 'I'm not stupid.'

"He patted the top of the skull and says, 'That's always the question—to be or not to be.' Then he glanced over and saw Howard Kinloch sitting under a palm tree reading a book. He set the skull on top of his backpack and sprang to his feet like a cat that just spied a wounded bird.

"Poor Howard, I thought. He's in trouble.

"Judd walked over to Howard and stared down at him. 'What're you reading, Kinloch?' he says.

"Howard lifted the book and says, 'The Bible.'

"Judd says, 'Is that where you're getting that *love-your-enemies* shit? Is that why you fire your rifle into the sky every time we're in a firefight?'

"Howard just looked at him.

"'You know what I mean,' Judd says. 'That pray-for-those-who-persecute-you shit.'

"Howard shrugged.

"'Then you better start praying for me,' Judd says. He reached down, snatched the Bible out of Howard's hands, walked over to a mud puddle, dropped the book into the slime and stepped on it.

"'What'd you do that for?' Howard says.

"'For your own good.' Judd says, 'and mine. If you don't learn to hate and kill the enemy, then my life's at risk. I don't want to die because Howard the Coward loves Jesus. To be or not to be, that's the question. The only good Jap's a dead Jap. You better learn that lesson or you're not going to live long on this island.'

"Judd stomped off toward the beach. I thought it was a helluva mean thing to do, desecrate a Bible like that. I walked over, lifted it out of the puddle, shook off the water, and handed it back to Howard. Tried to explain to him about Judd's moods and how Dunmore's death shook him up. Howard thanked me. He opened the book to the page covered with mud. There were only a few words you could still make out. After he read them he looked at me with the strangest expression. Kinda rattled me. He says, 'The first shall be last.'

"I'll never forget those words—*the first shall be last*. I didn't know what the hell they meant, but Howard seemed to understand. Almost like God gave him some kind of revelation right then and there.

"Early the next morning Marine Corsair fighters came zooming over our heads for the pre-invasion bombing and strafing of Ngesebus. Believe you me, they blew that little island to hell. They'd dive at the beach with machine guns flaming and rockets firing. Right when you thought they'd plow into the ground, they'd pull up and soar back into the sky. Then the ships offshore lobbed their huge shells, like flying refrigerators—KABOOMMMM! That little shit of an island got pulverized. We piled into amtracs and crossed the few hundred yards of water. No opposition whatsoever met us at the beach. The Fifth Regiment of the First Marine Division whipped Ngesebus in less than a day with very few casualties. That's something we never expected.

"The next morning orders came we certainly expected but didn't want to hear—it was the Fifth's turn to take on Bloody Nose Ridge. Like Chesty Puller's First Regiment during the first few days of battle, the Seventh had been shredded by the Jap's fortified positions on the hillsides. Attack one cave, and six emplacements on the opposite ridge would open up on you. Now the Seventh needed reinforcing. I felt like I was getting ready to attend my own funeral. What could we do? Had to obey orders. I wasn't no coward.

"The next ten days of fighting became a blur in my mind. Every ridge, every blasted canyon, every valley looked the same. The artillery, mortars and tanks would fire their rounds at caves and pillboxes. Then we rifle platoons attacked. The Japs were smart. They waited for the big explosions to stop, stepped out of their caves, and zeroed in on those stupid Marines charging up the hill with their measly M1s and a few grenades. I saw a lot of good men die during those days. The ridges had names like The Five Sisters and The Five Brothers. Some murderous family of hills, huh? Between The Five Sisters and The Five Brothers we lost about three-quarters of our regiment.

"Finally, we fought our way to the northern end of Horseshoe Valley. It looked like a scene from another planet. The vegetation had been blasted, burned and charred. Steep coral mesas and ridges surrounded a wide draw. By then, I guess it was October 5th or 6th, all the tanks had either broken down or been disabled by enemy fire. Unbelievable—rifle companies without tank support attacking mutually supporting fortified positions. Now I know how Custer felt, except the enemy wasn't shooting arrows.

"Lieutenant Preston commanded two platoons with about fifteen men left in each. He decided we'd cross the draw—about sixty yards—to a defilade of smaller ridges at the far end of the valley. Guess he wanted to be the hero and lead the first platoon across. He made Judd acting sergeant of our platoon. We'd provide cover fire if the Japs opened up on them.

"I lay next to Judd and Gator Snowfield at the top of a shell hole and waited for Preston and his boys to make the charge. Howard Kinloch crouched on the other side of Snowfield, the barrel of his M1 wobbling like an old man's cane. Judd told us to keep our eyes on the ridges to detect any gunfire and then shoot like hell once we found a target.

"Finally Lieutenant Preston took off, weaving across the draw. His men followed at five-yard intervals. Ten—twenty—thirty—forty yards—no sounds except for the footsteps of those fifteen Marines. Then with all of them in the open, the Japs let loose a firestorm. From twenty or more positions on the surrounding hillsides bullets hailed down. We fired, but it made no difference. All of the men in Preston's platoon fell, wounded or dead.

"About twenty-five yards away Private Gary Saunders squirmed on the ground, holding his belly and screaming for help. He was the closest one to us.

"Snowfield says, 'I'll get him.'

"'No, dammit!' Judd says. 'You don't have a chance out there.'

Snowfield jumped up and took off anyway. They cut him down a few yards before he reached Saunders. Now there were two men screaming in agony less than thirty yards away. I listened for about three minutes and then couldn't stand it anymore. Figured I'd die sooner or later. Now's as good as time as any. I jumped to my feet and went for Snowfield. Made it about five yards before a hot poker hit me in the quad. That's what it felt like anyway. Down I went. I yells, 'I'm hit!'

"Judd says, 'Stay down Stanley. We'll get help for you!'

"'Hurry up,' I says. 'I'm bleeding like hell.' Luckily I landed in a small ditch that provided some protection. After about five minutes I started to feel cold. That's not a good sign when it's over 100 degrees. As I was about to pass out I heard our boys let loose with a volley of gunfire. Someone grabbed me by the forearms and dragged me across the coral—the longest five yards of my life. When I glanced up, I couldn't believe my eyes—Josiah Jackson. Damn was I glad I didn't kill him over that stupid championship watch. The last thing I remember was Judd yelling, 'Doc! Doc! Need help! Over here! Doc Halleran!'

The tape ended and Byron hit the eject button. He glanced at J.J. and noticed an odd smile on his face. "We're not far from the hospital," Byron said. "Sorry we didn't find out what happened to your father."

J.J. pointed to the tape player. "Dad saved that man— Stanley . . . what's-his-name—Wilson or Wright? My father *was* a hero just like Momma said."

Byron nodded. "He had tremendous courage to face such intense enemy fire. Not many men would have done it."

"You're right."

As they entered the Wheeling Tunnel, Byron asked, "Do you think you're ready to face Judd Stone now? We could pull off somewhere and try to find the next tape."

J.J. shook his head. "I'm ready. Let's roll. I don't know what Judd Stone did to my father, but I have to admit, he was a courageous man too. They all were."

"No doubt about that. I never imagined the kind of conditions those men fought under for weeks, even months at a time. What's the old saying about freedom?"

"Three simple words," J.J. said. "Freedom isn't free."

* * *

Byron and J.J. walked down the fourth floor hallway, their hard-soled shoes scuffing on the white linoleum and echoing off the walls. They reached room 411 and stopped abruptly, confronted by the sign posted on the closed door: NO VISITORS PLEASE.

"I was afraid of this," Byron said.

In a low voice J.J. asked, "He's not about to die, is he?"

"Don't think so. He went through chemo this morning. It hits him pretty hard. Usually he makes a comeback the next day."

"What're we going to do? Hang out here a while?"

Byron sorted through his options. Perhaps they could seek out Stone's doctor or the head nurse and get permission to talk to him. If a visit wasn't possible, they could head to Byron's house for supper and return to the hospital that evening. J.J. had mentioned he could stick around until tomorrow afternoon if necessary. In that case, Byron would have more time to catch him up on the information about Josiah in Howard and Helen's letters. Hopefully Stone would be alert tomorrow. *Please, God, don't let the old Marine die now. Not without a confession.*

"Let me see if I can find the head nurse," Byron said. "Maybe we can twist her arm a little. Worst case scenario—we go back to my house and try again tomorrow."

J.J. tilted his head and closed one eye. "The worst case scenario—Stone kicks the bed pan before we talk."

Byron shrugged, smiling sheepishly at that possibility. As he turned to walk to the nurse's station, he heard a muffled voice, a few indistinguishable words. He stopped and faced J.J. They stared at Stone's door. The words came louder, clearer: "Doc! Doc! Over here! Need help! Doc Halleran!"

CHAPTER 19

Judd Stone stared at the crimson flow that soaked Wright's upper pant leg. *How much blood can a man lose before he dies?* "You're gonna be all right, Stanley. Doc's coming. He'll fix you up."

"I don't feel so hot," Stanley wheezed. "I'm dizzy. Can't see straight."

"Don't talk. Just lie still," Judd said. Stanley lay on his back halfway down the shell hole. Josiah Jackson and his litter partner, Leroy Parker, crouched at his feet, sweat pouring off their black faces. At the top of the shell hole, Howard Kinloch lay on his belly, staring at the bodies scattered across the blasted coral field.

"Is Jackson still here?" Stanley asked.

"Yeah. Right below you," Judd said.

Between short breaths Stanley said, "I want to apologize to him."

"Apologize to him? What the hell for?"

"For almost . . ." His breaths came with more difficulty. ". . . shooting him . . ." He swallowed, ". . . over that gaddamn . . .watch."

My watch. In the chaos of battle Judd had forgotten about the watch. He glanced at Jackson's wrist and noticed how it shone in the sunshine.

"I forgive you," Jackson said.

"Thanks. And . . . thanks for . . . s-saving m-me," Stanley managed before the muscles in his neck slackened, and his head fell back against the coral.

"It's his job to fetch wounded Marines," Judd said, but Stanley didn't respond. Judd twisted and peered down the hill. "Hurry up, Doc! He's lost a lot of blood!"

Doc Halleran, his face streaked with grime, climbed the slope on all fours with his medical bag slung over his shoulder. Two stretcher men scrambled behind him. Doc plopped his bag next to Stanley. "God Almighty," Doc said. "Looks like the bullet caught an artery. Cut the trouser leg off, Stone. Hurry."

Judd whipped his K-bar knife from the scabbard on his belt, inserted it into the cuff of Stanley's pant leg, and ripped upward, splitting the camouflage fabric. With both hands, he tore the cloth up the leg to above the wound. Blood seeped out of the bullet hole on the upper quad. Doc Halleran slapped a thick bandage on the wound and ordered Judd to apply pressure to it. Quick as a duck on a June bug, Doc slipped a tourniquet under Stanley's thigh, pulled it tight and cinched it. Then he wrapped the bandage tight with gauze and tape.

"We got to get him out of here now, or he's not going to make it," Doc said, glancing at his litter bearers.

"Me and Parker'll carry him back," Josiah Jackson said. "I'm the one who went after him."

"No!" Judd shouted. "We need you two boys here. Shultz and Hammer can handle it."

"We can help," Jackson protested. "Four litter getters can move a body faster than two."

"Dammit, I said, 'No.' I need you here."

"What the hell for?" Jackson asked.

"We've got wounded."

Jackson stepped up the slope and stared at the numerous bodies strewn across the draw more than twenty-five yards away.

Hammer and Shultz had already lifted Stanley onto the stretcher and crouched to grab the handles. "Hurry boys," Doc said as he finished inserting a needle into Stanley's arm and securing it. He raised a plasma bag over Stanley's chest and adjusted the flow. "We've got to get moving. He's critical." The two men lifted the stretcher and shuffled down the slope, Doc Halleran keeping pace with the suspended plasma bag.

"What wounded?" Jackson asked. "Those Marines are dead."

"I say they're not." Judd shifted his gaze to the glittering timepiece. "But first thing's first. Gimme my watch."

"The hell with that. Like I told your buddy, Wright—the only way you gonna get this watch back is to put a bullet through my heart."

Judd swiped his M1 off the ground and aimed it at Jackson's chest.

"Go ahead," Jackson said, "if you wanna go to prison. Unless you gonna kill Parker and Kinloch too. They my witnesses."

Judd glanced over his shoulder. Kinloch, sitting at the top of the shell hole a few yards away, stared, eyes wide and jaw hanging, as if he wanted to speak but couldn't get the words out. Returning his gaze to the stretcher-bearers, Judd noticed Parker trembling.

"Okay, you damn thief. You'll get yours and I'll get mine. Just a matter of time." Judd crawled to the top of the hole. "Jackson and Parker. I want you to go out there and bring back Snowfield."

"You crazy?" Jackson said. "Wright was only a few yards away. Snowfield's almost half a football field away. Besides, he's dead."

Judd eyed the bodies. "Do your duty, nigger. I said go get him."

"That's suicide. I ain't going out there to die for no dead man. I got a wife and a three-year-old boy at home. Anyway, who died and made you master?"

"Lieutenant Preston. He's lying out there with the rest of them. But he made me acting sergeant fifteen minutes ago. Ain't that right, Kinloch?"

Kinloch nodded. "Yeah, but . . .but . . ."

"But what, gaddammit?" Judd asked.

"I don't think Snowfield's alive either," Kinloch said. "I've been watching them. They're not crying or moving anymore. Just lying still."

"You shut the hell up!" With a swift shift of his body Judd jolted the butt of his M1 against Kinloch's helmet, flipping it onto the ground. Another thrust caught Kinloch on the side of the head. Down he went, limp as a KO'd boxer, sliding sideways to the bottom of the crater.

"We're down to one witness," Judd said, returning his aim to Jackson's chest. "Now I don't want to have to kill you for disobeying an order in the heat of battle, but I will."

Parker glared at Jackson with spooked horse's eyes.

"I know what you want," Jackson said. He pointed to the watch. "Let the Japs do your dirty work so you can strip it off me later. I'm tellin' you it ain't gonna happen. Go ahead. Shoot me."

"I will. But I think I'll kill Parker first. Then you." Judd slowly moved the barrel and aimed between Parker's wide eyes.

* * *

"He's calling for a doctor," J.J. said.

More words blustered from the other side of the door.

"Did you hear that?" Byron asked.

"Something like: 'Don't talk. Lie still.' Maybe there's a doctor in there already."

For several seconds Byron searched his mind to place the name *Doc Halleran.* Where had he heard it before? Stone's cancer doctor? *No. Halleran's the corpsman, the one that reminded Judd of me.* When Byron heard the words—*Apologize? What the hell for?*—he figured Stone couldn't be too close to Hades. He grabbed the knob, said, "Let's go," and shoved against the door.

As they entered, Stone babbled about fetching wounded Marines. Then he said, "Hurry up, Doc! He's lost a lot of blood."

"He's dreaming," Byron said. "He's on the battlefield."

"Should we wake him?"

"Shhhhhhh. Listen."

They edged to his bedside.

"No! We need you two boys here," Judd said and then mumbled several sentences with only a few distinguishable words—*thief . . . Jackson . . . bring back Snowfield.*

"He's talking about my father," J.J. whispered.

Stone's next words were very clear: "Do your duty, nigger. I said go get him."

"Son of a bitch," J.J. hissed between his teeth.

Stone's facial muscles tensed and writhed. His words became garbled.

Byron touched Stone's shoulder. His eyes blinked open and stared vaguely at the ceiling. His breathing accelerated, hands gripping his sheets.

"Are you all right, General?" Byron asked.

Stone glanced at Byron and said, "Doc?" When he saw Jackson, he sucked in a deep breath and raised his hands as if to ward off an attacker.

"Take it easy," Byron said. "You were dreaming."

"Jackson? Is that you?" Stone asked.

"I'm Jackson, " J.J. said.

Stone's lifted hands trembled. "Stay back," he gasped.

"I didn't come here to hurt you," J.J. said.

"You've come . . . back for it," Stone said with great difficulty. "That's why . . ." He took in two strained breaths. " . . .you're here."

"Huh?" J.J. glanced at Byron and shrugged.

"Relax, General," Byron said. "J.J.'s here because you asked him to come."

"J.J.?" Stone adjusted his oxygen tube, inhaling deeply.

"This is Josiah's son."

Several seconds passed as Stone stared at J.J., mouth agape, lower lip quivering. Finally he swiveled his head and said, "I thought you were . . . Josiah Jackson . . ." He paused to control his breathing. "—come back from . . . come back from the dead."

"I've come here to find out about my father," J.J. said.

Stone nodded. "I know . . . what happened . . .to your father." He coughed twice, swallowed, and repositioned the oxygen tube on his nose.

"Can you tell me anything?" J.J. asked.

Stone raised a finger. "What did . . . the preacher . . . tell me . . . about you?" he managed to ask between wheezes.

J.J. eyed Byron. "I don't know," he said as Byron shrugged.

"You run . . . some kind . . . of kid's program?"

"That's right. The Atlanta Center for Fatherless Teens."

"I'm glad . . ." Stone closed his eyes and spoke weakly. "I'm glad . . . you turned out good."

J.J. leaned closer. "Please, tell me about my father."

Stoned opened his eyes and met J.J.'s gaze. "I'm . . . responsible . . .for . . ." A sudden cough racked Stone's chest. He struggled for air between hacks.

"General, are you all right?" Byron asked.

Stone gasped, coughed, and swallowed.

With the sound of the door opening, light from the hallway brightened the room. "What are you two doing in here?" a woman barked as her bulk moved into the doorway, blocking the light. "This man was not to be disturbed. Can't you read? Who are you?"

"Sorry, Ma'am. I'm Reverend Byron Butler. I've been visiting Mr. Stone regularly. We were outside the door when we heard him call for help. I didn't know whether to . . ." Byron halted mid-sentence, scrambling for words to justify their intrusion.

"You should have came directly to the nurse's station," she said.

"Yes, you're right. We're sorry," J.J. said.

When the large nurse approached, Byron tried to step out of the way, but Stone grabbed his sleeve and pulled him closer. "Listen," Stone wheezed. "My house . . . the skull . . . bring the footlocker." He released Byron's shirt as the nurse swept Byron out of the way with a large forearm.

"Mr. Stone is very sick. He's been through a difficult treatment today. You'll have to leave," she said as she checked the monitors next to the bed.

"But . . . but this man has come from Atlanta . . ."

"Yes," J.J. said. "Mr. Stone requested I fly up to visit him."

"I *said* you'll have to leave." She turned and glared at Byron and then J.J. like a disgruntled bulldog. "This man needs rest. No visitors."

"May we come back this evening?" J.J. asked.

"No chance. Maybe tomorrow if he's feeling better." She pointed to the door. "Now leave, please."

Like two boys escaping the principal, they exited the room and hurried down the hallway. They slipped through the closing doors of an empty elevator. Byron hit the first floor button and said, "Tough nurse. Sorry about that. I tried to claim pastor privileges, but she wasn't impressed."

"Don't worry about it," J.J. said. "Tomorrow's another day."

"Let's hope tomorrow comes for Judd Stone."

"Hey, what did he say to you when he pulled on your elbow?"

"That was the strangest thing. He said, 'My house . . . the skull . . . bring the footlocker.'"

J.J.'s mouth pursed and eyebrows knotted. "What's he talking about?"

Byron rubbed his chin for several seconds. "There must be a footlocker somewhere at his house, but how do we find it?" Then he stiffened, his jaw dropping. "The skull. I know exactly where *the skull* is."

CHAPTER 20

When the elevator doors parted, Byron gawked at the familiar man wearing overalls and a plaid shirt and tried to change mental gears. "Earl," he said. "How's . . . How's . . .Eric?" Stone's final few words had entrenched Byron's line of thought, but he jolted himself away from the skull and footlocker to focus on the boy's condition.

Earl glanced up and eyed Byron as if he didn't recognize him at first; then his expression unleashed amazement along with a torrent of words. "Pastor Byron! You're not gonna believe this! He's out of the comma. Just got the call. Eric's awake! Come with me. It's a miracle! Let's go see him!" Earl lunged and bear-hugged Byron, pinning him against the back of the elevator.

Byron embraced the man and regained his balance. *Eric's conscious? Thank God. They thought he might be a vegetable.* "That's wonderful, Earl. When did you find out?"

"Twenty minutes ago. Got here as fast as I could." Earl released his grasp and turned towards the buttons as the elevator doors closed. When he saw J.J. standing there, he said, "Sorry. Didn't mean to trap you in here with us."

"No problem," J.J. said. "What floor?"

Earl hesitated, his eyes flitting from J.J. to Byron before he said, "Sixth."

"He's with me," Byron said. "My new friend, J.J."

Earl extended his hand. "Earl Waller. A buddy o' Byron's a buddy o'mine."

J.J. shook his hand. "Good to know you. Sounds like you just got good news."

"The greatest," Earl said, his weathered face beaming. "The greatest."

On the ride up to the sixth floor and walk down the hallway, Earl related to J.J. that Byron saved his son's life, insisting Byron's visit to Eric that day had been divinely timed. Earl didn't go into the details of the suicide attempt, and J.J. didn't pry—he only nodded, smiled, and uttered a few encouraging phrases: *Is that right? . . . Uh huh . . . That's really something.*

As Byron listened, he realized for the first time that Earl viewed him differently now, held him at a new level of admiration and appreciation. He recalled Snowfield, Jackson, and Wright as they dashed across the draw into enemy fire to rescue the wounded. *Am I like them? Willing to lay down my life for another? No. I didn't even think about it. Just reacted.* Byron broke into the conversation, denying the act was heroic and claiming anyone in his shoes would have responded the same way.

"No way," Earl said. "That was a courageous thing you did. A rare thing."

Byron shook his head, the flush of embarrassment restraining any words that tugged on his tongue.

"Here we are," Earl said as he halted in front of a room with the door slightly ajar. He spoke softly: "Eric's been in a coma for three days. Don't know how alert he'll be. I guess it's better to try to stay calm."

"Good idea," Byron said. "Lead the way. We'll hang back a little."

The door swung wider, and a nurse appeared with a clipboard in one hand and a blood pressure wrap in the other. "Hey, Mr. Waller," she said. "Doctor Irving just left. Said he'd be back in twenty minutes."

"How's Eric?" Earl asked.

She smiled, her eyes lively above chubby cheeks. "I think he'll be all right. He's having a hard time remembering. Don't be surprised if things aren't clear to him—names, events, places. At this point we still don't know the extent of memory loss. Dr. Irving will be able to give you more details as soon as he gets back."

"Can we go in?"

"Sure."

With the blinds closed, the room was dark except for the shifting glow of the television suspended on the wall not far from the foot of Eric's bed. Eric stared at the screen where Big Bird balanced a tray of cookies while Cookie Monster gobbled them as he counted to ten. A white bandage encircled Eric's head like a Swami's turban. A cable hanging from a pulley suspended his right leg. The casts on his left arm and other leg displayed colorful graffiti—names, racing logos, doodling.

"How's my boy?" Earl asked as he approached.

Eric slowly shifted his attention from the television to Earl. His eyes narrowed and mouth dropped open.

"It's me, son, your father." Earl leaned to within a couple of feet.

With his good hand Eric reached and touched Earl's cheek, his fingers gliding along the deep crevices of his face. "Daddy?"

"That's right, dear old dad."

Eric lowered his arm. "You're so . . . so wrinkled."

Byron stepped to the bed railing next to Earl. Eric's usual expression, the rebel-without-a-cause look, had been replaced by a softer, childlike quality.

"Wrinkled?" Earl said as he swiped his hand across his jowl. "I'm nearly fifty years old, boy. Not a young buck like you."

"Fifty?" Eric said.

Earl chuckled. "That's right. Turned forty-eight three months ago. Don't you remember? You bought me that Charlie Daniels CD and then borrowed it the very next day."

Eric swiveled his head sideways then met Byron's gaze.

"Look who came to see you," Earl said.

"Hi, Eric," Byron said.

"Who . . . who are you?" Eric asked.

"You know this guy," Earl said. "Pastor Byron. He saved your life."

"Saved my life?"

Byron smiled and leaned on the railing. J.J. moved to his side.

"I don't remember." Eric pointed to J.J. "Do I know you?"

J.J. shook his head and held out his hand. "I'm J.J., a friend of Pastor Byron."

Eric tentatively gripped it and shook hands. When he let go, his eyes returned to the television. On the screen Ernie splashed in the tub with his rubber ducky as Bert held up a bright orange letter "D."

Earl stepped back, glanced at Byron, and in a low voice said, "I don't think he knows what happened."

Byron shrugged.

"Why are you watching Sesame Street?" Earl asked. "You haven't watched that show since you were a kid."

"I don't know," Eric said, eyes fixed on the screen.

Earl reached and turned off the television. They stood in the dim glow filtering through the blinds until Earl managed to turn the florescent light on above the bed.

Eric stared at his casts. "What happened to my legs?"

"Don't you remember?" Earl asked.

Eric slid his fingers over the cast on his left arm and shook his head sideways.

"You were in an accident. On your ATV."

"ATV?"

"That's right," Earl said. "Your four-wheeler."

Eric frowned and scrunched his nose. "My bicycle's a two-wheeler."

Earl backed up a couple of steps and motioned Byron to join him. He pitched his voice low. "He's like a child again. Doesn't remember the accident or the shooting."

"Probably some form of amnesia," Byron said. "It'll all come back to him eventually."

"You're probably right," Earl said, "but I'm not sure that's a good thing."

As Earl stepped to the bed, Byron wondered if not remembering *was* better. Isn't the truth better? *You can only grow by facing your past, not forgetting it.* He thought about all the years Judd Stone tried to quash the guilt of his offense against Josiah Jackson. The transgression became a millstone that weighed upon his soul until he could no longer bear it. How could forgetting your wrongs be better than facing them? If Stone could have forgotten, would he have died peacefully? *Maybe. Maybe you can forget your sins on this side of eternity, but they're bound to catch up with you on the other side.* Then it occurred to him that Eric's circumstances were totally different than Stone's. *He's not trying to forget. Can you be responsible for something you honestly can't remember?*

"Byron," Earl said over his shoulder. "Could you say a prayer for Eric?"

"Of course." Byron moved to the head of the bed, reached and took Eric's hand, and offered his other to Earl.

"May I join you?" J.J. asked.

"Sure," Earl said, gripping J.J.'s hand. "The good book says, 'For where two or three have gathered together in my name, I am in their midst.' Isn't that right, Pastor Byron?"

"That's pretty close, Earl." Byron bowed his head and prayed for Eric. He asked God for healing, guidance, and strength for both Eric and Earl to face the future, finishing with an analogy about seeking the light that guides one to the firm foundation of the truth.

After the prayer Byron reasoned Eric might adjust better to his new surroundings with fewer people to keep track of. He promised Earl he'd stop back and check on his boy after church tomorrow. "I'll make sure the congregation gets updated. We'll keep both of you in our prayers," Byron assured him.

"I appreciate that, Pastor. Don't know where we'd be without all the prayers that have been offered," Earl said.

On the way out to the car, Byron filled J.J. in on the details of Eric's situation—the ATV accident six weeks ago and the more recent self-inflicted wound.

"That's too young to give up on life," J.J. said as he opened the car door.

Once inside the vehicle Byron said, "I have a hard time understanding how a sixteen-year-old can lose all hope. Life begins at sixteen—cars, sports, girls, your first job—so much to experience and learn." He started the Caravan, backed it out of the parking space, and headed toward the exit. "Have you dealt much with teen suicide at the youth center?"

"Haaaell yes," J.J. said. "Several incidents over the years. Sometimes teens have a hard time seeing the big enchilada of life. Most kids that attempt suicide don't really want to die."

"They don't?"

"Haaaell no," J.J. said in his deep baritone.

"Why do they do it?"

"They want to escape. Take Eric for instance. He wound up in a situation he couldn't deal with. He lacked the ability to see beyond his current circumstances. Can you imagine lying on that bed day after day, unable to move, trapped in that broken body?"

"I see what you mean," Byron said. "He wanted out—to get away from everyone who knew what happened. To get away from himself, really."

"Uh huh. He didn't have any options. In Eric's mind, dying was the only way to escape that terrible place."

"But why can't kids understand that life goes on? Things change. That the bad memories fade with time?"

"Have you ever been depressed?" J.J. asked.

"Of course. Preachers are human like everybody else."

"But have you ever gone into a deep depression?"

"Nothing serious, I guess."

"I've worked with kids who were scraping the bottom. That state of mind is like blinders on a horse. They can only see their failures and mistakes—how they've let everyone and themselves down. Kids battling severe depression believe things will never go right again. They can't imagine a positive outcome for their lives."

"Then how do you help them?"

"It's not easy. They have to decide to live. You can't do it for them. Being there helps. More than anything they need to know you love them unconditionally—no matter what they've done."

Byron wondered about J.J.'s statement. *Where does responsibility for your behavior come in? Should you sweep everything under the rug? How can a person change unless he owns up to his reckless ways?* "Do you think it's better not to mention past mistakes? Forget they ever happened?"

"I wouldn't go that far, but I wouldn't be in a hurry to bring them up either. Sooner or later the kid'll want to talk about it. That's why being there's important. No judgment. No condemnation. Just ears willing to listen. Let the kid face his mistakes when he can handle it. He'll work through it at his own pace."

Byron nodded, knowing sooner or later Earl would ask him to counsel Eric again. J.J's advice seemed sound—the kid has to decide he wants to live. *Just be there and listen. Don't worry about being a hero. You can't save someone who doesn't want to be saved.* He tucked it into his memory files.

As Byron pulled into the left lane and slowed to turn off Route 7 and up Mackey Avenue, J.J. said, "That is one helluva steep hill. Stone lives at the top?"

"That's right. Along the ridge."

"How do you know Stone? Are you his pastor?"

Byron laughed. "No way. Stone probably hasn't set foot in a church for decades."

"What's the connection then?"

"Several days ago he requested spiritual counseling, but I've known him for many years. We met when I was a senior in high school. It's a long story."

"Give me the Cliffs Notes version."

Byron chuckled. "Okay. One night a buddy and I were hanging out in an abandoned house on Wheeling Island. A couple of dope dealers stopped in to smoke some grass and didn't know we were hiding in the shadows. One of them lived across the alley from Stone. He claimed that Stone hid a ton of money somewhere in his house."

"A ton of money? Why would he keep it at his house?"

"The General doesn't like bankers. His father lost his entire savings during the Depression and blamed those 'greedy banking bastards.' Anyway, we overheard these two hooligans scheming to rob the old Marine, so we took some mental notes. My friend's father was Stanley Wright, the man on the tape. Stanley and Judd were best buddies. We felt obligated to head up to Stone's house and let him know about it. Well, that wasn't too smart. He recruited us to help foil the robbery. What a night. I'll never forget it."

"So he's got money stashed away, huh? What's his place like? Nice?"

"No. Stone's house is pretty creepy—camouflage carpeting, a big Japanese flag hanging from the living room ceiling, rifles and swords all over the place. And the skull."

J.J. shifted in his seat, facing Byron. "That's right. You said you knew where the skull was."

"Yes. It's sitting on a shelf in his bedroom. Stone shot the Japanese soldier right between the eyes. You can see the bullet hole." Byron pointed to his forehead.

"What did he do? Cut the man's head off after he killed him?"

Byron slowed the car, pulled along the curb and came to a stop. He gazed at J.J., nodded slowly and said, "You guessed it. Then he boiled off the skin and dug out the brains."

"Good Lord. What kind of man is Judd Stone?"

"He's a man with a guilty conscience who's about ready to meet his Maker. That's why he wanted you to come here. I'm not sure what he did to your father, but it must have been bad. He doesn't want to die until he has a chance to make things right with you."

J.J. took a deep breath and blew it out slowly. "Let's get rolling. Which house is his?"

Byron pointed to the right. "There's the beast."

They climbed out of the car, strode up the sidewalk and stopped when they reached a dented mailbox. Crumbling concrete steps led down the hill to a decrepit house covered with the tattered skin of brown-brick shingles. The front porch and overhanging roof sagged with age. From the posts and railings, pale yellow paint peeled, revealing rotten wood. Weeds and thistles infested the small yard, vines and ivy creeping up the steps and entangling the balusters.

"You got the key?" J.J. asked.

Byron shook his head.

"How we getting in?"

"Good question."

They descended the steps and climbed the few creaking wooden planks to the front porch. A rickety storm door without panes or screens hung open. Byron jiggled the knob to the heavy wooden door, but it didn't budge.

"Now what?" J.J. asked.

"Let's go around back and break a window."

J.J. swiveled his head, inspecting the other homes in the neighborhood. "Dey probly don't take kindly to tall black dudes breakin' inna houses 'round heh, do dey?"

Byron grinned. "Don't worry. If the cops come I'll flash my clergyman's I.D. and tell them were on a mission from God."

"Gotta get me one of those," J.J. said.

* * *

Around back Byron found a large screwdriver in the lawnmower shed. He angled it between the door and frame, managing to retract the latch with minimal damage. The door creaked open releasing the smell of stale air from the kitchen.

J.J. sniffed. "You can tell an old bachelor lives here. It has that certain odor."

"Yeah," Byron said. "Smells like my running socks after they sit in the bottom of the hamper for a week."

Byron led the way up the stairs to the living room and found the light switch. The first thing he noticed was the huge Japanese flag tacked to the ceiling. It had a large red ball in the middle with red rays extending to the edges. "That's a souvenir from Peleliu. Stone found it on the first day of the battle in one of the aeronautical buildings."

"Very impressive," J.J. said. "But why tack it to the ceiling?"

Byron shrugged. "He must enjoy looking at it."

"He loves his swords and guns, doesn't he?" J.J. said, pointing to the numerous racks mounted on the walls.

"It's like an armory in here. And check out the floor—a camouflage shag carpet. This room hasn't changed in twenty-five years."

"Kinda like a time capsule, isn't it?" J.J. asked. "Keeping old things around helps him maintain a comfort zone. We all do it to some extent."

"Don't see any footlockers in here, do you?"

J.J. shook his head.

"Follow me," Byron said. "The bedroom's this way."

They walked down a shadowy hallway and stopped in front of a closed door. Byron turned the knob and shoved the door open. The late afternoon light through a small window cast a sepia tone that faded into the dark corners of the room. The muted shaft illuminated the end of a king-size bed. On the bedpost hung a holster with a pistol. J.J. circled the room glancing at several framed photographs of Marine platoons hanging on the walls. He stopped and inspected a large dresser with a mirror. Bottles and papers were scattered across the top.

He turned to face Byron. "Nothing over here. Where's the skull?"

Byron reached for the switch and flicked on the light. "There," he said, pointing above the bed. From the center of a shelf mounted on the wall, the yellowed skull grinned. A gold front tooth sparkled in contrast to the black hole in the middle of the forehead.

"Why would Stone want us to bring that wretched thing to the hospital? And where's the footlocker he mentioned?" J.J. asked.

"I'm not quite sure." Byron edged to the side of the bed, planted his knee on the mattress and reached for the skull. With his fingertips he gripped the top of it and carefully withdrew from the bed. He held it up to the light and turned the skull to look on all sides. "I don't see anything written on it. No codes. No clues."

"Wait a minute," J.J. said. "Angle it this way again." J.J. pointed into the eye socket. "I can see something in the brain cavity. A balled up piece of paper."

Byron tilted it to let the light enter the sockets. "I see it." He shook it and the paper rattled inside. "How are we going to get it out?"

"I've got an idea," J.J. said. He walked to the dresser and picked up a small object. "Tweezers."

Byron held the skull with both hands while J.J. operated. After several minutes of adjustments and unraveling, J.J. managed to extract the wrinkled paper through the eye socket without tearing it.

Byron set the skull back on the shelf.

J.J. held the paper up to the light.

"What's it say?" Byron asked.

"Looks like a map. No words at all. Just a few numbers at the bottom."

"Huh? Let me see." Byron grasped the edges and examined the strange shapes and markings. "What in the world?"

J.J. pointed to the line that circumscribed all the other symbols. "I think it's a map . . . a map of an island. And look. He put a red circle right there."

CHAPTER 21

Byron pointed to the crisscrossing lines on the center of the map. "It *is* an island." His finger traced the surface. "These are landing strips. Buildings. A mountain to the north. Jungle areas and swamps over here."

"Which Island?" J.J. asked.

"Must be Peleliu. The bottom part is shaped like a lobster claw. Stanley Wright mentioned that on the tape. Why would Stone stuff a map of Peleliu inside a skull?"

"Could it have something to do with this red circle? Did you say this symbol must be some kind of building?"

Byron examined the red line circling a small rectangle. "Yes. Wright mentioned there were aeronautical buildings on this side of the airstrip. On the first day of the battle when things quieted down, Stone took off across the field to check these buildings for souvenirs."

"He must have been crazy."

"Look around this place. It's a cuckoo's nest."

J.J. chuckled, but then his eyes sobered. "Did he find anything worth keeping in that building?"

"Sure," Byron said. "Japanese flags. Bunch of small ones and a couple of big ones." Byron's eyes widened.

"Big ones? Like the one tacked to the ceiling in the living room?"

Byron nodded. "One and the same. He told Will and me the story about that flag when we came to inform him about the dope dealers who planned to rob him."

They rushed out of the bedroom, down the hallway, and into the middle of the living room. Byron folded the map, put it into his breast pocket and pointed to the red circle in the center of the flag. "This is one of the regimental flags he found in that building. It's got to be covering something."

J.J. pulled a coffee table to within several feet of Byron and stepped up on it. He reached for the corner of the flag and tugged downward releasing a loud, "rrrriiiiiipppp!"

"Velcro?" J.J said. "This thing's velcroed to the ceiling."

"Easy up. Easy down," Byron said.

The border of the cloth separated from its anchored strips as J.J. carefully peeled it away until it hung like a curtain from one end. A square seam, approximately three feet by three feet, etched the ceiling. Located a few inches to the left of one of the sides was the round knob of a combination lock, inset flush with the surface.

"A safe?" J.J. said.

"In the movies it's always behind an old painting."

"Unfortunately, we don't have the combination."

"Wait a minute." Byron pulled the map out of his pocket. "There are three numbers at the bottom—9-15-44. Try it."

J.J. reached for the knob but hesitated. "Can't quite see the numbers. Bring that floor lamp over here and take the shade off of it."

Byron dragged the lamp as far as the cord would allow. Removing the shade brightened the ceiling.

"Okay. Here we go," J.J. said. "Nine to the right. Fifteen to the left. Forty-four to the right . . . Nothing." He pressed against the square with his hand and jiggled it. "No luck."

"Try it the other way," Byron said. "Go left instead of right."

J.J. went through the numbers again in the opposite direction. "Nope. Not happening."

Byron held the paper in the light and studied the digits. "I just noticed something. There're three short lines next to the numbers like you see in that game—what's it called? — hangman."

"Three missing numbers?"

"Yes. Maybe it's some kind of mathematical puzzle."

J.J. stepped down from the coffee table and rubbed his chin. "Nine, fifteen, forty-four . . .I don't see a pattern. Wait a minute. Nine plus fifteen is twenty-four . . .No. That doesn't make sense."

"Maybe it's not a mathematical pattern," Byron said. "Could it be a date?"

"September 15th, 1944."

"That's it! That was the day the Marines landed on Peleliu."

"When did they leave?" J.J. asked.

"I'm not sure, but I'd bet we could find some World War Two history books around here."

"In the bedroom," J.J. said, "there's a shelf next to the dresser with books on it."

They headed back to the bedroom and within five minutes found a paperback with a red and blue cover entitled *With the Old Breed at Peleliu and Okinawa* by E.B. Sledge. Byron turned to the contents page and found a chapter called "Brave Men Lost."

"It's got to be here," Byron said. "It's the last chapter in the section about the Battle of Peleliu." He quickly thumbed through the book until he came to the end of the section. After flipping back a couple of pages he found a date. "Listen to this: *Next morning, 30 October, we squared away our packs, picked up our gear, and moved out to board ship. Even though we were leaving bloody Peleliu at last, my mind was distracted by an oppressive feeling that Bloody Nose Ridge was pulling us back like some giant inexorable magnet.* That's the day they left—October thirtieth."

"10-30-44. Let's roll," J.J. said.

J.J. led the way to the living room and stepped onto the coffee table. After spinning the combination lock several times to prepare for a restart, he precisely turned the knob, stopping at each number then reversing the direction. When he finished, the hatch fell open against his hands. He ducked and allowed it to swing down. "Puzzle solved," J.J. said.

Byron gazed into the hole. "I can see a light with a pull string on it mounted on the rafters. We'll need a ladder."

"Wait a minute," J.J. said. "There's something on the edge. I can barely see it." He ran his hand along the opening and grabbed the end of an object. When he pulled on it, a rope ladder with wooden rungs fell from the hole, clattering at his feet on the coffee table.

"'Ask and ye shall receive,'" Byron said.

J.J.'s smile widened and brightened his face. "'And it shall be given unto you, good measure, pressed down, shaken together, and running over.' Luke chapter six, I believe. Great verse for a fundraiser like me."

Byron grabbed a rung and tugged to see if it was solidly anchored. "Feels secure."

"Do you know the military term for this kind of ladder?" J.J. asked.

"No clue."

"It's called a Jacob's ladder. They were used to board ships."

Byron bobbed his head, eyeing the opening. "In the Old Testament, Jacob's ladder led to the gates of heaven."

J.J. stared into the dark chamber. "Not quite the heaven I expected. Let's get rolling." He ascended the rungs with a wobbly struggle and then used the sides of the opening to steady himself until he could crawl onto the attic floor. Immediately he stood and pulled the string on the light, sending a beam through the hole onto Byron.

When Byron reached the top of the ladder, J.J. offered a hand and pulled him up through the opening. About a foot above their heads the main beam stretched the length of the room with rafters slanting down like the ribs of a whale. Tacked to the wall at one end was an American flag. Below it sat piles of equipment—helmets, rifles, swords, canvas bags, various size shells, hand grenades, and even a machinegun mounted on a tripod.

"Wow," Byron said. "There's enough firepower up here to invade Mexico."

"Look there." J.J. pointed to the other end of the room. Against the wall sat a large dark green box about half the size of a coffin. Rusted metal corner strips trimmed its edges, and a padlock secured a large hasp.

"That must be the footlocker Stone wanted us to get," Byron said as they neared.

J.J. pointed to lettering on the top left side. "PFC Judd H. Stone, Fifth Marines, Easy Company. He must have brought it home from the war."

Faded symbols covered the rest of the top—a blue diamond with four white stars and the word *Guadalcanal*, an anchor and globe with an eagle on top, an American Flag, a bulldog with the letters U.S.M.C. underneath.

"I wonder what could be in there?" Byron asked.

J.J.'s jaw tightened, radiating his cheeks with creases. "You don't think he'd put my father's remains . . ."

Byron reached out and grasped his shoulder. "No. He wouldn't do that. At least I hope he didn't. Why would you keep a man's bones in your attic?"

"You said he was crazy."

* * *

Byron drove the van around the block to the alley and backed into the yard to within a few feet of the steps. After opening the hatch on the rear of the vehicle, he hurried to rejoin J.J. in the attic. The footlocker was heavy but not unmanageable. By holding one of the metal handles, Byron lowered it through the opening in the attic floor to J.J., who stood on the coffee table. They carried it down the steps, into the kitchen, and out the back door to the Caravan. The contents made muffled noises as they'd tilted and shifted the box, but Byron couldn't fathom what it contained.

As they drove away, J.J. asked, "Do you think anybody noticed us?"

"Maybe. Neighbors keep their eyes out for each other in these close-knit communities. Hard to say if we aroused enough suspicion to warrant a call to the police. Guess if we hear a siren, we better do some quick thinking."

"Just pull out your clergyman's I.D. Didn't you say that works every time?"

"Right. Cops know we preachers never lie to authorities or embezzle funds or consort with women of ill repute."

J.J. chuckled. "Uh huh. Cops around here must never watch the national news."

"Now that we've got the box, what do we do with it? Pry open the lock?"

"I assumed Stone wanted us to bring it to him."

Byron slowed the van and stopped at the bottom of the hill. He checked the oncoming traffic. "You're probably right. Guess I'm just curious." After a pickup truck flew by, he accelerated onto the four-lane highway. "I could hear stuff jostling around inside. What did it sound like to you?"

"Old bones."

"Really?"

"I don't know. Guess not. They never sent my father's body home—just some of his belongings. Nothing of any importance. I always wondered what happened to the watch. Momma had no idea. Stone must know something. Why else would he want us to tote this thing to the hospital? Whatever's in there must have something to do with my father's death."

"The War Department never gave your mother the official notification—cause of death, where he was buried, that sort of thing?"

"Just that he died bravely in battle and his body wouldn't be returned to the States. I did find out some more details when I was about ten years old."

"How?" Byron asked as he slowed to turn left onto a county road.

"A big man drove up to our house in an old Cadillac. A black man. At first I thought he must be a professional football player, but when he opened the car door, I knew that was impossible."

"Why?"

"He had prosthetic legs. Didn't seem to bother him much, though. After pulling a couple of crutches out of the back seat, he planted his feet on the ground, lifted himself up onto the crutches, and hobbled over to the porch. I was strumming my father's guitar, an old beat-up acoustic. He asked me if I could play, and I shook my head 'no.'

"He sat down on the banister and said, 'Gimme dat ol' six string, boy.' I handed it to him. Within a minute he had that pitiful thing tuned up and sounding like a Les Paul. He played 'Swing Low, Sweet Chariot,' and sang with a deep voice that made my insides quiver. And he just didn't play chords but picked out the melody and harmonies, his fingers fluttering up and down the neck of that guitar. When he sang the chorus, he closed his eyes and lifted his head toward heaven: *Swing low, sweet chariot. Comin' for to carry me home. Swing low, sweet chariot. Comin' for to carry me home.* I thought God had sent an angel to see me. One of the big ones that sang solos in heaven."

The quality of J.J.'s singing voice stunned Byron, reminding him of Lou Rawls. "Whooaa, J.J. You've got some great pipes there."

"I've been known to warble a tune or two at the First Baptist on Sunday morns. Anyway, my momma came out onto the porch. She didn't recognize him. When he finished, he opened his eyes and smiled. Introduced himself as Bill Robinson. Said he promised my father he'd stop by and visit us if he ever got to Atlanta."

"Bill Robinson?" Byron said. "Big Bill Robinson?"

"That's right. How'd you know?"

"Stanley Wright mentioned him on the tapes, and another fellow, Howard Kinloch, wrote about Big Bill in one of his letters to his wife."

"Well, Big Bill claimed he was my father's best friend. He told us about all the boxing matches Dad won, and how they volunteered for combat on Peleliu. Up until then black soldiers had to serve in the rear echelon as cooks or laborers. Because my father was thin, strong and fast, they assigned him to a medical unit as a stretcher-bearer. Big Bill didn't see any fighting until the last week of the battle. By then most of the white Marines had been killed or wounded. The officers were desperate for help. They formed several platoons of black volunteers. Bill said they did themselves proud. He lost his legs on the last day when he stepped on a mine."

"Did he mention what happened to your father's body?"

"My momma asked him. He said my father died trying to save a wounded Marine. Because the Japanese could fire down from caves on the surrounding hillsides, they couldn't retrieve the bodies for several days. Finally, planes came through dropping napalm all over the place. He told us my father's body was never found. Said God took him to heaven in a chariot like Elijah—Swing low, sweet chariot. I believed him when I was a kid. Once I started reading about these Pacific battles, I realized what probably happened."

Byron swallowed and cringed. "The napalm?"

"That's right. The dead went up in flames. Nothing left but charcoal and ashes. But now I'm not so sure."

"What do you mean?" Byron glanced at J.J. for a few seconds then returned his gaze to the country road.

J.J. shifted in his seat and stared at the back of the van. "That box back there. I can't shake this feeling—the feeling there's a part of my father inside that footlocker."

CHAPTER 22

At the Butler dinner table, J.J. stabbed a breaded pork chop from the meat platter. "I hope you don't mind me taking another, Mrs. Butler, but these are delicious, and I'm hungrier than a tiger with a toothache."

"There's plenty, J.J. And please, call me Lila."

"Thank you, Lila. Hard to hold myself back with cooking this good."

Lila beamed. "I'm used to whipping up big meals for hungry teenage boys. They eat twice as much as normal folk, so I just double the amount the recipe requires for a family of four."

After swallowing a huge gulp of mashed potatoes, Matt asked, "How long has your son been playing for the Richmond Braves?"

"'Otis has been with Richmond for about a month," J.J. said.

"Sweet. That's on the screws," Matt said.

Lila pointed her fork at Matt. "Watch your language, young man."

Byron chuckled. "Don't you know what 'on the screws' means, Hon? It's baseball talk for 'right on' or 'that's a solid hit, man.'"

"It just sounded off-color to me." Lila shrugged and fluttered her eyelashes. "I guess I whiffed that one, eh?"

Byron shook his head, catching a glimpse of J.J.'s wide smile.

"What position does he play?" Mark asked.

"He's at the hot corner," J.J. said.

"The hot corner?" Lila asked. "Let me guess. He's the catcher."

"No, Ma," Matt said. "The hot corner's third base."

Lila rolled her eyes. "Forgive my baseball lingo ignorance." She picked up a large plate of chocolate chip cookies. "Here, Matt, pass this around the horn."

Everyone laughed as Matt scooped up three cookies and handed the plate to J.J. For thirty minutes the twins plied J.J. with questions about the minor leagues, his son's stats, weight training, off-season conditioning, and batting and fielding drills. J.J. talked about Atlanta Brave players he'd met personally through fundraisers for the youth center, and the boys listened, enraptured. Lila kept replenishing the men's coffee cups until the pot emptied. Mark and Matt polished off what was left of the cookies. Finally, Byron put a halt to the discussion, stating he and J.J. needed to go to his study to do some serious World War II research before it got too late.

* * *

"You've got a wonderful family, Byron," J.J. said as he sat down in the wooden armchair across from Byron's desk.

"Thanks. I warned you about the twins. Once they found out your son played triple-A ball, I knew the barrage would start. If I hadn't put an end to it, you'd be answering questions 'til midnight." Byron turned and reached for the war memorabilia box on the shelf to the right of his desk.

"I enjoyed it. Nothing like kids and sports. I played some baseball and boxed a little in my younger days. Wasn't that good, though. Not like my father or my son. The talent must have skipped a generation." He balled his hands into fists and circled them in front of him. "But I loved the physical part of it—the training, the sweating, the disciplining of the body. Can't remember feeling more alive than when I was in top shape, circling that ring."

Byron set the box in the middle of the desk. "I know what you mean. When I was a kid I loved to compete too—mostly at distance running. That's one reason I think you'll be interested in these letters. Couple of them mention your father's boxing match against Judd Stone. The information revealed here helped me get a better handle on the circumstances that led to your father's death."

"Interesting. Now who wrote these letters?"

"A man by the name of Howard Kinloch. His wife, Helen, is a member of my congregation. She gave me this box of war stuff a few days ago. Thought her husband's letters may shed some light on Stone's confession. Howard belonged to the same platoon as Stone and Wright. He befriended your father when those two had it in for him."

"Really. This Kinloch wasn't afraid to stand on a black man's side of the fence, huh?"

"Well, I wouldn't say he stood up to Stone and Wright. Howard wasn't the bravest man in the war. He had courage issues when it came to facing the enemy—whether it was a couple of bigots or a company of Japanese soldiers. But he did care about your father."

J.J. pointed. "How many letters do you have there?"

"'Bout twenty. I've read through most of them." Byron placed a stack in front of J.J. "I've ordered them by date. You'll notice that Helen wrote on one side and Howard on the other. Lots of couples did it that way because of a paper shortage. Besides that, it helped them keep a record of their communication."

J.J. picked up the first letter. "What're you going to do for the next two hours while I'm reading these letters?"

Byron lifted three yellowed envelopes. "I've got a few more to read. Then I need to review my sermon for tomorrow's worship service. By the way, would you be willing to sing a solo for us?"

"In church or in the shower?"

"In church of course. Even I can sound like Lou Rawls in the shower. Just pick out a good old hymn. The congregation will love it."

J.J. agreed to do his a cappella version of "Amazing Grace." Then he opened the envelope and started to read the first letter.

Byron pulled out the pages of the next one on the yet-to-be-read pile and turned them over to find Helen's opening lines.

My Darling Howie,

It's been almost four weeks since I heard from you. You still haven't answered my last two letters. Although my heart is aching, I'm going to do the best I can to change my tune. You must be getting tired of reading pages and pages of my problems and complaints. That's not really me. It's just that I get grouchy and depressed when I don't hear from you. From now on I'll assume that you haven't had a chance to write back because of your circumstances on the battlefield.

The radio has been keeping me company a lot lately. Right now Bing Crosby is singing "I'll Be Seeing You." It's a new song, but the kind you fall in love with the first time you hear it. The first line goes—"I'll be seeing you in all the old familiar places." It makes me smile and cry at the same time. Doesn't that sound silly? But it's true. Sometimes when I'm lying here in bed, half awake and half asleep, I swear I see you out of the corner of my eye lying next to me. Or I'll hear a noise downstairs and my first thought is that you just got home from work. Then reality hits. I come to my senses and try to buck up. Every old song brings back a memory. Driving along in that old Ford, we always sang those ditties together just like Judy Garland and Gene Kelly. Well, maybe we didn't sound that good, but it sure was fun. The words and music somehow connected us— opened up our hearts to each other. Maybe that's why I've been listening to the radio so much. It connects me to you.

I hate how the war has separated us, Howie. I've been thinking about the critical words I wrote in my last letter about America entering the war, and it makes me feel ashamed. Although I can't stand this war, I still love my country. Please forgive me for writing those things. I've thought a lot about the events that drew us into this conflict. We didn't go looking for a fight. They hit us first. Maybe they figured they could wipe out our navy and will to win with one big blow. The enemy made a huge mistake. America is more than just a country. It's a way of life. Germany and Japan don't understand freedom, how it sinks its roots deep down inside of you. No wonder they underestimated our determination to defend what we hold dear—something bigger and truer and more important than an emperor or the Fatherland. I'm proud that you are an American soldier who answered the call to defend Lady Liberty. But please, be careful and come back to me.

There. I feel a lot better now that I have confessed. You won't hear me complain any more about my country or the hard times this war is putting us through. I want to be brave and hopeful. Let's agree to be courageous together. This war can't last forever. We've got to hang in there for each other. Be strong for me and I'll be strong for you.

Besides listening to the radio, I've been reading the Bible a lot. I keep getting the same message—the trials of life refine us and make us better people. We're both traveling a long and difficult road. I believe our paths will lead back to each other. Along the way the hard times will turn us into the people we want to be—upright, caring, and faithful. Together we'll make a wonderful home for our babies. I hope we have lots of them.

It's getting late, Howie, and I'm tired. Tomorrow's another day. I need a good eight hours sleep to make it through a ten-hour day at the can factory. That alarm will go off before you know it. Please, please, please write me soon. I need to hear from you. You are everything I ever wanted in a man and more. I love you so much that I can't come close to expressing it with this pen. I'll end this letter with my heart's hope:

I'll be seeing you in all the old familiar places,

Helen

Byron glanced up and noticed J.J. reading intently. Apparently J.J. got drawn into the passion of those letters as quickly as he did. They held something special—something rare in today's shallow world. Considering Helen's words he'd just read, Byron sensed the reverberations of truth deep within like the bonging of an old church bell. Love, war, loneliness, suffering, and sacrifice shaped the deepest parts of that generation. Toughened them up. Refined them like molten steel in a blast furnace used to build ships and planes and tanks. The men and women of those days experienced an inner strengthening that sustained them through one of the most difficult times in history.

His generation, the baby boomers, enjoyed the spoils. They drove cars that were more expensive than their parents' houses and spent more on vacations in one year than their parents did in a lifetime. *No wonder life has such a hollow ring for* most people nowadays. My generation has never had to suffer for all that's been handed us.

Byron turned the pages over and read Howard's side.

My Dearest Helen,

I just opened your third letter. Sorry about falling behind. I've been writing like crazy today to try to catch up. Please be patient with me. Within the next hour I promise to finish this letter and put all three back into the outgoing mail this afternoon. I pray the ship hauling these letters back to the states won't be sunk by some Nip sub along the way. More than anything, I want these words to reach you.

You are right, Helen. War changes people, but I'm not sure if it has changed me for the better. I don't want to become like some of the men in my platoon, filled with hate and the craving to kill. Sometimes, though, I understand why they have become so hard-hearted. I've seen many terrible things the enemy has done—too terrible to mention in this letter. Seeing these horrors plants a black hard seed in a man's soul. The more you see the more it grows. The more it grows, the more you want to hate, destroy, and kill. The only thing that helps me is going off by myself and thinking about you or finding a quiet place to read my Bible. You and God keep me going.

Something very strange happened this morning. When I got up I found a nice palm tree to sit under and read the Gospel of Matthew. I decided to get through as many chapters as possible before some sergeant came along to recruit me to dig a latrine or bury the dead. No one bothered me for almost two hours. In chapter twenty I was reading Jesus' parable about the landowner who hired workers to labor in his vineyard. He told the ones hired in the morning he'd pay them one denarius. Every hour throughout the day he hired workers at the same wage. At the end of the day he paid them all one denarius. The ones who worked all day complained, but the landowner insisted they agreed to one denarius. Then Jesus said, "So the last shall be first, and the first shall be last." I didn't quite get it. Didn't seem fair. Then Jesus told his disciples he was going to Jerusalem where he would be betrayed, mocked, flogged, and crucified.

Just then Judd Stone came up and asked me what I was reading. I wanted to crawl in a deep hole somewhere and hide. During the last skirmish with the enemy he caught me firing my rifle into the air again. When I told him I was reading the Bible, he really blew his stack. He claimed reading God's word taught me to love the enemy and pray for my persecutors. Then he said something that threw me for a loop—a line from Shakespeare: "To be or not to be, that is the question." He reached down, grabbed my Bible, walked over to a mud puddle, and dropped the Good Book right into the muck. Can you believe that? After Stone walked away, Stanley Wright picked up the Bible and tried to apologize for him. Here's the strange thing. It fell open into the puddle at the very page I was reading. When Wright gave it back to me, I noticed the only words I could still read on the page was, "the first shall be last."

Right then, Helen, God spoke to me. I swear I could audibly hear his voice. He said, "To be or not to be, that is the question. To be last means not to be first." I know that sounds crazy, but it all makes sense. The workers in the parable got angry because they wanted more for themselves. To be last means to not be selfish but to be glad when others are blessed. To be last means to be willing to go to Jerusalem and be mocked, flogged, and crucified. To be last means to put your own needs aside to help someone else.

I'm not sure why God revealed this to me, but I know I have to be ready. Did you ever get that feeling that something is going to happen? Remember last winter when we walked down to Patterson's Pond to watch the kids ice skating? All that morning I had the feeling something was about to happen. Wouldn't you know it, two minutes after we got there Franky Logston fell through the ice. I panicked when I saw him struggling in that freezing water. My mind went blank. Instead of jumping in after him, I just stood there watching him splash and holler. Luckily you knew what to do. By the time I snapped out of it, you had already found a fallen branch on the edge of the woods. Somehow we managed to pull Franky out of the pond with that branch. If his life depended on me, he would have drowned.

That's why I want to be ready, Helen. When it's my turn to help someone, I don't want to panic. I want to be able to think fast and do whatever is necessary. I know my turn will come again. The first shall be last. Pray that I have the courage and clear mind to know what to do. I feel like I've let so many people down in the last ten days. I don't want to be known as Howard the Coward the rest of my life. God help me, I want to do my duty and not stand there shaking in my shoes like a scared kid. Keep me in your thoughts and prayers.

With all of my love,

Your husband, Howie

P.S.   Lord willing, I'll be seeing you in all those old familiar places.

"The first shall be last," Byron mumbled.

J.J. glanced up from the pages he held. "What'd you say?"

"I . . .I'm a little stunned. In this letter Howard Kinloch quoted the same passage of scripture that I'm using as my text for tomorrow's sermon—Matthew chapter twenty."

J.J. nodded. "What do you think? Coincidence or providence?"

"I'll go with providence."

"It's all part of God's big ball of yarn."

Byron tilted his head. "What?"

"Sometimes the Lord takes a piece of old thread and ties it to a new one. It's all part of one big ball of yarn."

"Hmmmm. That's a neat way of looking at it."

"So did Howard give you any good insights to use in tomorrow's sermon?"

Byron sat up. "Yeah, he did. He said the first shall be last. According to Howard, people who are first in God's eyes must be willing to put their own needs aside to help others. I always interpreted that verse the other way—that selfish people who always try to be first will end up last on God's list."

"There's always more than one way of looking at things. Howard's interpretation reminds me of an old friend named Don Trotman. Back in the mid eighties during a blizzard in January, Don's plane waited to take off from the Washington National Airport. They sat on the tarmac for an hour hoping the storm would pass. When the pilot finally got the clearance for takeoff, no one checked the wings for icing. The extra weight caused the wing of the plane to dip and catch the top of the bridge over the Potomac River. It crashed into the water. Terrible tragedy. Seven survivors crawled out onto the wing of the plane. Don was one of them. A helicopter showed up about fifteen minutes later and dropped a basket. Don was in his late sixties and should have been one of the first to go. But he always grabbed the basket, held it steady, insisting someone else get in. He wanted to be last. One by one he helped secure the survivors onto that lifeline."

"Bet he got a hero's welcome when he finally got to shore," Byron said.

J.J. shook his head. "When the helicopter returned for Don, it was too late. The plane had sunk. He drowned in the icy water."

"My Lord, J.J." Byron said. "Sorry to hear that."

"Sometimes there's a price to pay for being last."

CHAPTER 23

During Sunday morning's worship service, J.J.'s soulful voice resonated in the old church like the slow hum of a bow across the strings of a double bass. The congregation sat mesmerized, the words of "Amazing Grace" so familiar to them yet born anew by the masterful rendition. Sunlight filtered through the stained-glass windows casting colorful shafts across the rows of listeners.

Byron, sitting to the right of the pulpit, gazed at J.J. and sensed that rare flame of inspiration born in the presence of spirit and truth. After J.J. finished, an awed silence persisted for several seconds followed by thunderous applause as if an invisible hand had stayed the eruption until the impact had been felt to the core. Byron rose to the pulpit on the wave of exhilaration and read the scripture passage from the Gospel of Matthew, chapter twenty. He delivered the sermon with the verve of an impassioned storyteller, ignoring his notes for the most part and finishing with the account of Don Trotman, the plane wreck survivor who chose to be last.

After the service the Butlers and J.J. returned to the parsonage for a hearty lunch of Reuben sandwiches, potato soup and tossed salad. J.J. bid goodbye to Lila and the twins, insisting he had to head to the airport after visiting Judd Stone. He suggested the family plan a trip to Atlanta that summer and stay at his house, embellishing the offer with promises of tickets to a Braves' game and an excursion to Richmond to see his son, Otis, play. Mark and Matt demanded the invitation be accepted on the spot, but Lila needed time to check schedules and make plans.

On the way to the hospital J.J. wanted to talk about Howard and Helen's letters. According to J.J., because Howard was a misfit in his own platoon, he became a link to the black soldiers—the one trusted to hold the watch during the fight. After losing the fight, Stone became obsessed with the watch. His compulsion to possess it warped his already war-damaged value of human life. What J.J. didn't understand was why the watch consumed Stone. Byron brought up Stone's competition with his brother for his father's attention.

"His brother was a Navy corpsman," Byron said, "an overachiever who outshone Judd at every endeavor except for one—boxing."

"I get it," J.J. said. "The watch was Stone's only hope of winning his dad's approval."

"Right. And it might have worked for Judd if something terrible hadn't happen."

"What happened?"

"His brother got killed on Iwo Jima trying to patch up wounded soldiers. He was awarded the Navy Cross. Next to that medal, Judd's golden watch lost its shine. His father stuck the watch in the back of his sock drawer. Total rejection."

"Makes me wonder what's worse," J.J. said, "—growing up without a dad or being rejected by him."

"I know what both sides of that face look like. Believe me, it isn't pretty."

"You told me you didn't discover your father's identity until after he died. If you didn't actually know him, how could he reject you?"

"Easy," Byron said. "I knew from talking to Mom that my father was still around. She just didn't want me to know who he was. He lived in my hometown, less than a mile from me. He knew I was his son but never told me he was my father. Every day of my life he rejected me until the day he died."

After a few moments of silence J.J. said, "I can see your point. That would be tough. I grew up without my father, but at least I knew who he was. I saw his picture on the wall every day. Momma always bragged on him."

"That you grew up to be successful doesn't surprise me. Your dad was a hero, a natural leader. Your mom made sure you knew that."

"Hmmmm." J.J. rubbed his chin. "Yeah, that's true. She expected the same of me. That's what you call a self-fulfilling prophecy. I became what Momma kept reinforcing. You've done well for yourself too, huh? A man of the cloth with a wonderful family."

"Guess so," Byron said. He often wondered why he turned out to be a so-called "good man," dedicating his life to serving others. Perhaps rejection affected people different ways. Throughout his boyhood he always wanted to meet his father and prove he was a worthy son. Maybe in his case, rejection intensified that desire. After his father died, that drive to be worthy became a spiritual journey, but a difficult one. "Hang around me long enough, and you'll find out I'm far from perfect."

J.J. smiled. "You've got some faults too, huh?"

"Oh yeah."

"My biggest problem is my temper. I don't lose control often, but when I do, ya betta get outta my way."

"Long fuse to a stack of dynamite, eh?"

J.J. chuckled. "That's right. In my younger days when I flipped out, I'd break something or hit someone. Not a good pattern of behavior. I've definitely mellowed. Can't say I''ve conquered my anger, but I haven't hit anybody for twenty years."

"I tend to do the opposite," Byron said. "Hold it all inside, retreat to my study, and shut everyone out."

"That's not good either."

"Guess you could say we're both a work in progress, huh?"

J.J. chuckled. "Haaaell yeah. The good Lord ain't finished with us yet."

Byron veered off the interstate onto the ramp that led to the hospital and stopped at the red light. His mind returned to the contents of the box. The sheer weight of the thing widened the possibilities. *Why did Stone insist they haul it to the hospital?* Glancing at J.J. he said, "That footlocker's got me wondering. It's too heavy to contain just one person's remains. He's loaded it with something else."

"I've had a strange feeling about that thing ever since we hauled it out of Stone's attic. The man kept the head of his enemy for a souvenir on a bookshelf. That's gruesome. What if Stone had psychopathic tendencies? What if that box is filled with human remains? His war trophies. Now he's ready to let go of it. He wants us to hear his confession," J.J. raised his hand, thumbing toward the back of the van, "and remove this . . . heavy weight from his life."

Byron considered J.J.'s speculation. *Could be—a footlocker full of bones.* "Stone did serve a long time—World War II, Korea, and Vietnam. He retired on a military pension."

"Lots of battles and lots of trophies."

The light turned green and Byron eased off the brake and onto the gas. *Lord, let that not be the case. What would we do with a box full of bones? Bury it? No, we'd have to report it to the authorities. But who? The military? The police?*

After pulling into a parking space near the front entrance of the hospital, Byron turned off the engine, craned his neck, and glimpsed the footlocker in the back of the van. "Guess we better lug it up to his room."

"That's what the man wanted, right?" J.J. said.

Byron took a deep breath and blew it out. "General's orders."

* * *

On the way to the elevator whenever anyone gave them a strange look, Byron smiled and said, "Special delivery."

The footlocker, about three and a half feet long, strained his upper body, sending a dull ache down his arm muscles, and numbed his fingers.

"What do you think?" J.J. asked. "At least a hundred pounds."

"Seems like two hundred."

"If it's not full of bones, what else could be in here?"

"Who knows," Byron grunted. "Maybe grenades or green stamps."

J.J. half-smiled and shook his head.

On the elevator, Byron managed to hold onto his end with one hand and press the button with the other. Sweat trickled down his back. When the doors parted, he hustled to get down the hall and around the corner to Stone's room before he lost his grip.

Three steps inside they lowered the box to the floor, stood, and shook out their arms, both huffing as they turned to face Stone. He sat on the raised bed by the window in the light of the clear day. The sunshine, bright against his pale forehead, cast cavernous shadows across his sunken eyes and darkened his hollow cheeks with deep valleys.

Stone's voice rumbled like a landslide. "Couldn't talk too good yesterday. Lucky to get out a few words. Didn't know if you'd find it or not. "

"Wasn't easy," Byron said, approaching the bed. "Had to do some problem solving and map reading."

"Well . . ." Stone's lips tightened almost into a smile. "Figured you'd remember the skull from your visit twenty-five years ago. Didn't know if you'd find the map or remember the story about the flag."

"As soon as I saw the red mark on the map I recalled the story. You crossed the airfield and found the Japanese flags in the aeronautical buildings on the first day of the battle."

"That led us to the flag attached to the ceiling in the living room," J.J. said.

"Mission accomplished," Stone said. "You boys would have made good raggedy-ass Marine scouts."

"Just one thing, General," Byron said. "You never gave us the key to your house. We had to break the lock on your back door to get in."

"Who gives a shit?" He coughed several times and swallowed. "I may never get out of this place alive. If I do, what the hell? I'll spring for a new lock."

"One other thing, Mr. Stone," J.J. said, drawing nearer. "You never gave us the key to the padlock on that footlocker either."

Stone appraised J.J., eyes narrowing, the striations across his cheeks deepening. "I didn't give you the key because I didn't want the box opened . . . yet, anyways. That key I always keep with me. It's in my pants pocket in the closet yonder." He pointed to the other side of the room.

Byron gestured toward the box. "Are we going to open it now?"

"Not yet. More important things to do now."

"Like what?" J.J. asked.

"Well . . . You want to know about your father don't you?"

"That's why I flew eight hundred miles to get here."

"Your father and me weren't friends. You know that don't ya?"

J.J. nodded.

Stone cleared his throat and swallowed. "In truth, we were enemies. He hated me. I hated him. On Pavuvu we faced each other in a boxing match. The Negro troops put up five hundred bucks and I put my championship watch on the line. Your father was a good fighter. I admit that. But I swear he didn't whip me. Someone threw in the towel before I was ready to quit. The preacher here tells me my best friend, Stanley Wright, admitted to it on some war memoir tape. Hell, I could have fought another twenty minutes. My greatest strength is endurance." Stone paused, taking several deep breaths. "Could outlast anyone."

Byron glanced at J.J., noting his solemn expression, a subtle tensing around his eyes and mouth. *Hope Stone didn't call J.J. up here to defend his right to the watch. That would be unconscionable. Come on, old man, it's time to fess up.* Byron almost told Stone to forget the fight and get to the point, but Stone started up again.

"Anyway, maybe Stanley did throw in that towel, but something else has made me change my thinking lately. I've been having nightmares . . . nightmares about your father."

"About my father?"

"Yeah. Like he's come back from the dead to either get even with me or warn me, or maybe both."

"What do you mean 'get even' with you?" J.J. asked. "What did you do to him?"

"I confess on Pavuvu I played a practical joke on him to get my watch back. Tied him up in a cave and threatened to decorate the walls with his innards. We left the cave then tossed in a dud grenade. Scared him shitless at the time. That was wrong of me. But that's not the worst of it.

"When we got to Peleliu I gave the watch to a friend of mine for safe keeping. That good ol' boy stepped on a mine and got blown to bits and pieces. Later I discovered your father stripped the watch from my buddy's corpse. That's no lie. He took a gaddamn watch off a dead American soldier."

"Yes," Byron said, "but Josiah believed the watch was rightfully his."

"Well . . . that's true, but at the time I thought that was the dirtiest deed a man could do—strip a souvenir from one of your own boys. Anyway, I vowed to get that watch back one way or another.

"The opportunity finally came. During the fourth week of battle we were fighting our way to the end of Horseshoe Valley. My company had been decimated, probably seventy-five percent casualties. For days on end I expected some Jap to put a bullet between my eyes or launch a mortar shell to blow my balls off. Battle puts a constant strain on a soldier—screws up a man's mind.

"Our new lieutenant got the crazy idea to charge across an open field to a defilade on the other side where we could start cleaning out the caves at that end of the valley. Big mistake. My platoon gave them cover fire. 'Bout twenty Marines sprinted across the draw. Japs didn't open up until they were out in the middle. Must have been eight or nine gun emplacements still left in those hills. Bullets poured down like a cloudburst.

"Couple of my buddies tried to go after the wounded. Senseless thing to do. Emery Snowfield made it about thirty yards before he went down. Stanley Wright took a bullet in the thigh after a few steps. Lucky sonovabitch fell into a ditch.

"That's when your father and his litter partner, Parker, showed up. I told him to go get Stanley. He didn't want to at first. Hell, the man was only five yards away. I promised that Kinloch and me would cover his ass. Finally he got up the nerve to do it. Have to give your old man credit. He saved my best friend. Doc Halleran showed up a few minutes later with a couple of his boys and hauled Stanley out of there. That's when I realized your father was wearing the watch."

Stone shook his head, his eyes losing their focus. "I just wanted it back, that's all. I promised my . . . I promised my father I'd bring it home. So I told Jackson to hand it over, but he wouldn't. I raised my rifle and aimed at his chest. He said, 'The only way you're gonna get this watch back is to put a bullet through my heart.' That's when I ordered him to go get Snowfield."

Stone lowered his head and stared at his hands in his lap.

"But Snowfield was out in the middle of the draw," J.J. said.

Stone nodded. "That's right. A suicide mission. I knew he'd get killed."

Byron glanced at J.J. and noticed his eyebrows tensing, jaw muscles tightening.

Stone blinked as if focusing on a scene from the past. "Your father said, 'I ain't goin' out there to die for no dead man. I got a wife and a three-year-old boy at home.' Then Kinloch piped up and claimed that he believed Snowfield was dead too. I whipped the butt of my M1 around and knocked Kinloch out cold.

"Then I said, 'Now I don't want to have to kill you for disobeying an order, but I will.'

"Parker was shaking in his boondockers, but your old man wasn't fazed. He said, "You just want to let the Japs do you dirty work so you can strip the watch off me later. Go ahead. Shoot me."" Stone lowered his head and closed his eyes, as if the story had ended.

J.J. stepped forward and gripped the bed railing. "Did you shoot him? Did you kill my father?"

Stone raised his head, slowly swiveling it sideways. "I turned my rifle on Parker. I said, 'I'm killing your partner first.' Parker begged for his life. Said he'd go get Snowfield by himself. I knew that would do the trick. No way would Jackson let Parker go it alone. Two men could lug that corpse twice as fast as one.

"'Get a move on,' I ordered. They both took off across the draw. The Japs waited until they lifted the body before shooting. Both men jerked and twitched as the bullets hit them then collapsed into a heap on top of Snowfield.

J.J.'s breathing became audible as if he strained each breath through his teeth.

"Jackson didn't move," Stone said, "but Parker flopped around like a catfish on land 'til they plugged him with a half-dozen more rounds."

Byron stepped closer, ready to jump between them. J.J. lifted a trembling hand from the rail and formed a fist. "You despicable bastard."

"I'm not finished," Stone said. "If you want to hit me, wait 'til you hear it all."

J.J. glared at him but lowered his fist.

"They didn't send in reinforcements that day. Had to be 105 degrees in the shade. Within two hours those bodies started to rot. The odor was unbearable. I lay at the top of the shell hole and watched the blowflies gather. In the midst of the tangled limbs I could see the watch. It glittered in the sunshine.

"The next day about noon I saw your father's arm move. I thought what the hell? Then he rolled over."

"My father was still alive?"

Stone nodded. "He looked at me and called for help. Somehow he kinda half stood and stumbled in my direction. Course the Japs opened up on him and down he went. Then he started crawling across that sharp coral. I knew the enemy wanted me to run out and get him. They let him crawl. He made it to that ditch Stanley fell into."

"Was he safe from their fire in that ditch?" Byron asked.

"More or less. He kept saying, 'Help me, Stone. I've got a wife and kid.' Just then a runner came by and told me to clear out. Said the Hellcats were flying over in five minutes to drop napalm. I knew the Japs would duck back into their holes when they saw the aircraft. As soon as the first plane came over I jumped up and ran to Jackson. He reached towards me with his hand. That's when I stripped the watch from him and took off running before the fire fell from the sky."

CHAPTER 24

J.J. lunged at Stone, clutching at his neck. Byron pulled back J.J.'s shoulder and forced himself between them. In the struggle Byron's back jostled Stone's emaciated body. Byron grabbed one of J.J. wrists and yanked him toward the foot of the bed. "No J.J.! Don't do this!"

"I'll kill him," J.J. said.

Byron managed to stand, blocking J.J. from Stone's bedside. "Calm down."

"Go ahead." Stone coughed and swallowed. "Strangle me if you want to."

J.J. tried to step around Byron. "I will, you bastard! You're a murderer. You could've saved my father."

"Let him go, Preacher," Stone said. "I deserve it."

"Maybe you do. But J.J. doesn't deserve to go to prison for killing you."

J.J. stepped back, breathing harshly. He blinked his eyes, the anger-etched lines in his face fading with realization. "You're right, Byron." He dropped his arms to his sides and took deeper breaths. "That son of a bitch is not worth going to jail over. Give me a minute. I'll get control of myself."

A nurse entered the room. "Is everything all right in here?"

"Hell yes," Stone growled. "Everything's fine. Give us some privacy, would ya?"

The nurse shook her head, exited, and closed the door.

Stone rubbed his neck. "Figured I might die like that."

Byron faced Stone. "Like what?"

"Just like in my nightmares. I'd dream Jackson was choking me. When I'd wake up, I'd be choking myself."

"Those bruises on your neck?" Byron said.

"That's right. My own hands. Jackson was getting back at me with my own hands."

J.J. spread his fingers and stared at his palms. "Did you think my father wanted to get back at you through *my* hands? Is that why you called me up here? To be your executioner?"

"No," Stone said. "I just wanted to give you the chance if that's what you wanted."

"Huh?"

"I understand what he's saying," Byron said.

J.J. knotted his brow. "I don't get it."

"Either you were going to kill him or forgive him." Byron put his hand on J.J.'s shoulder. "He figured it was your call—your decision. His death or life. Judgment or grace. Am I right, General?"

Stone nodded. "You ring my neck, and I get what I deserve."

"But if you forgive him," Byron said, squeezing J.J.'s shoulder, "he gets what he doesn't deserve—grace. But that's the nature of grace. No one deserves it."

J.J. leaned on the bed railing. "So you're asking for my forgiveness?"

Stone swallowed. "I don't feel right asking for it. It's too much to ask. But it's the thing I need most."

J.J. glared at the old man, and Stone lowered his head, chin almost touching his breastbone. "And if I don't want to forgive you?"

Stone glanced up, his dark eyes watery. "Then I don't think I'll survive another nightmare."

J.J. stepped back from the bed and took in a deep breath. His exhale hissed between his teeth as he eyed Stone from head to foot. "I feel sorry for you. You are a man to be pitied."

Stone looked up, his voice quavering as he spoke. "I know what kind of man I am—a murderer and a thief. I need more than pity. If that's all you want to offer me, fine. But it doesn't help." Stone blinked and wiped his eyes.

J.J. shifted his gaze to the floor, the lines on his face softening. He rubbed his chin and smoothed his mustache.

Seconds passed interminably into minutes. Byron felt the urge to mediate, utter some spiritual platitude, but managed to keep his mouth shut. Don't panic. *Let them work this out.* He closed his eyes and said a quick prayer for his own patience and their reconciliation.

Finally J.J. said, "Okay." He bobbed his head slowly. "I forgive you."

"Do . . .you . . . do you really you mean that?" Stone asked.

J.J.'s facial muscles tensed again. "I wouldn't say it unless I meant it."

"I'm sorry," Stone said. "I don't doubt your word. Forgiveness . . . it's hard for me to get a grip on it," Stone said. "I haven't given or received it much in my life."

"In your case, it's not easy to give. Hating you would be easier, but I wasn't brought up to take the easy way."

"I want to give you something." Stone shifted his gaze to Byron. "Preacher, do me a favor."

"Sure, General. Whatever you want."

He pointed to the other side of the room. "There's a ring of keys in my pants pocket in that closet over there. Bring 'em here, would ya?"

"Sure thing." As Byron crossed the room he felt ten pounds lighter, as if someone had lifted a weight from his shoulders. The words of J.J.'s solo echoed in the sanctuary of his mind: *Amazing grace, how sweet the sound.* Deep inside he felt a rare confirmation. *Maybe I am in the right business.* He opened the closet and saw the old jeans hanging on a hook. Reaching inside the pocket, he grasped a mass of cold keys and extracted them. *One of these opens that footlocker.* He looked at the case on the floor. *Surely after the battle, Stone didn't sort through Josiah's charred remains and find his skull.* The thought sent a shiver through him as he passed the box. *Maybe opening this thing right now isn't the best idea.*

At Stone's bedside, Byron's arms dangled, the keys jangling in his hand.

"Well," Stone said, "hand them over."

Byron glanced at J.J. and then at the keys. *Here we go again. Get ready to referee.* Slowly he reached and dropped the keys into Stone's hand.

Stone's bony fingers filed through the keys, found the right one, and worked it around the ring. Holding it up, he stared at J.J. and said, "Everything in that footlocker now belongs to you."

"What's in it?" J.J. asked.

Stone shook his head. "You'll find out soon enough."

J.J. reached for the key. "Do you want me to open it now?"

Stone pulled the key away. "I know this sounds like an odd request, but I'd rather you open it when you get home."

"When I get home?"

"Please." Stone stared at the footlocker. "There's something in there I don't want you to see until you get home."

"That means I'll have to rent a car and drive home," J.J. said. "Airport security won't let something like this slide by. They'll want to know what's inside."

"It won't pass through security," Stone said. "They'll be too many questions you can't answer."

Byron met J.J.'s questioning eyes.

"Is there something illegal inside of it? If so I don't want it," J.J. said.

Stone held out a trembling palm. "You've got to trust me on this. I'll pay for the rental." He waved toward the far corner of the room. "Get my wallet out of those pants, preacher."

J.J.'s lips tightened. His eyes shifted between the footlocker and Byron several times.

"There's an Enterprise Rent-a-Car in downtown Wheeling a few miles from here," Byron said.

J.J. rubbed his fingers across his mustache, inhaled deeply and said, "Damn. That's a twelve-hour drive. Guess that's the only way to do it. All right, Mr. Stone. I won't open the footlocker until I get home."

Stone handed J.J. the key and said, "Thanks."

"For what? I'm the one that's getting the box." J.J. said.

"For freedom." Stone stared at the footlocker. "That thing has been my master for decades. You're setting me free."

Stone extended his hand. J.J. hesitated but then shook it.

"One more thing," Stone said before letting go of J.J.'s hand.

"Now what?" J.J. said.

"I'd like to talk to the preacher alone before you haul that box out of here."

"Sure," J.J. said as they released their hands. "I'll wait in the hallway."

J.J. stepped away from the bed, motioned Byron to take his place beside Stone, then walked to the door, opened it, went out, and closed it behind him.

Byron handed Stone the wallet.

"Here's a couple hundred bucks," Stone said, pulling out the cash. "That should cover the rental car."

Byron accepted the money and slid it into his pants pocket. Then he leaned on the railing, and Stone clasped his hand over Byron's. "Thanks, Preacher," Stone said. "You did good. But there's one more thing I want to confess."

Byron studied Stone's expression, wondering what the old man would say next. Was he serious? Stone's eyes watered, and he blinked several times. "Is it something you did during the war?" Byron asked.

"No. It's something I didn't do."

"Didn't do?"

"There's a Bible in my suitcase. Same closet where my pants are hanging." He waved toward the other side of the room. "Get it for me, Preacher."

Byron made his third trip to the closet and found the old, brown leather suitcase. He placed it on the floor, unfastened a strap and lifted two clasps. Under several pairs of boxer shorts and a flannel shirt he saw the Bible, the once-black cover torn and stained with brown splatters. He carefully lifted it, noticing the warp of its pages as if it had been dropped in water at one time. It felt alive in his hand and smelled musty. He carried it to Stone and placed it in his lap.

"Is it yours?"

Stone shook his head sideways. "It belonged to a soldier in my platoon. He died during the last day of fighting on Peleliu. Our new lieutenant gave it to me along with a letter from the guy's wife. At the time I was acting sergeant. Guess he figured I should take care of contacting next of kin."

"May I take a look at it?" Byron asked.

Stone's hand trembled as he gave the book to him. Byron opened it to the New Testament, Matthew chapter twenty. There he found the only legible words—*the first shall be last.* "What were you supposed to do with this?"

Stone lowered his eyes, staring blankly at the floor. "Lieutenant Hobbs wanted me to send it back to his wife along with the letter she'd written. He told me to give her an account of how her husband died—you know what I mean—bravely, sacrificing himself for freedom. That kind of thing."

Byron handed Stone the Bible. "So what did you do?"

"Nothing. I was messed up. Peleliu screwed my mind. I wanted to write out the whole story and send it back to her. At the time I couldn't find any decent paper. I opened her letter. Figured I'd use the back of it. Shouldn't have read her words. That's what did me in—the words she wrote to her husband. After reading her letter, I readdressed the envelope and sent it back to her—blank."

"What did you do with the Bible?"

"I stashed it in the bottom of my sea bag. Figured one day when I got my head straight, I'd do a proper job of telling her how her husband died. Maybe even personally deliver the Bible to her." Stone braced his forehead against his palms. "Never got around to it. Guess I didn't want to face that responsibility—look her in the eyes. When it comes to those kinds of things, deep down . . ." Stone glanced up, blinking, chin quavering, ". . . deep down I'm a coward."

"Do you want me to take the Bible to her?"

"Yes . . . I think she's still alive."

"That letter she wrote, would you know what to write on the back of it now?"

Stone raised his head, met Byron's gaze and nodded. "I'd know exactly what to write."

* * *

After J.J. and Byron lugged the footlocker back to the van, they headed to downtown Wheeling and found the car rental company. Byron pulled the wad of cash from his pocket and handed it to him. J.J. counted the money and declared the expense shouldn't be half that amount.

"Stop somewhere in Virginia or North Carolina and get yourself a gourmet meal, compliments of the General," Byron said.

"I've got a better idea. I'll hit a McDonalds whenever I get hungry, spend four bucks on a quarter pounder and large coffee, and put whatever is left over into the youth center fund. Won't do much to this year's deficit, but at least it's something."

Byron chuckled. "Probably the first time Stone has ever donated to a worthy cause."

J.J. got out of the van and walked to the office. Ten minutes later he pulled a shiny red Ford Taurus into the space next to the Caravan. Byron popped open the van's hatch, and they loaded the footlocker into the trunk of the Taurus. After J.J. slammed the trunk, they faced each other and shook hands.

"Make sure I'm the first person you call as soon as you open that thing," Byron said.

"If that's what you want." J.J. glanced at his watch. "You'll hear from me about three a.m."

"Three a.m.?" Byron rolled his eyes and let out a long whistle. "My wife might complain, but it'll be worth it."

"Remember, you're heading my direction this summer for your family vacation. Free room and board. Lot's of things to do in Atlanta."

Byron slapped J.J. on the shoulder. "Nothing sounds more inviting to a poor preacher than the word 'free.'"

Byron explained the quickest way to get back on Interstate 70. They embraced and thanked each other. Then J.J. climbed into the Taurus and drove away. As the car disappeared around the corner, Byron felt like he'd just said goodbye to his closest friend. *That's odd. I've only known the man for two days. Doesn't take long to connect to a kindred spirit. That's the way it's been all of my life. The older I get, though, the fewer I meet.*

Before climbing into his vehicle, Byron slid open the passenger door and picked up the tattered Bible. He examined the brown splatters. Had to be the residue of old mud from when Stone dropped it into the puddle. *Wow. Helen will be shocked to see this.*

Byron opened the driver's side door and got in, placing the Bible on the passenger seat. On the ride home he recalled the last two letters he'd read the night before. The first was the two-page letter from Helen without Howard's response on the back. He'd guessed Howard's death to be the explanation for the blank sides. The second correspondence was from the war department, what Byron assumed to be the official disclosure to the spouse that the loved one had been killed in action.

Why did Helen's letter rattle Stone? He remembered Helen mentioned a strange dream that had upset her—something that occurred on her father-in-law's farm concerning the livestock. Was it the sheep? At the time it didn't make a lot of sense. Now, after speaking with Stone, Byron wondered if his cursory reading had missed something important.

As soon as he pulled into the manse's driveway, he grabbed Howard's Bible and headed straight for his study. On the way up the stairs he heard the vacuum cleaner droning from the living room. He hesitated, thinking he should check in with Lila to see if anyone had called and give her a kiss hello, but the urge to read the letter quashed that notion, and he double-timed up the remaining steps.

The letter sat on top of the stack in the war box, which he'd left on his desk. Quickly he slid out the envelope flap, extracted the page, and started to read.

My Darling Howie,

It's three o'clock in the morning. My heart is pounding. I hope and pray this letter gets to you quickly. I've just awakened from an odd dream. I don't know what it means. It was one of those dreams that seem more real than life itself. I wanted to write it down now before I forgot any details. God always gave dreams to people in the Bible. Some prophet like Daniel or Joseph would figure out what they meant. Maybe you can figure this one out.

I dreamt I was at your parent's house out on the farm. Your mom was crying and I didn't know why. I asked your father and he said because the holidays were coming—Thanksgiving and Christmas. Then I understood. She was missing you. When someone you love is far away, it's hardest during the holidays.

Then your father asked me to walk with him across the hills to the north pasture. I said, sure I'd go. On the way he kept saying we have a lot to be thankful for. Of course, I agreed with him, although I miss you terribly.

When we arrived, I saw a huge flock of sheep—spotted ones, dirty white ones, black ones. Your father told me to wait there. Then he waded out through the herd. I wondered what in the world he was doing. He tried to pick up one of the sheep, but it bit him and kicked him, squirming out of his arms. He gave up on that one. Then he bent down again, turned around and came back carrying a lamb. It wasn't dirty like the other ones and had a blue ribbon around its neck. Then I recognized it. Remember Joshua, the little lamb your Uncle Matt gave you to raise when you were twelve? We were just junior high buddies back then, but I went out to his farm with you to pick it out. It was the cutest thing, and I took the ribbon out of my hair and tied it around its neck. You kept it as a pet for a year before releasing it into the herd.

I said to your father, "What's the lamb for?" But he just walked right by me back toward the house. I couldn't keep up with him, but I kept calling out, "What's the lamb for? What's Joshua for?" Finally, he turned around, looked at me and said, "Thanksgiving." Something inside of me began to ache like when you want to cry real bad but can't. I wanted to catch up and take Joshua away from your father, but my feet were stuck in mud. That's when I woke up. Howie, I think this dream has something to do with you. That's why I'm sending this out as soon as I can tomorrow morning. Maybe it's a message from God. Maybe it's nothing. I don't know.

Please be careful. I love you more than I could ever express,

Your one and only,

Helen.

Byron folded the page, stuck it back into the envelope, and placed it on top of Howard's Bible.

CHAPTER 25

Lila stood in the study doorway, dressed in baggy gray sweats, her hand grasping the sweeper handle. "When did you get here?"

"'Bout ten minutes ago." Byron walked around the desk, crossed the room, embraced, and kissed her.

She pushed him back with her free hand. "Thanks for letting me know."

He studied her eyes, hoping she really wasn't irritated with him. "I was in a hurry to do something."

She smiled, relieving his slight anxiety. "You're always in a hurry to do something."

Byron shrugged, knowing she was right.

"How'd it go with J.J. and Mr. Stone?"

"There were some . . . tense moments. Overall, I'm pleased with the outcome. They parted on peaceful terms, but I'll have to tell you the whole story tonight at dinner. I've got a couple more visits to make today."

"That reminds me. You got a call from the hospital about an hour ago."

"Earl Waller?"

"Close. Eric."

"Eric? Eric has never called me before. Yesterday he could barely remember me."

"Sounded pretty urgent," Lila said. "Wanted to see you as soon as possible."

"I was headed over there anyway to see Judd Stone again. I'll stop in and talk to Eric first."

"Hey." Lila beckoned him with her forefinger.

He stepped closer, and she reached around his backside and pulled him tight against her. With lips almost touching she said, "I'd like to see you real soon too sometime."

"I can arrange that." Byron kissed her, gently at first and then more aggressively, growling like a cartoon tiger between smooches.

She placed her fingers on his lips. "That's enough for now—a few lively sparks."

"We'll start a fire tonight," Byron said, sliding his hand down her back and across her nicely rounded rear.

* * *

As Byron merged onto the Fort Henry Bridge, he checked the side mirror for oncoming traffic. He slowed to time his maneuver—drop in behind the first car, allow the two vehicles in the passing lane to get by so he could accelerate into the outer lane, which proceeded through the tunnel, before the other lane peeled off to the right into downtown Wheeling. He scooted in behind the first vehicle easily enough, but the two cars in the far lane took longer than expected. By the time the second car passed, he had barely enough lane remaining but managed to swerve into the flow. He took a deep breath, let it out, and relaxed. If only he could move in and out of the lives of people as deftly. Meeting with Eric Waller, Judd Stone, and Helen Kinloch in the next few hours would be much more mentally challenging and emotionally demanding.

Driving into the tunnel, he blinked, trying to adjust to the loss of light. *What had happened to Eric? He must be regaining his memory quickly. Yesterday he had the mentality of a nine-year-old, watching Sesame Street, hardly recognizing me. And why does he want to see me? We never hit it off before. Always a little uncomfortable around each other when I came to counsel him. Maybe Earl pushed him to call me.*

Emerging into the bright daylight, Byron tried to organize his thoughts concerning Judd Stone and Helen Kinloch. He took a quick peek at the Bible and envelope next to him on the passenger seat and shook his head. He never would have guessed Stone held on to that Bible all those years. It had to have been a source of guilt, a reminder of the way he treated Howard. And how had Howard died? Did he finally raise the courage to face the enemy in a firefight, or was he a victim of a random mortar shell? Byron hoped Stone could offer more details concerning Howard's demise. *Wait 'til the General sees Helen's letter. This is a day of restitution for the old man. First he set things right with J.J., and now he'll have another chance to write Helen about Howard's death.*

Byron looked forward to seeing Helen too. They had a lot to talk about now that he'd read through all her war letters. With Stanley and Stone's accounts fresh in his mind, he could answer some of her questions. But the information she really wanted—details of Howard's death and Stone's involvement—depended on what Stone had to say.

Now he needed to focus on his visit with Eric. After pulling into the hospital lot and finding a parking space, he glanced at the Bible and letter on the passenger seat. After picking up the letter he hesitated. *Should I take the Bible? I don't really need it.* He inhaled deeply and blew the air out. *Take it.* The two words sent a chill through him, as if someone else spoke them audibly. He lifted the Bible and glanced into the back seat before heading out.

* * *

The door to Eric's room was open but the lights were off. Byron stepped in and peered into the corner.

"Eric?" Byron said softly.

"I'm awake, Pastor Byron."

And shaky, if his voice was any indication, Byron thought as he pulled the privacy curtain back. Below the bandage swathing his head, Eric's eyes glistened in the meager light that sliced in from the blinds.

He blinked several times and waved his good hand. "Thanks for coming."

"Hey, Eric. Where's your dad? Figured I'd see him here."

"He hung out all morning. Left a couple hours ago. I wanted to talk to you alone. Hope you don't mind."

"Not at all. Your memory must be making a comeback."

"Big time."

A tremor of uneasiness stirred Byron's chest and drained into his stomach. Recalling the day Eric attempted suicide, Byron feared too much memory recovery might not be a good thing. "Yeah, you barely knew me yesterday."

"Things are coming back to me. I'm having a hard time sorting out what's real and what's not. There're pictures in my mind, but they're not making sense. Kind of like a puzzle."

"Did you speak to your father about these new memories?"

Eric nodded. "I tried. But Dad doesn't want to talk about it."

"I see."

"If it were up to Dad, I'd be five years old again. Can't blame him. I didn't get in so much trouble back then."

Byron edged to the front of the bed and put his free hand on the railing.

"What'd you bring with you?" Eric asked.

Byron lifted the objects into the sparse light. "Just an old beat up Bible and a letter."

"Why'd you bring them here?"

"I'm stopping by to see someone else after I visit you. The Bible belonged to a Marine who fought and died in World War II."

"Oh," Eric said, slowly nodding.

"The man I'm visiting is facing some memories like you. Some difficult ones."

"Was he a soldier?"

"Yes, Eric, he was. He did some things he wasn't very proud of during the war, but now he wants to make it right."

With his good hand Eric reached for the Bible. "Can I see it?"

"Sure." Byron took the letter in his other hand and gave Eric the mud-splattered book.

He opened to the inside cover and pointed at the inscription. "Someone wrote a note on this first page."

"That was the soldier's wife, Helen."

"Can I read it?"

"Go ahead."

Eric cleared his throat as if preparing to read out loud in English class. *"My Darling Howie,*

"I miss you terribly. Without you there's a lonely aching inside of me. We both will need God's help to get through these difficult days. I pray this Bible gives you strength, comfort, and hope. Read it whenever you can.

"Remember Psalm 23:4. 'Yea, though I walk through the valley of the shadow of death, I will fear no evil: for Thou art with me; Thy rod and Thy staff, they comfort me.'

"My grandfather always told me there's nothing wrong with being afraid. The important thing is to face your fears. May God grant both of us the courage to face our fears.

"I love you more than words could ever describe. Please come back to me.

Helen"

Eric placed the book in his lap and thumbed through the pages, watching the words flip by. "Did he get killed in combat?"

"Yes," Byron said. "He died on the last day of the battle."

Eric met Byron's gaze. "He must have faced his fears."

Byron nodded. "That's not easy to do."

Eric handed Byron the Bible. "I tried to shoot myself, didn't I?"

Byron hesitated, thinking Earl should be here to answer that question or perhaps some psychologist. The Bible felt like a lead weight. He swallowed the knot that had formed in his throat, but it came back instantly. Do your duty, preacher. Face the question. Byron reached and grasped Eric's hand. "Yes. You tried to commit suicide."

"And you stopped me."

"That's right."

Eric squeezed Byron's hand tightly. "I was afraid."

"There's nothing wrong with being afraid."

"I can't remember why I did it. For some reason I didn't want to live anymore."

"You were going through a very tough time."

"I remember being in some kind of accident. Getting hurt." He motioned to the casts on his legs.

Byron considered mentioning the ATV wreck and the death of Eric's friend, Johnny Owens. No. Not now. Let the memories come back at their own pace. One step at a time. "Eventually you'll remember everything that happened. The important thing now is to face your fears. You have a lot to live for. You need to be courageous."

Eric blinked and a tear slid down his cheek. "I want to be brave."

"You don't have to face it alone. I'll be here. We can talk whenever you want. You have a lot of people around who love you."

Eric nodded. "Pastor Byron . . ."

"Yes."

"Can a kid like me . . . someone who's screwed things up so many times . . . get it right? You know, make something out of himself? Make people proud instead of disappointed?"

A series of images from Byron's teen years flashed across his mind—fights with his mother, breakups with girls, angst concerning his father's rejection, running away from home, bouts with depression. Then, a sentimental wave swelled in him as he considered his life now—a close-knit family, great kids and a loving wife. He couldn't speak for several seconds.

Finally, he said. "The truth is, Eric, it's up to you. You could have a great life. Make lots of people proud of you. Or you could stir up a world of trouble. Every person possesses something that determines his future. Do you know what it is?"

Eric shook is head.

"The power to make decisions. You decide what happens from here on out. People can help you, but no one can live your life for you. God Almighty could shine a beam down to light the path of success, but God won't take your freedom of choice away from you. It all comes down to what you decide."

Eric stared into a dark corner of the room for several moments. "So if I screw up again . . ." He met Byron's gaze. ". . . I'm responsible."

"That's right."

"And if I turn things around and get it right . . ."

"It's because that's what you decided to do. Good or bad, you make the choices."

Eric reached and grasped Byron's hand. "Thanks for stopping to see me."

"You're welcome." Byron squeezed Eric's hand firmly. "I'll stop back tomorrow."

"And thanks for stopping me from committing . . . you know . . . from blowing . . . blowing my . . ."

"You don't have to say anything. I know, Eric, I know."

Eric smeared a tear across his cheek. "One more thing."

Byron blinked, his eyes watering.

"Could you say a prayer for me before you leave?"

"Of course."

CHAPTER 26

When Byron handed Stone the yellowed envelope, he eyed it warily. "What's this?"

"Does it look familiar?"

"Somewhat. Where'd you get it?"

"From Helen Kinloch, Howard's wife."

Stone's hands tightened on the envelope. "I'll be damned. She gave this to you?" He fumbled with the flap.

"Yes. She gave me a box full of letters and war memorabilia just a few days ago."

"This takes me back a long ways." He read the first few sentences. "Yes sir, the same letter Lieutenant Hobbs handed me. He wanted me to write her on the back of these pages. Tell her how Howard died."

"And you sent it back as is."

Stone bobbed his head, continuing to read.

Byron pulled a pen from his breast pocket and held it in front of Stone's face. "Well, General, you've been given a second chance."

Stone slowly raised his head and pointed at the words. "It was this dream she wrote about. When I read it back then it stunned me like a hard left hook to the noggin."

"Why would a dream about some sheep shake you up so much?"

"It just did." Stone reached for the pen. "I understood what the dream meant. That's why it bothered me."

"What did it mean?"

Stone averted his eyes and drew in a raspy breath. "Don't want to talk about it now." He gently touched the letter. "Got some writing to do."

As Stone stared at the blank page, pen poised to write the first word, Byron rubbed his chin and studied the man's wizened face. You understood the dream, huh? Never would have pegged you as a Daniel or a Joseph, General—an interpreter of dreams.

Byron lowered himself into the cushioned chair next to the hospital bed and waited patiently. Occasionally he glanced at the television where the Pittsburgh Pirates struggled to come back in the late innings against the Cincinnati Reds. The sound had been turned down. Only loud cheers and occasional outbursts from an enthusiastic announcer could be detected.

His thoughts drifted from the game to Eric and the change that had transpired in the boy's thinking since the shooting. Byron felt optimistic about Eric's future. He wondered if the bullet somehow damaged a part of Eric's brain in a beneficial way. Was that possible? Could an injury to part of the brain result in the elimination of a self-destructive tendency? If so, then Byron's redirection of that fatally aimed bullet had been heavenly guided. Or else it was one hell of a coincidence.

He glanced at his watch. Almost four o'clock. He still had plenty of time to run over to the nursing home, see Helen and then return home before six. Sitting back in the seat, he gazed at Stone, who leaned on the over-bed tray and focused on the tip of his pen as he drew out each letter. What was he writing? Hopefully Helen would be willing to share those words later.

Finally Stone completed the task, folded the pages, stuck them back into the envelope, and tucked in the flap. He held it out and said, "Here. Make sure she gets this."

"Of course, General. I'll take it to her after I leave here."

"Good. One more weight off my soul, huh, Preacher?"

Byron smiled. "Before long you'll be floating in the clouds."

"Yeah," Stone snorted. "I'll believe that when I look over my shoulder and see an angel strummin' a harp."

Byron grinned. Stone appeared to be in better spirits, as if a debt had been paid for him. But something dark remained—a sadness, a regret, a thorn still lodged in the paw of the old lion. "Before I leave, General, I've got a question for you."

Stone glanced at his palms, as if studying the lines and creases like a fortuneteller. "I know what you're gonna ask. What did that dream mean? Right?"

"I am interested in the dream, but I was going to ask you how Howard died."

Stone peered out the window and took several deep breaths. Meeting Byron's stare he said, "That's another story I wanted to tell you, Preacher."

"Good. I'd really like to know."

"All right. I'll tell it like it happened. The ugly truth. One more confession to lighten my soul." He cleared his throat and gulped. "By the end of October we had corralled the Japs into what was called the Umurbrogol Pocket on the eastern border of the island. We'd heard the Army's 81st would come in soon to replace us and finish the cleanup work. Knowing we were about to head back to Pavuvu, all we wanted to do was stay alive. Japs didn't care, though. They still hoped to make us permanent residents.

"By then all the rifle companies had been shot completely to hell. We had maybe ten percent of our original guys left. Howard and me and a few other lucky ducks were lying in a long trench across a draw from a cliff side, keeping our eyes on the caves. Every once in a while one of them yellow bastards would get loaded on Saki and come charging at us with a sword or pistol. We'd see who could knock off the asshole first. Kinda like target practice. 'Cept for Howard, of course. He didn't want to kill anybody."

Stone took a deep breath, his eyes becoming distant. "The brass had become desperate to shore up our lines until the army got there. They were asking any Tom, Dick, or Harry to volunteer—mechanics, typists, aides, laborers, dishwashers. Late that afternoon I looked over my shoulder and couldn't believe my eyes. Here come a squad of black cooks up the hill toward us carrying rifles.

"'What the hell they doing here?' I said to Howard. "Now I've seen everything—niggers totin' M1s like they're actually gonna use 'em.'

"Howard told me they have a right to fight too, and then he waved to one of them—a big one by the name of Robinson. Bigger than a grisly bear.

"'Bout half a dozen of them plopped down in the trench not ten feet away from me. They all said hi to Howard like he was their second cousin. Between us and them was a spic named Comacho and a Jew named Rubin. I thought, Chriminey, what's next? A Chinaman?

"'What're you boys doing here?' I said. 'They run out of potatoes to peel behind the lines?'

"'We ain't 'fraid to fight,' one of the Negroes said. 'I'd be fightin' the whole battle if they'd let me.'

"'Shit,' I said. 'You'd be dead the first day.' He shot back some smart-ass answer. Hell, he had no idea what it was like. Nobody did 'cept for the soldiers who went through it.

"Then the big one, Robinson, says to me, 'Where'd you get that watch, Stone?'

"'None of your damn business,' I said. I can remember the look on his face like a panther about to pounce—those angry eyes and that yellow-toothed snarl.

"He said, 'Hell it ain't. That belongs to Josiah Jackson.'

"I said, 'Yeah? Tell Jackson to come get it.'

"Robinson said, 'You know he's dead. But he's got family at home. I could send it to them.'

"'Like hell,' I said. 'Jackson gave it to me before he died.'"

Stone hesitated, shaking his head. "In all our squabbling, no one paid attention to the caves. A drunk Jap had come chargin' out with a hand grenade. He tossed that thing at us right before Comacho drew a bead on him and cut him down. I'll be damned if that pineapple didn't land right between me and Kinloch. It rolled down the slope and stopped at our feet. For a split second I looked at Kinloch. The way he stared at it you'd a thought a goose had just laid a golden egg. Didn't look scared either, like he usually did."

Stone gripped at his sheets, his legs squirming underneath. "I knew I had to do something or both of us were goners. I reached with my foot and gave that grenade a kick. It didn't go far enough—'bout ten feet to where Camacho and the cooks were lying. Kinloch looked at me like I was Judas counting my silver coins. Then he leaped like a deer and landed right on that grenade. The explosion was terrible, but Howard . . . Howard took the full brunt of it.

"I scrambled to his side, turned him over and pulled him up to me. The last few beats of his heart pumped spurts of blood all over my face and chest. I was covered in Howard's blood. Then he died in my arms, coughing and gagging. I lowered him to the ground and looked at my red hands. I must have been a sight. Those black cooks, Camacho, and Rubin stared at me. Thought one of them might raise a rifle and shoot me dead. So be it. I deserved to die. But none did. Just looked at me like I was some kind of monster. Maybe I was."

Stone refocused his gaze on Byron. "Right then and there I thought about pulling out my pistol and shooting myself in the head. But I didn't. I looked down at Howard. He was a mess of blood and guts. I cradled him in my arms and picked him up. He wasn't that heavy, maybe a hundred and forty pounds. Then I walked down the slope and away from the battle."

Stone paused and lifted his hands in front of his face. "There are times when I can still see Howard's blood on my hands." He swiveled his head, his eyes meeting Byron's. "Sometimes I look in the bathroom mirror and see my face dripping with his blood. Preacher, there's always been an ugliness inside of me, but I never knew how ugly until that day. Carrying Howard back to the medical tent, I realized I had it all wrong—Howard Kinloch wasn't a coward." Stone pointed at his chest. "Here's the coward. The fact that I'm still here is the proof. I never could raise the courage to sacrifice myself. Or kill myself for that matter."

"Killing yourself is never the answer, General," Byron said. "It takes much more courage to go on living."

"No, Preacher. My still being alive has nothing to do with courage. I learned to lie to myself—learned to deal with the guilt and shame of it all. Learned to blame others for my mistakes. I even convinced myself I deserved that watch. But then the nightmares started. And the truth came to me."

"That's when you called for me?"

"That's right."

Byron eyed the sparse gray strands on top of Stone's head, the thin pale skin, and spidery veins. He felt an aching in his chest, a sensation of empathy for a person suddenly exposed to the pain of reality. It was the same sensation that bore through him only fifteen minutes earlier in Eric's room.

"Maybe the most courageous acts of our lives don't happen on a battlefield."

The old man's eyes softened. "What're you saying, Preacher?"

"Maybe the bravest thing we can do in life is face the truth—the ugly truth—confront it, confess it and then leave it behind. Make a new start. A better start because of what we've learned."

Stone rubbed the white stubble on his chin and let out contemplative sigh. "Kinda like a snake, eh?"

"A snake?"

"Yeah. Slide out of the old skin, leave it behind and go a new direction."

"That's right," Byron said. "Even snakes start again."

Stone unhooked the oxygen tube from his nose, sat straight up, stretched his arms toward the ceiling and smiled, a wide smile. "Yeah. Maybe I'll do that."

CHAPTER 27

Byron steered into an empty space in the McGraw Nursing Home parking lot, put the vehicle in park, and glanced at his watch. Almost four-thirty. Sunday was supposed to be a day of rest. Not for preachers. He'd been going strong since six this morning. Usually by now he'd be done with the day's work, probably napping on the family room couch while Lila watched a romantic comedy on the classic movie channel. Although fatigue had settled on him during the drive over, the prospect of visiting Helen and talking about the letters and Judd Stone sent a new surge of adrenalin into his system. He scooped the Bible and letter from the passenger seat, wondering how Helen would react when he presented them to her, then exited the van and walked briskly to the front entrance.

After buzzing in and entering the patients' quarters, he saw Rita standing near the counter at the nurses' station. She put her hands on her wide hips, back arching, ample breasts lifting.

"Back again already, Pastor? Twice this week. Can't keep away from me, can you?"

Byron reached and touched her shoulder. "That's right, Rita. You're a hard woman to resist."

"Don't I know it." Her gleeful laughter exploded, echoing down the hall. She slapped him on the back. "You better keep walking before you get in trouble."

Byron smiled. "We don't need any scandals, do we?"

Rita raised her eyebrows. "I wouldn't mind one, but you couldn't handle it."

Byron shook his head and headed down the hallway.

Halfway down he turned and peeked into Helen's room. The light was out but the late-afternoon sun streamed through the window and across a desk, dresser, and a bed neatly made with a red-plaid quilt. "Helen?" He stepped in and glanced around, seeing no one. *Must be down in the lounge.*

Half the time when Byron visited, he would find Helen sitting in the sunroom—or the Room of Light, as she called it—a lounge at the end of the hall with windows on all sides.

When he entered from the darkened hallway, the brightness caused him to squint. On the left a mid-sized television sat on an in-table, and a dozen empty chairs with flowered cushions lined the walls. Helen sat in her wheelchair on the other side, gazing out the window.

"Hey, good buddy," Byron said.

Helen gripped one wheel, spun the chair, and flashed a wide smile. She wore a forest green sweater that contrasted with her almost-white hair. Raising her hands, she motioned him to her with her fingers. "Pastor Byron. Come give me a hug." She held out her arms. "This is a treat. Two visits this week."

Trying to keep the Bible and letter from being noticed, he bent down and embraced her, holding them against her back as she kissed his cheek. She felt warm but fragile.

"What are you carrying?" she asked as he inched away. "A box of candy? Chocolates?"

Byron slipped the Bible and letter behind him. "Something you haven't seen for a long time. You'll be surprised."

"Really?"

Byron nodded. "Close your eyes and I'll put it in your hands. See if you can guess."

"This better be good," she said as she held out her hands and shut her eyes. Byron carefully lowered the Bible into he grasp. "It's a book, isn't it?" Helen asked, eyes still closed.

"A special book. Go ahead. You can look."

She opened her eyes and said, "Great gravy. It's a mess." Then she gasped, carefully lifted the cover to the first page, and read the inscription she'd written almost sixty years before. "Howard's Bible," she said, barely a whisper. A couple of tears trickled down her cheeks. "Where did you get this?"

He knelt next to her, gently placing his hand on her arm. "One of Howard's platoon members asked me to give it to you."

"Who?"

"Judd Stone."

"Judd Stone? He had it all these years?"

Byron nodded.

"Great gravy, he only lives five miles from me. Why didn't he bring it to me long ago? Certainly he'd have realized what this would have meant to me."

"He's a hard man to figure out."

"You don't have to tell me. I know. You read the letters— how Stone picked on my husband. Howard was a good man, but Stone wouldn't give him any credit." She wiped her cheeks with one hand, using the other to secure the Bible. "A bully and an ignoramus—that's what he was. I can't believe he didn't at least send this to me by mail."

Byron pointed to the Bible. "Do you see that letter between the pages?"

With the tips of her fingers Helen pinched the end of the envelope and slid it out. "This is one of the letters I wrote to Howie. Did you find it in the box I gave you?"

"Yes. That's the last letter you wrote to him."

She nodded. "Howard's side is blank. He got killed before he could respond."

Byron shook his head. "No. Now there's a message on the back that should have been written long ago."

"A message? From who?"

"Judd Stone. When Howard got killed, the Lieutenant gave Stone the responsibility of informing you and returning the Bible. He couldn't raise the courage to do it until now."

Helen shook her head and fumbled with the flap. "Better late than not at all, I guess. Getting that Bible back is a blessing I never expected. What in God's name did Judd Stone write me about after all these years?"

"Could you . . ." Byron tightened his lips then started again. "Could you read it out loud? I'd really like to know too."

"Of course." Adjusting the pages to a good reading distance, Helen cleared her throat.

"Dear Mrs. Kinloch,

"Please forgive me. This is way past due. I was the acting sergeant of Howard's platoon. Lieutenant Hobbs asked me to write to you and tell you how Howard died. By now you know Howard died heroically, sacrificing his life for others. He dove on an enemy hand grenade and saved nine men including me.

"Back then I couldn't handle the responsibility. I sent the letter to you without writing a word and stored Howard's Bible in my sea bag. I hoped some day I could raise the courage to visit you and tell the whole story, but I kept putting it off.

"The truth is I should have died that day. I tried to save myself instead. My reaction led to Howard's decision to fall on the grenade. I'm responsible. For years I blocked the incident out of my mind. I couldn't face you because I knew what I had done.

"When we left Peleliu I figured the worst battle of my life was over. I was wrong. Facing myself in the mirror every morning since has been much worse. I saved my own skin but lost my soul. For years I lied to that face in the mirror. I'm tired of lying.

"I'm sorry for what I did. I'm sorry he never returned to you. I'm sorry I robbed you of the chance to live out your life with Howard and have his children. I'm sorry it has taken me this long to face that man in the mirror and tell him to go to hell.

"Now that I have faced the truth, there is one thing I know for sure—Howard Kinloch was the bravest man I ever knew.

"Sincerely,

Judd Stone"

Helen sat back and took a long, tremulous breath. Releasing it, she couldn't hold back the tears. Byron embraced her as she cried, her thin frame so delicate beneath his grasp. After several minutes she released her grip on him and gained control of her breathing.

"I'm okay," she said. "It's just that his words reminded me of all . . . of all that was lost."

"I understand," Byron said.

"Don't get me wrong. I've lived a good life. A fulfilling life." She laid her hand on her breast. "But there's still an aching right here. I still miss Howie."

"I'm sorry."

She fluttered your hand. "Nothing to be sorry about."

Byron watched as she pulled a tissue out of a leather satchel on the side of her wheelchair and dried her cheeks.

Seeing her pain, he wondered if he should change the subject, try to end the visit on a positive note. But then a smile returned to her face.

"Do you mind talking about these things?" Byron asked.

"Not at all. It's good for me. A few tears never hurt anybody. Anyway, I learned something from this letter."

"What did you learn?"

"A few more details about how it happened. You know . . . Howie's death."

"No eyewitnesses ever gave you the full story?"

She shook her head. "I knew Howie dove on a hand grenade to save his fellow soldiers. The officer at the ceremony told me that."

"Ceremony?"

"Yes." She reached into the satchel and pulled out the blue-velvet case.

"I remember now," Byron said. "You promised to show me what was in that case when I finished reading the letters."

Helen smiled and held it up. "I always keep this near. Congressman Fedderline presented it to me at a memorial ceremony in Washington D.C."

She opened the case to reveal a gold medal in the shape of a cross with an old sailing vessel in three-dimensional relief in the middle. Attached to the top was a blue ribbon with a narrow white stripe down the center.

"The Navy Cross?" Byron whispered.

Helen nodded. "It's one of the highest medals given for bravery in combat."

Byron grazed his fingers over the surface, envisioning Howard's final act of sacrifice. "Stone told me exactly what happened that day. I know why he blames himself for Howard's death."

Helen's eyes widened. "Tell me."

"Stone, Howard and two soldiers, a Jew and a Hispanic, were holding the line that day. Just about everyone in their platoon had been killed or wounded. The army hadn't arrived yet to relieve them, so the officers recruited every able-bodied man to help defend the front line. A squad of black cooks showed up with guns to give support."

Helen raised her hand. "Wait a minute. You said a Jew, a Hispanic, and a group of black soldiers were there with Howard?"

"Yes. They were lying in a trench across from some caves."

Helen turned over the letter and glanced at the side she had written on—the side describing the dream. Looking up, she said, "Go on."

"While Stone and a couple of the black cooks argued, a Japanese soldier charged out of a cave and threw the grenade. It landed right between Howard and Stone and rolled to a stop at their feet. Stone believes he should have jumped on it right then. He was the acting sergeant, responsible for the lives of those men. Instead, he kicked it toward the others. That's when Howard leapt to his feet and dove on it. He took the full force of the explosion and saved all of them."

Helen held up the pages. "The dream."

Byron filed through his memory and retrieved the image of Howard's father wading through the sheep—white ones, dirty ones, spotted ones, dark ones. "What about the dream?"

Helen's eyes glazed over, unfocused, staring above him. "Now I know . . . now I know who those men were."

"Who?"

"The sheep."

A chill prickled down Byron's back. "And Howard . . . he was . . ."

"The lamb."

Hands clasped behind his head, Byron lay on the bed and stared at the plaster swirls on the ceiling. With a pillow propped behind her back, Lila supported her paperback novel against her raised knees, reading intently.

"Hon," Byron said, "do you remember our wedding night down in that lodge at Black Water Falls?"

She peered over her glasses at him. "Of course, By. How could I forget? You ordered the fresh mountain trout, and they cooked it with the head and tail still on. I almost died laughing, watching you eat with that fish staring up at your every bite. Then you began talking to it and I peed myself."

Byron chuckled. "Yeah, I wanted to make you laugh. Help you relax."

"It worked."

"We had fun that night, didn't we?"

"Lots of fun. Why are you thinking about our honeymoon night?"

Byron inhaled deeply and blew the air out audibly. "Reading Helen and Howard's letters got me thinking. They had an incredible love for each other—the way we felt when we were first married."

Lila laid the book on the nightstand and turned on her side to face Byron. "You don't think we love each other as much now?"

"I didn't say that. It's just different now."

"Of course it's different, By. We've been married twenty years. We've gone through a lot together."

Byron turned onto his side, reached and caressed her cheek. "I know. I just want to keep that flame of passion burning between us. I could see it in Helen's eyes today. That flame still burns for Howard even though he's been gone sixty years."

Lila scooted closer and twirled his chest hair with her finger. "They had something very special. Something rare."

"Those letters helped me realize something."

"What's that?"

"The things I get obsessed with aren't that important." He leaned closer until their lips were almost touching.

"What is important?"

He kissed her softly. "You are."

"By, I'm starting to feel some flames of passion of my own. I might need some help getting them under control."

"Should I put on my fireman's hat and red suspenders?"

"I don't think they'll help keep your pants up."

* * *

Byron rolled off of Lila onto his side, breathing like he'd just sprinted a hundred-yard dash. He draped his arm over her back and drew her to him. She also breathed harshly, eyes closed.

When their respiration slowed, Byron asked, "Did I put the fire out?"

Lila giggled. "It took mighty effort, but you finally put it out."

Byron grinned. "That was a five-alarmer. Took everything I had."

They both laughed. Lila nudged her head against his chest. "Now I feel energized. Mind if I read for a while?"

Byron pretended to snore until she slapped his rear. "Huh? . . . What? . . . D'you say something?"

"Do all men fall asleep thirty seconds after making love?"

Byron rolled onto his back and stared at the ceiling, clasping his hands behind his head. "I don't know. Maybe I could conduct a survey from the pulpit this Sunday."

Lila slugged him playfully in the ribs. "I'm sure the session would love that." She sat up and turned on the nightstand lamp.

Byron eyed his wife as she pulled her nightgown over her head. "Hon?"

"What, By?"

"After all these years I can still hit it outta the park, can't I?"

"You put all the wood on that one. Deep to centerfield." She picked up the war romance she'd been reading.

"Hon?"

"What?"

"Love you."

"Love you too, By."

Warmed by the effort and calmed by a deep sense of satisfaction, he allowed every muscle to relax and stared at the ceiling, amused by Lila's "thirty-second" comment. Certainly he would stay awake longer than that, pondering the experiences of the day. But his mind grew sluggish, the images and thoughts draining away. Sleep came quickly

* * *

When the strident ring pierced his ears, Byron reached for the snooze button on the digital alarm clock. The noise halted for several seconds but started again. On his second attempt to turn off the alarm he realized the sound originated from beyond the alarm. The phone. Who's calling at this hour? What's the matter with me? It's got to be J.J. He extended his arm slightly farther and lifted the receiver. "Hello . . . "

"Byron?"

"Yeah. J.J. That you?"

"It's me."

Lila turned over and mumbled, "Who's calling this late?"

"It's for me, Hon. Go back to bed."

She grunted, turned onto her side and pulled the sheet over her head.

"Just a second," Byron said as he got out of bed and took the cordless phone down the hallway to his study. "Okay, go ahead."

"You wide awake?" J.J. asked.

"Now I am. Unless I'm dreaming." He glanced at the clock: 3:37. "You make it home all right?"

"Took a half gallon of coffee, but I made it."

"Well, I'm dying to know. What's in the trunk?"

"Don't know yet."

"Why not?"

"Wanted you to be with me when I opened it. I'm standing in my driveway with a flashlight and cell phone."

"I'm with you, man. Go ahead." Byron heard fumbling noises.

"Okay. The key fits. I'm taking the padlock off."

The next sound he heard was a loud thump and rattle. Did J.J. drop the phone? Then, from a distance the words: "Oh my God."

After another clattering sound came J.J.'s rapid breathing. "Byron, you still there?"

"Still here. What's going on?"

"This thing's full of . . . and I mean to the top—full of cash."

"Cash!"

"Stacks of fives, tens, twenties. I can't believe it."

Byron closed his eyes, remembering Stone's words from their first meeting almost a week ago—*Gaddamn bankers. My old man brought back a small fortune from Europe after the First War.*

During the Depression he lost every cent he'd ever put into that vault. The bastard bankers stole it. This was Stone's personal vault.

"What am I supposed to do with this?" J.J. asked.

"Whatever you want. At the hospital Stone told us everything in that trunk now belongs to you."

"The youth center—of course. It's an answered prayer. Byron, I gotta go. Gotta haul this thing into the house and count the money. This could solve our financial problems for the next five years."

"Hey! Before you hang up, make sure you call me back later and let me know how much is in there."

"Will do. Talk to you in a few hours. Bye."

After Byron hung up, he walked downstairs and put water on to boil for hot chocolate. He felt his heart thudding against his chest and pictured J.J. in frenzied excitement, counting and stacking the money. Then he imagined Stone lying in that hospital bed, a wide smile creasing the wrinkles on his cheeks. *Judd Stone, you sly snake, you. For decades you must have deposited a good portion of your pension into that footlocker. But why? Guilt? Hope for redemption? A chance to make up for past mistakes?* Byron contemplated the complexities of the old man's decision to hand it over to J.J. *Maybe it was just his way of sliding out of that old skin.*

Byron took the phone and cup of hot chocolate into the family room and stretched out on his recliner. The minutes slipped by as he reviewed the events of the last week. The faces and words of J.J., Stone, Helen, Earl, and Eric faded in and out of his mind like a kaleidoscopic newsreel. He had confronted each circumstance and done his best, offering a part of himself—compassion, wisdom, kindness, whatever he could muster—in an effort to help. What more could he do? *Maybe that's all God expects from me—to face the circumstances and do my best. Fight the temptation to withdraw from people's pain and offer to help bear the burden.* A sense of weightlessness flowed over him, as if he were rising toward the ceiling. He knew something had changed within.

The ring of the telephone brought him back. He checked his watch—six-thirty. Almost three hours had passed since he'd talked to J.J. Had he fallen asleep?

He picked up the receiver. "Yes. Byron here."

"Are you sitting down?" J.J. asked.

"Stretched out on my recliner."

"Good enough. I counted the money."

"And?"

" . . .Three hundred and twenty-five thousand, two hundred and fifty dollars."

"Whooooooweeeee! Some gift from above, huh?"

J.J. chuckled. "Just like the old saying—A treasure in the attic."

"Congratulations. I know you'll put it to good use. Spend a little on yourself. Take your wife to the Bahamas."

"No. It's all going to the youth center. Besides, there was something else in the footlocker I'm keeping especially for me."

"Something else?" Byron sorted through the possibilities but drew a blank. "What did you find?"

"Let me give you a hint. I'm wearing it. Right now it's 6:33 and a new day is about to begin."

"The watch?"

"The watch."

Printed in the United States
126703LV00003B/71/P